His American Classic

To
Charlotte
Enjoy

G J Morgan has been a Chef, a fashion graduate and now works in finance. His unpublished novella "Miss B Tee" has recently been adapted into a short film. His and Her American Classic are his debut novels.

HIS

AMERICAN

CLASSIC

G J MORGAN

Matador
9 Priory Business Park,
Wistow Road, Kibworth Beauchamp,
Leicestershire. LE8 0RX
Tel: 0116 279 2299
Email: books@troubador.co.uk
Web: www.troubador.co.uk/matador
Twitter: @matadorbooks

ISBN 978 1788038 607

British Library Cataloguing in Publication Data.
A catalogue record for this book is available from the British Library.

Printed and bound in the UK by 4edge Limited
Typeset in 11pt Adobe Garamond Pro by Troubador Publishing Ltd, Leicester, UK

Matador is an imprint of Troubador Publishing Ltd

Thank you to all those at Matador and Troubador Publishing. You made the process of turning stone to diamond far less daunting than I thought it would be.

Thank you to my early readers: Taya Nicholls (my little Romanian pocket rocket/Business partner), Sarah Lawson (my cinema girlfriend) and Gina Hewitt (my lifestyle coach).

Thanks to Phil Burman (Dad number 2) for constantly being my technical support and turning childlike scribbles into a front cover. Thanks to Paul Burman for being the only person who could relate to the struggles of being a writer and when best to laugh or cry (mostly cry).

Thanks to Barbara Middleton-Chappell for telling me straight and making me realise I'd ran out of excuses not to start writing again.

Thanks and love to Jodi Ellen Malpas for taking time out from being a New York bestselling author and giving me invaluable advice on what to do when the last word has been written (turns out more writing).

Thank you most of all to my wife Krissy, my friends and family, for giving me hours and evenings and mornings and years to type away at my laptop. Without whom the novel would still be an idea on a hotel napkin.

PART ONE

TOM

The Valley/Feb/Shot 7

1

"*Ladies and gentlemen, boys and girls. Welcome to Hollywood Star Tours. My name is Tom and I'll be your guide today. How are you all? You all happy? I want to see bigger smiles than that, guys. Come on, days like today don't come around often. Now straight off the bat I know what you are all probably thinking. Milk-skinned, sunburnt, funny accent. Hardly who you would typically be expecting to be driving you around this beautiful city. And I tell you, it is beautiful, and some of the beauty you'll see today you will recognize from movies and magazines. But my job today, ladies and gentlemen, is to show you its hidden beauty, its little gems, its secrets. Don't worry, you'll get to see your Rodeo Drive and your Hollywood sign, you'll get your postcard moments, that is a given. But trust me when I say that today you are going to see a hell of a lot more than you were probably expecting. Closer than you could ever imagine to the real thing. So, buckle up those seatbelts, apply those suncreams, get those cameras ready as the next two hours are gonna be jam-packed and I wouldn't want you to miss a thing.*"

It was mid-August, busy season; the boss called us all in for her daily pep talk. It was no room for five people, it wasn't even a room, it was a cupboard space. Paperwork loomed floor to ceiling, fans surrounded her desk as she rattled a keyboard at speed. Normally either ill, stressed or pissed off, that Thursday morning she was all three.

"Tommy. How did yesterday go?" Not yet looking up from whatever she was reading.

"Went well. No hiccups."

"Manni is settling in," she said, as I worked out a reply to neither a question nor a statement.

"Where is Golden boy? Romancing married women again?"

"Day off, smart-ass. He deserves one after nine days straight. Did you hear he got another $100 tip? Got within twenty yards of Aniston over at Runyon Canyon, walking that little white dog of hers."

"Norman."

"What?" She looked up.

"Norman. Her dog is called Norman."

"Who gives a fuck. Where were you when all this was going on? Showing some old fucks where Ginger Rogers used to live. You could do well to take a leaf out of Manni's book."

"The guy's a sex pest. He hits on anything."

"The guy gets tips."

"I prefer my way of doing things."

"Well I don't, and I don't reckon the customers do either."

"I get no complaints."

"What is it with you Brits?" She fed herself a handful of pills. "You judge a service by whether or not some poor bastard has complained or not. Do you think my business survives based on no hiccups? Do you think I get repeat custom based on no hiccups? I don't know what to do with you. You work hard, I'll give you that. People like you. God, I even like you, don't do me much good, but you're likeable. But in this job, that ain't enough to cut it, you hear me?"

"Look. If you want me to flirt more, I'll do it, just like Manni. I'll flirt with the old, ugly, women, kids, men. I can flirt with anything if that will keep you off my back."

"I just want you to wow them. This is America. I know it's a struggle for you to understand. But we expect pearly whites and razzle-dazzle as standard. We expect and I expect the best. Tourists haven't travelled across oceans and drove across state lines for 'no hiccup' service. They've come here to see the dream. Do you understand, you lump?"

"Crystal-clear."

"I hope so. Back to work. There's a group of eight outside. Departing in five."

"I'm on it."

"Oh, it's Halle Berry's birthday today, she's just been spotted up at Maxfield with her kids. Pattinson is out and about too; seen an hour ago over at Melrose Trading Post. Antiques shopping. Vampires have to eat too, so be on the lookout."

"And there was me thinking we just show the tourists houses and landmarks."

"Don't push my buttons today. This is last-chance saloon for you, boy."

"As much as it pains me to say this, Pattinson eats over at Surs on North Robertson."

"Sounds a good place to start. Right, off you go to the mob, look restless. Remember: teeth and gums."

"Can't I be mysterious and aloof?"

"You can be unemployed if your tips get any smaller."

She laughed, as much as she fought it. That was the trick, I guessed. Keep her smiling.

The rest of the day was pretty standard. Met some nice people, newly-weds, retired folk on vacation, met a few rude ones too, nothing out of the ordinary. I even managed to track down Pattinson, not where I predicted, but I found him, that was the main thing. Gave a couple of *Twilight* fans the best day of their lives, something signed to take back home. Not that Pattinson was best pleased, though they never were.

Halle Berry. I decided to ignore my boss's orders on that one, left that to the others to fight and squabble over. Me, I drew the line at mothers and their children blowing out birthday candles. Some moments aren't to be shared with others, even the ones that tip well.

★ ★ ★

At home, I played catch with Molly, not that she caught much, as Cassie set the garden table, waving at next door who were doing the same. Next door was always broiling or singing, they didn't speak English too good, but always smiled and waved. Their cooking always smelt better than ours too.

We rented in Glendale, far away off the tourist route and our house wasn't anything camera-worthy. Damp, wallpaper ripped and curled, furniture borrowed or bought cheap, but we tried our utmost to make the best of it. Admittedly, we weren't the tidiest, and despite our best intentions, over time it became accepted that we lived in a permanent state of tidying, a party that neither me nor Cassie had attended. Every day Cassie would curse at the mass of shoes and boots piled up by the front door, the stack of bills and statements left to pile up in the kitchen unopened. Despite all our combined efforts we never quite kept on top of it. We'd both rather be roller-skating or at some zoo or gallery than be sweeping floors or mowing lawns. That was us, in a house that was ugly but loved.

Cassie served up dinner, as we talked and ate. It was nice, the evening sun less harsh; meant I could come out of the shade finally, we talked about something and nothing. Somehow, over mouthfuls of ice cream, me and Cassie had now fallen out and it was my own fault for bringing it up, not that I thought I had. I just said that we didn't need a three-bed and could make do with renting a two to save on bills. The conversation escalated quickly, and it was a debate we'd had time and time again: she wanted a second child and I didn't, least not yet, so it was a disagreement that would not go away and would either end in separation or pregnancy, probably the latter. Molly was between us, eating and humming, so the difference in opinion we kept to angry whispers across the table and then later silent baths and early bedtime for everyone except me.

I decided to go back downstairs; it was early, time to myself was rare. For a few hours I did very little, sank myself in front of the TV, reruns of *Seinfeld* on NBC. I started to watch an old samurai movie, but I wasn't in the mood for subtitles and decapitation. So I grabbed the keys off the side, drove off through the street lights west towards Mulholland. Towards a friend and bar I knew would still be awake.

★ ★ ★

The friend was Mick and as predicted he was still on his feet. He was all gut, his belly filled most of his work station. He leant back against the array of liquor, his belly nearly touching the cash register. There were glasses to be cleaned and tables to be cleared but this was his bar and his rules. His arms crossed, making his way for a bowl of cold nuts. He worked seven days a week, in his eyes his shift ended about five hours before.

Night hours had always been a constant running battle for me, and America was worse. Cassie, although warm and soft, freely admitted to being a shocking bed companion, and Molly's bouts of apnoea and wheezing, and the humidity of LA, all contributed to me struggling to get to sleep and even more importantly stay asleep. I'd tried all manner of things, pills, lavender oil, infomercials about award-winning food blenders and new expensive and elaborate ways to get stomach muscles; even tried jazz. Eventually bored by all I'd tried, I started to take myself out of the house.

I'd say a few nights a month, guaranteed, when all else had failed me, I'd take the Jeep out for a drive, off on my own private tour. A silent tour, one without me having to narrate or perform. Up past the Methodist church maybe, Pyramid Lane, east on Sunset possibly, up Porn Valley, (yes exactly what it sounds like). I just drove, chased colours and sights, no real direction or destination; most times I ended up in downtown bars, mixing with the kinds of people you'd expect to see as the rest of the city slept. Bars that looked empty but gave you enough company to feel welcomed and loved. I had friends around the city that I would not dare tell Cassie about. Men with loose sets of principles, people at the bottom end of society, dependants, dependent on welfare, violence and all other manner of vices, but it never scared me off, in fact I found the downtrodden a welcoming bunch.

The Hollywood bars I frequented suited my objective just fine and it made for more interesting conversations. I'd talk with them of course, but I'd listen too; watch Nascar, drink my soda, watch the odd fight or scuffle, nothing the bar staff couldn't sort out. LA was full of crazy, just depended on how crazy you wanted it and where you drove your car. One way to fight insomnia at least, gave me a smile, made me go home and hug the family a little tighter knowing how others had it.

So far, all the talk at the bar that night had been about Mr Jackson. Around that time, Mr Moonwalk's death was all over the city and Bel Air was busier than ever in his absence. I'd taken my Jeep up at least six times a day, on Boss's orders, so the grieving could take photos, pay respects, gasp at the drama unfolding. What a mess, and a mess that would only get messier; it was a hell of a shame. I was born too late to be a real fan but he deserved a better death and showed just what fame could do to someone. Death had only made the fanatics more fanatical and they showed no signs of slowing down. There would be court cases, law suits, a doctor would most probably go to prison, not to mention splitting his estate. A sad state of affairs and it felt wrong to watch, and it felt even worse to be the one paid to show people where to watch it.

I'd been there a good while. Mick had gotten himself a measure of bourbon, the good stuff high up on the top shelf; without prompting he gave me another soda. I must've been the only one not drinking. The bar had emptied, the few remaining drinkers sat in their company, men in their own personal space, drinking for their own personal reasons.

"When I die I'm doing it my way." Feeding himself more nuts, staring at the TV, newsreaders reporting, fans crying. "Just gonna eat and drink myself to a point my body gives up."

"Sounds like suicide to me, Mick."

"If it is then I've been killing myself since I turned twenty-one," patting his belly.

"Can you leave the bar to me? Would be a nice gesture."

"I wouldn't give it you. I like you too much. This place is a fucking curse. All it has ever given me is debt and a bad heart."

"Who would you leave it to?"

"No one. Let the city fight over it."

"You wouldn't leave it to your kid?"

"He wouldn't want it. He wants nothing to do with me, let alone some beat-up bar with fucked plumbing and an endless lease."

"How old were you when you had him?"

"He was born 1989. I'm fifty-two," as he served a couple of guys a pair of beers.

"You were quite old then."

"It wasn't planned."

"Nor was mine."

"Yes but at least you love your wife. I hated mine then as much as I do now."

"I never thought I'd be a dad, especially not a dad at twenty-four. Always thought I'd travel forever. No fixed abode. Answer to none but myself."

"That's not a reality; that's a dream, kiddo. Every man needs a place to nest, a woman to call his own. Some just take longer than others."

"I know. I just didn't think it would happen to me so young. Is this what life's like? Constant fear of letting someone down. Not doing enough. Chasing money so the bills don't catch up with you."

"It's not all bad. Most men would die for what you got, including me."

"Are you happy, Mick? Single. Free to roam. Sow your wild oats."

"Do I look fucking happy? Look at me. I want what you have, Tom. Don't take it for granted. Don't waste it."

"She wants more children."

"All women want more children."

"But life is hard having one. I'm piss-poor. It seems ludicrous to have another right now."

"Money should never be a reason to have or not have children. Unless there is another reason?"

"Like what?"

"Maybe you are with the wrong woman."

"Maybe."

"Do you want to be with her?"

"I can't leave her, Mick. Not with Molly how she is."

"That wasn't the question. Is she the right woman?"

"She used to be."

"And now?"

"I don't want to make Cassie a single parent. I don't want to be a single parent. I don't want Molly to have that life."

"Is she the right woman? Yes or no?"

I didn't answer, sipped my drink.

"Well, you won't find the right woman here that's for sure and hanging out with dropouts like me isn't going to help either. Go home and start asking yourself some big questions. It's too late for such topical conversation."

"Can I have another soda first?"

"Hell no. I ain't running no charity. My advice is free, my livelihood isn't."

"Thanks, Mick. Thanks for listening."

"Hey, you ain't the first man to ask a barman for his opinion and you won't be the last. Now get out of here, King of the Road, before I set the locals on you."

I decided to take his advice, finished my soda and drove home to my warm wife and bed. I never knew why but I always felt like I'd done something wrong after a night out on my own. My nights were so spontaneous and so filled with neon; a different life than my daytime self, a world away from nappies and cartoons and routine. I always felt in the middle, always felt like half was never enough of either.

Cassie said once that most girlfriends would worry about my new hobby and I agreed. I assured her it was nothing like that, and that wasn't a lie, my adventures were never that sort. Even though I was torn I wasn't a bastard, though I'd nearly been one. The other night, few months back, some girl at a bar made a move on me, was quite blunt about it, outright asked me if I fancied hooking up. She was the complete opposite of Cassie, short, curvy, breasts hard not to stare at. Of course, I declined, though I knew a lot of husbands who would've jumped at the chance of a one-night stand or potential affair. But that husband wasn't me.

But I was having an affair, that was for sure. An affair with the city, so whatever time I eventually got home, my hair stinking of smoke, my fingers salty from cashews, I always felt like I'd cheated, like I was lying to everyone, including myself.

★ ★ ★

Next morning was like our previous night's disagreement had never happened. We didn't have time for apologies, and arguments always resolved themselves as we attempted to get everyone fed and out of the house on time.

I envisaged families who did it better than us. Men who had time for a run round the block, a long shower, before joining his family at a laid table, hot toast, halved grapefruits, his children reading quietly, his wife at the griddle pan, as he read a big newspaper. There would be a lightness about it all, a casual levity.

Already my Friday morning had sucked. Couldn't find my shades, Cassie couldn't find the urgent letter I was supposed to post. She asked me if I had money for groceries, I gave her the little change I had in my pocket, knowing it would only be enough for milk and bread. We kissed cheeks at the doorway, daughter in her arm, Hoover in the other. A look to suggest she wished I didn't have to go, and a smile which made me not want to leave.

11

The journey to work stuck to its familiar trends, Alt 97 on the radio, Highland Avenue traffic, palms as tall as ladders, blue skies; always blue skies. Despite the endless jams I still loved to drive, top down, music up, just driving in the open air was enough for me. For an Englishmen like me, starved of such weather, just not seeing grey was a minor miracle.

Got to the office, Roger treated me to a quick breakfast burrito, quick machine coffee to beat off the night before, the boss then set us off to work. A new audience, the same old tired lines, my little drum roll, my rousing speech, more celebrity houses, more celebrity spotting.

End of my shift, Boss called me over.

She was letting me go.

I was being fired.

Fed me a yarn about streamlining, efficiencies, unstable financial climate; it stank of industry protocol, this had been practised, this had been Googled and she had done it many times before and despite her saying it wasn't personal and giving me a hug, her affection was purely for display. Still I listened and she talked, I listened again and she talked some more, culminating in her giving me an envelope full of crumpled cash and a pat on the back. In the Jeep I counted it; although a wad of notes it would barely last a fortnight. Thank God, she said I could work my notice, six weeks to sort my shit out, at least she had the decency to buy me some time.

* * *

Even now I couldn't quite fathom how it had ever come about, this career. It was always my intention to one day live in America, that was always the plan all along, but it was never my intention to be a tour guide. Guiding strangers around a city I barely knew myself. I was as lost as they were, a tourist just like them. I remember when I first landed the job a couple of years before, I phoned home across the pond. I expected Mum to be a tad underwhelmed by it, the fact that after a half decade of higher education and a year of backpacking, my career had led me to that of a glorified cab driver. But she didn't say much, for the most part she was surprisingly enthusiastic. Think she was just glad I was employed finally.

Even the night before my first day as a tour guide, I still wasn't sure it was the right thing to do. Lying on the bed, me and Cassie debated my new career move. She asked me, if I could do anything, what would it be, and we got talking about my options, realistic options. No talk of journalism, movie work, space exploration, just realistic options. She tried to narrow the choices down, fired questions at me.

Do I like to work in a team, prefer to work alone, office job or on my feet? And although it didn't make my choice any clearer, I could tell she was enjoying the process, so I played along. It went on for a good half hour, until it became silly, asking me if I'd prefer to work with animals or food. She agreed it had turned far-fetched and after, analysing her findings, she concluded that a tour guide ticked all the boxes. We ended up in a play-fight, cushions were thrown by both parties and we did end up making out on the floor of our kitchen. We'd made a mutual decision, I was desperate and underqualified. I had no other choice.

So, I began my new job. Excited at first, but the glitz and glamour didn't last long. I was, as predicted, a cab driver. I was a back of a head, a baseball cap and a name badge, a curator of the rich and famous, a peeping Tom, literally. It was never a career, it was a rut, a comfortable rut, but a rut that paid the bills.

★ ★ ★

After I got fired I drove around for a bit, found somewhere high and quiet. The Hollywood sign looked different that day and forty-five feet was a long way up, and a longer way down. Peg Entwistle sprang to mind.

I think a lot of people in LA were like her, me included. I'd seen them on my daily routes, forgotten actors, sidewalk pop stars, performing to a moving audience. All of us sold the idea of what it might be like to make it in Hollywood. I looked down, the carpet of rich and poor, success and failure, for all to see. There was nothing really in-between in Hollywood and I wasn't sure exactly what camp I sat in.

Actually, that wasn't fair. I'd had successes. I fell in love, a lot of guys searched for that their entire lives, I'd class that as a success. Met Cassie on a tour bus funnily enough, still you can't help where and who you fall in love with and I fell for Cassie and I fell for the city, although I don't think the city has ever loved me back. Not long after we'd met, we found out she was pregnant; after that things moved fast, deposits were put down on a house, joint accounts were set up, futures were planned. Seven months later, a little earlier than everyone expected, we had little Molly.

She turned two September just gone and I still can't quite believe she made it. Her start in life was full of headlines, five weeks premature, 3lb 14oz, special care unit. My memories of that time were and still are clouded. Transfers between hospitals, doctors giving us worst-case scenarios, nurses with paperwork, waiting rooms, visitors' hours. Cassie was discharged after five days, Molly had to wait another twelve days till we could finally bring her home.

Not an ideal start for little Molly. She'd seen more doctors than I'd seen the Beverly Wilshire and from day one she'd either been on a ventilator or in a hospital waiting room. We were assured it wasn't serious, a side effect of being premature. Still, when you see your firstborn strapped to wires and machinery, the only way we could see it was very serious. And those things weren't cheap, not that I was putting a price on my daughter, but in the cold light of day healthcare in the grand old United States was a luxury not a right. Money meant medication. Money meant she might reach her next birthday. I'm being dramatic of course, the doctors had always assured us it wasn't critical, but in my eyes, that was the value of every dollar I earned. That's why I always worked so many long hours, for Molly; worked the hardest I could, just not hard enough.

Times would have to be tough for a while, I thought. I was confident I could find work, I just didn't know when or what it would pay. In the meantime, I would need to cut back, make a few changes to save a few bucks, though we already lived hand to mouth, not sure what else we could cut back on.

Fuck! The Jeep, I thought. I'd have to give the Jeep back too.

How the hell was I going to get the money for new wheels?

How did this happen? How did I get myself into this mess?

I always thought I was a pretty decent tour guide. The stupid thing was I actually loved being a tour guide for the most part. I didn't even mind the boss; for all her flaws and despite her firing me, we always got on. She was never built for LA, she was all Vegas, a feisty little pit bull, but I liked her honesty, her laugh that cackled and coughed.

I genuinely enjoyed showing people the city, enjoyed telling them stories, loved how excited they got, like I did when I first arrived. It was only when the job changed for the worse that I started to unknowingly lose interest; when it became a matter of routine. That's when the boss knew my cards were marked. I'd become disillusioned by it and the boss must've seen that and started to look out for reasons to let me go.

I never said I was the model employee. I was a hard worker but yes, sometimes I might have read my *LA Weekly* in the Roosevelt car park, had the occasional coffee with a couple of superheroes from Grauman's Theatre sometimes, but I never took advantage of my employer. I just think I'd changed and what was expected of me had changed too. The audience in the back of the Jeep had become hungrier and more aggressive in what they expected from a tour, and from me as a guide. No longer interested in locations or legends, they now wanted reality and were relentless in getting it. They wanted their pound of flesh. Boss called it 'safari', and I hated it ever since she coined the phrase, but that was in truth exactly what it was. "The bigger the meat, the bigger the buck." She actually said this, I'm not even kidding. Mistimed, I remember I sniggered and was given the look I'd become all too familiar with, which was very similar to the look I was given when I was canned.

She even had radios installed, to keep all Jeeps in the loop, and had us all measured up with matching khaki shirts and pants. We looked ridiculous, but the tourists lapped it up, every day more dollars, every day a new hunt. It was laughable but lucrative. But like on safari, waiting for a pride of grazing lions or the emergence of a rare bird by a watering hole, my role had become that of a hunter or stalker. And LA has a lot of watering holes, and a lot of rare birds, and lots of alpha males. And I knew how and where to find them. A socialite's favourite bookstore on Sunset. The newest heart-throb with a six-pack at a bar, a designer's local grocery store. I tell you, hang about anywhere with either food, drink or clothes long enough and celebrities will come to graze and socialize. And when they come, our Jeeps are there; mine included. So, the magazines, the internet, became a necessity and the pursuit regrettably addictive. The radio, the gossip, the Jeep, all tools of the trade.

I was going to miss that Jeep. It was the only car I had ever owned and I didn't even own it, not technically. Most of my significant memories, good and bad, have involved that vehicle one way or another. I even thought Molly was conceived in the back of that Jeep momentarily until Cassie's journal proved I was out by three days. One late night when Molly was first born, and neither I nor Cassie had any other ideas on how to get her to sleep, I took us all for a drive. Thought the humming engine and bad suspension might help her nod off, when in fact it had the reverse effect and heightened all of her other senses.

Cassie had not been in my Jeep for a long while and on that particular night the city was in good form. I drove a bit, we stopped, I drove a bit more, we stopped. We whispered about our plans for the future, I took her to my favourite houses on Roxbury Drive and restaurants on West Malibu I would love to take her to.

But mostly we talked about Molly, about being prepared for an uncertain future, about worst-case scenarios if her health didn't improve. We both cried a bit, even me as much as I tried not to. When our daughter eventually did fall asleep, as the sun was coming up over Wattles Garden Park, I asked Cassie to marry me and she said yes. Unprepared, I didn't have a ring so instead I slipped on an imaginary one, before going to Wendy's to share a garden salad with literally the last few dollars we had between us. God, I even made her sign a napkin, the terms of the marriage. Meal on the table by six, house tidy, sex every night. Two out of three wasn't bad I suppose, it was a great day, in every which way it was perfect. The imaginary ring had since become a running joke between Cassie and myself. The longer the wait for the real stone, the bigger the imaginary one became.

"This ring is getting so heavy I may have to take it off," she always joked, but deep inside it hurt that I couldn't afford it and I hoped she knew if I'd had the money I'd have been the first person down Rodeo Drive with my wallet. Until that time she was still my wife, just not in the official sense, but in the way that mattered most. She's always deserved more and there were men out there who would do better than me.

I looked at the sky, looked at my watch. It was time to head home. It was in the traffic I decided not to tell Cassie about today, about me losing my job. I had plenty of time to fix it. Later after dinner and a shower Cassie chatted on the phone, an old friend with a lot to tell, meant a ten-minute chat turned into a lot longer, so instead I updated my CV online, which made for pretty light reading. University then travelling then tour guide. I was hardly qualified for much, but I was a hard worker and willing to do anything as long as it paid. There were plenty of jobs like that in Hollywood. I was sure I could get myself sorted without the need to worry Cassie. She had enough on her plate already and it was a problem I could sort out on my own.

An hour later my CV was done. As I started to pack away the dishes and pans, I could hear Cassie from the other room, laughing, talking fast the way girls do. I overheard her being invited out, someone's birthday, a chance for a rare night off, but I could already hear Cassie decline, a lie about already having plans, when I knew we had none.

★ ★ ★

Over the weekend I tried my best not to panic. Did family stuff, free stuff like walks and baseball, stuff that I knew wouldn't damage the bank balance. Monday, I sent out my CV, hoped somebody would bite, but no one did. Spent a couple of lunch breaks talking to some big lady across a big desk as she looked for jobs on her computer; she said I'd hear from her but I never did.

More days passed, they felt like weeks. I begged the boss to change her mind, give me another chance, but she'd already hired my replacement. I was screwed, I would've spoken to my bank, but I knew the sorry state of my finances. Molly wasn't great either, had a few bad nights, couldn't get her breath. Another hospital visit and another big medical bill. Things didn't look great for her or for us.

I realized I needed help. I decided to ring home.

My cell had no credit so I rang her from a phone booth. She sounded startled, I'd forgotten the time difference, I apologized. Told her I didn't have many quarters, which was partly true. Gave her the rundown on my situation, she listened, told me what I needed to hear, the 'everything will be OK' speech, said she would send money. I told her not to, but she insisted. I wasn't in a position to refuse, and was man enough to resort to begging if it meant looking after my family.

I'd changed a lot. Before I'd always lived a way of life where I made myself accountable for my own actions, an almost blind stubbornness to refuse a handout, to do things on my own, to be dependent on no one. There were so many times when I was travelling when I knew it would've only taken a phone call to Mum and Dad and I'd have had money wired into my account. Koh Chang, Cambodia, I had some rough times where I was reckless with my resources, left myself vulnerable. There were things I did on that trip I'm not proud of, slept on too many floors, pushed broom, ate meat that made my insides churn. But it was a shit I'd got myself into and a shit I had to climb out of. And I always did.

But my willingness to accept charity all changed with Cassie and Molly. When I became accountable for three and when recklessness affected more than my back and stomach. Still didn't feel right asking Mum for money, it was money she probably didn't have herself; she wasn't wealthy. She wasn't when Dad was alive, less so now. Made me feel sick I had to ask, well I didn't even ask, but I rang with that intention in mind, so it was no surprise when her help was offered.

★ ★ ★

Another week went by and still no job, working my notice had gone quick, too quick. And the search for new employment, which at first glance had been painless and optimistic, had spiralled into blind panic. End of September and I'd be officially jobless, so I only had a few days left at work till I would have no choice but to tell Cassie the truth.

I'd only had a handful of interviews, most were a complete waste of time. One interview I had to sneak out of the house in my shirt and tie before the girls woke up. I wasn't expecting much, the interview was over as soon as it began, and I got the impression the position wasn't mine once they looked me up and down. I had to apply really as one of the girls on the counter had a friend, who knew a friend, who knew of an opening. It was embarrassing actually. I was the oldest in the waiting room by a long shot, and the salary they offered was meant for someone just out of grad school rather than someone with a wife and kid.

The guys took me out too, a farewell lunch. There weren't many of us, but it was a nice gesture. The Grub girls presented me with a bottle of import beer and a box of Yorkshire Gold. I drank the first and hid the second in the Jeep. As we started to walk back to work I found myself alongside Roger, who was ever keen to offer his words of wisdom, regardless of whether the advice was wanted or required.

"How many interviews you had?"

"Including yesterday, three. I've got one tomorrow, so technically four."

"Uniform or desk job?" We both stopped at the lights.

"Insurance company."

"You got experience?"

"I got a British education, if that helps. Best in the world."

"What you study in?"

"You'll laugh."

"Hit me with it."

"American Studies, little bit of Photography but I dropped out."

He laughed.

"You're shit out of luck, pal."

"Just have to flirt and charm."

"Hey, it's worked for me," winking at a girl half his age as she walked past, oblivious to his gesture. "Probably best you make something up, Tom. Some bank in London that doesn't exist."

"Why does everyone assume I'm from London? I'm up north, hours away."

"Everyone here likes you, Tom, customers like you. Even the boss likes you."

"I don't think that's enough these days. I'm glad, deep down I'm glad. This isn't the job I'd applied for. We're supposed to be tour guides, not vultures."

"Hey, it worked for Vince."

"How so?"

"Sorry, Tom, I thought you knew."

Vince I hadn't seen in a long while. We were briefly very good friends, very close and for a short while we spent most of our time with each other. Vince was on the same induction of new recruits as myself, we liked the same things, same movies, taught me how to drive an automatic. Taught me how to drive like an American, how to bully the road, how not to get lost. Streets go sideways, avenues up and down and all that. I liked him, but I could see why others didn't. I even invited him over for dinner one time, him and his current girlfriend of the month. But it never happened again, Cassie didn't much care for his company, or the company he kept. He didn't last long as a tour guide either, the boss saw to that. Vince was never shy about his plans for world domination; he left abruptly and defiantly and our friendship ended equally as abruptly with his resignation.

"No, last I heard he'd moved across to Pasadena to live with a cousin. So, what's he up to? Cali Prison? Bond villain? CEO of Apple?"

"He's finally gone to the dark side, to the world of scandal."

"What, mob boss now is he? Looting?"

"No, worse. Paparazzi."

"Fuck no, that is worse. Well, he always said he had it in him. How did it come about?"

"No clue."

"Fuck."

"Obviously working for him. Saw him the other day, but he was in a hurry. He must have dropped twenty pounds, he was driving an Escalade as big as a tank."

"Traded in his rusty coupe."

"Yes, sir, he did."

"Thinking about it now, he mentioned the idea to me a few times. I nearly sold him my camera, but it never came about."

"Never know, if things don't work out, could be a Plan B for you."

"That would never be a Plan B."

"It's not too far removed from what we are doing now."

"Yes, one the reasons I'm glad I'm getting out, and so should you."

"Hey, man. My moral compass broke a long time ago. Four kids and real estate can do that to you. All I'm saying is, it's an option."

"All I'm saying is, it's not."

"Let's agree to disagree."

"Let's."

"So back to work. Are you sure your morality can stretch a bit longer, that queue is looking pretty darn long."

"Boss won't be pleased."

"She never is."

"Come on, let's make a move. Those celebrities won't find themselves," as we reached tour guide country.

Roger later told me the real reason I was sacked, he'd heard it through Manni. The boss heard I chose not to hunt down a mother and her buggy, a customer complained apparently. Turns out all moments are in fact meant to be shared, nothing is private in the world of celebrity. I actually found it funny, indirectly Halle Belly had gotten me fired, I should have known the boss would've found out. I suppose she had to set an example, she couldn't be seen to be allowing employees to break rank, defy orders, but I didn't regret anything I'd done previously. It didn't make me sad or happy. It just made me shrug.

★ ★ ★

Me and Cassie had not been getting on great either since I found out I was being let go, a constant series of shit to deal with, nothing big, just broken kitchen appliances, bills we hadn't expected. That, together with me keeping my unemployment secret and lack of sleep, meant either me or Cassie were always on different extremes, either going hell for leather, or giving each other the silent treatment.

After another big fight, I found myself grabbing the keys off the side again, took myself on a drive, further and higher, towards a more palatable view, parked the car, opened a pack of smokes, looked out across the valley. I checked the clock, it was gone one.

England had never boasted horizons, too flat – well, that wasn't fair, London's skyline was equally as grand, even my mum's village sometimes, but it was a view that wasn't accessible, not for people like me. In London you looked up and it made you feel small, whilst in Los Angeles you had the means to reach the top, which gave you the ability to look down and attempt to grab some perspective. American views always brought me out in hope, made me reflect. Cassie joked it was the place I went to get all deep and meaningful and she was right. Cassie joked a lot, it was her way of dealing with things I suppose, dealing with Molly. I just worried one day the hurt would build and build and would have to eventually spill out. Till then she kept up the smiles, we both did, we both felt that was what our daughter needed more than lab results and hospital corridors.

I was in the mood for pot. I did smoke some pot up here once. Me and Vince, it was his idea, never again, it got way too deep and meaningful, even for me, there was talk of the cosmos, the afterlife. But San Fernando valley can do that to you, take you off somewhere, make you look at things on a grand scale. The city lit up for miles to see.

February just gone Cassie bought me a camera for my birthday, said it would be nice to see all those skies I told her about so much. It actually wasn't a bad camera, but I'd never used it, took a few shots of her and Mollie over at Griffith Park when I first tested it out and it's sat in the glovebox since. Still got the photo though, pride of place in my wallet, the three of us together, my two girls and me. To look at it now I never knew what she saw in me, bad teeth, a lobster in shades. Mum had the same photo, she said I looked like a musician, although I'm guessing it wasn't meant to be a compliment.

We've had our ups and down, me and Cassie, mostly ups. We nearly split up once, stayed on a friend's floor for two nights, we made up, things went back to normal, then she got get pregnant. When I met her of course there was instant attraction, a physical one, it is hard to resist a girl like Cassie, an electric combination of blonde and tan. We never had anything in common as such, different tastes in music and film, different opinions on the world. But what I loved and still love most about Cassie is her energy, her spontaneity, she was reckless. Molly changed that.

Don't get me wrong, Molly changed us both, and I'm not dumb enough to think that having a child doesn't impact spontaneity and without a shadow of a doubt removes any thought of recklessness. But she was changing even before Molly – the longer we were together, the more she wanted stability, a structure, and all that free spirit Cassie had before was replaced with just settling. Settling rather than chasing.

I didn't know if I was explaining it right, I couldn't quite put words on it. The only way I could describe it is, I don't think we would have been together if we hadn't had Molly. We actually talked about it once, I think we both knew it, and we both accepted that it was most probably true. We loved each other, and we would never choose to split up, but because of Molly and not for ourselves. I don't know if that was wrong or right, but for us it was the only way at the time. So, it was love, the biggest love, just not the love that would last forever, just the kind of love we felt Molly needed. I told her I loved her every day, and her back. And we both meant it, truly meant it. You can love someone for the wrong reasons, can't you? As long as it's love then surely that was OK? That's what I thought.

What me and Cassie really needed was a date, some time for ourselves, get drunk and talk about anything apart from parenthood. Though a babysitter was unlikely, family were an aeroplane journey away and our friends weren't quite trustworthy enough to care for a child, too busy being young and spontaneous to be sat staring at a cackling baby monitor. So, until then we were on our own, surviving, being OK parents and an OK couple, taking both for granted and not particularly enjoying either.

I lit another smoke. It was gone in seconds, put my head back and closed my eyes, tried to free my head of all the noise.

★ ★ ★

I don't know exactly when but I must've fallen asleep as I sat at the wheel, the sound of tyre on gravel made me come around. I don't know how long I'd been out for, all I remembered was being cold and thirsty.

The noise of tyre on gravel was a Mustang that had parked a few spaces across from me. I couldn't make out the colour or the front as it was dark and parked at an angle away from mine. It was beautiful though, the car, and it had been looked after, had money spent on it. There were two of them inside, a man and a woman. Oblivious and certainly not quiet, they drank from champagne bottles like no one was watching. With my lights out, they probably thought my car was one that had been abandoned or broken down.

I recognized the girl. Not entirely sure where from.

Valley girl. That was my first reaction, took me a while to remember who she was, get a glimpse of her face. When I did, I knew who she was instantly.

Amanda Lebowitz.

Actress, made a handful of forgettable teen comedies back in the late nineties, since then she'd been on the decline, physically and emotionally. Bad movie decisions, surgical mistakes too. I couldn't quite make out what was happening in that car, but it looked like it involved unzipping the driver's fly, putting things in her mouth.

I shouldn't have continued to watch. Watching them didn't feel exciting, I wasn't turned on. I felt nothing but curiosity about the situation, not excited or pulsated. I just felt tired, still cold, and ready for home. I went to twist the car keys, but I stopped.

My heart raced and in a mad moment I grabbed my camera from the glovebox and aimed the lens towards them.

★ ★ ★

When I woke up that next morning, as Cassie cuddled her coffee and daughter, I decided to tell her about me being fired. I just came out with it. I told her what money we had left, told her about my mum sending me money, told her I would keep looking for work, no matter what it was, told her I loved her, told her I was sorry.

Cassie just smiled, said we would all be fine, gave me a kiss followed by demands for *Spongebob* and congee. I told her she was taking advantage of me, I only cooked congee on very special occasions, birthdays and Valentine's. It turned out losing my job was now an occasion too. That was our relationship, nose to nose, romance then rage. That was why I would never leave her, no matter how bad it got, there was always too much good to ever want to let go, even if it meant putting myself last.

I never did tell her about what happened the night before though, when I was in the Jeep. Because at the time it didn't feel like a big thing. If anything it felt embarrassing and an incident I wanted to forget quickly and erase from my memory. Once or twice I thought about the money it could've made, there were people out there who would pay big money for the photos I'd taken, but it didn't sit right. The money would be tainted and anything it funded would be tainted too. The camera stayed in the glovebox till I had to return the Jeep, and I shoved it in the back of the closet.

★ ★ ★

Not long after, it turned out I did get that job for the insurance company, don't know how I ever managed it – luck, I assumed. I can't tell you how relieved I was, and although the excitement was for the security rather than the job itself, it gave us all a lift – it wasn't a job for me, it was a job for us. I took us all out to celebrate at our favourite coffee shop, omelette cheese sandwiches all round, a belated birthday stack of cookies for Molly. Cassie even presented me with a new tie, warned me not to become the next Gordon Gecko, said she finally got the husband who wore a tie to work.

It was a great day, we talked about a house of our own, pets, having another baby came up again and I agreed we should start trying. We even shook hands on finally going to Coachella next year rather than listening to it on the radio. We talked about visiting her folks over in Clearwater – they've only seen Molly the once when she was first born. I agreed, once I'd passed my probation at work, we would book a surprise flight for the following summer. Mickey Mouse-land here we come. I'd ask her to marry me there, that was the plan. I would ask her dad first, surprise her, do it right, with a real ring this time.

With the rest of Mum's money, I even ended up buying myself a new car, nothing fancy, out-of-state plates, an old '91 Wagoneer, dependable, mostly; just affordable. Gave back the Jeep, cleaned it out of all the suncreams, 7 Eleven receipts, magazines, Advil. Handed the boss the keys, she apologized, which I didn't expect, wished me luck. I'd miss her, weirdly enough.

But hey, life went on and things returned to relative calm. My new boss was OK; the average age of my office was mid-fifties, it was quiet, repetitive, but I wasn't complaining. At home Molly wasn't getting any worse, but she wasn't getting any better, me and Cassie were much the same. Things were normal, the arguing didn't stop, got worse in fact, no matter what we did it always ended with slammed doors and the rattle of my car keys.

End of October we decided to head down to the coast for a

few days, just the three of us. We'd had a big chat about where things were going wrong, agreed things had to change, we fought too much about big things and silly things, agreed it wasn't a good environment for Molly. It was much needed and we both agreed that we both could do things differently, treat each other better, try to remember the people we were before, be more selfish with our free time, go on dates, hold hands more, take it in turns to have Molly, trust I could be a parent without worrying I'd do something wrong. Felt good to get things off our chests, say some home truths, put all the cards on the table, it wasn't an easy conversation, but it was one that had to be had. The little holiday was a fresh start and although I felt a little pressure, knowing it had that make-or-break finality to it, the mood as we packed up the car was all positive. Felt like how me and Cassie were when we first met, she had that look in her eye again, like she was ready for adventure, the look that made me fall for her the first time.

★ ★ ★

On the way there, an oncoming pickup truck hit us at speed off San Diego Freeway. I don't remember anything about the crash. The car rolled, I had to be cut out, so I'm told. I remember, moments before, Molly singing 'Oranges and Lemons', Cassie's hand on my lap as she talked bathroom colours. After that, it was screams and sirens. After that, things went dark. And stayed dark.

2

Most people have probably never heard of Peg Entwistle, unless you'd been on my tour. If you had, you definitely knew, she had a whole two minutes dedicated to her. Every tour, same time, delivered on the approach, the gasps as Mount Lee comes into sight, as I told them all about Hollywood land, Holy weed, Holywood, all its various names, before they'd all rush off with their cameras to have their photos taken and I could have five minutes to stretch my legs, take a few sips of water, stop talking.

Peg Entwistle was a sad one – escaped the grey of England like myself, dreamt of making it big on stage and screen. In a last-ditch attempt for fame and notoriety she jumped off the big H. She achieved that at least, became a name and a story. Still sad.

She was twenty-four, two years younger than me, no age to give up.

Funny what those nine big letters on a hill could represent. Drives people to do the grandest of things.

★ ★ ★

The letterbox woke me up. Took me a while to come around, stretching and yawning. Felt like morning, but it clearly wasn't. Outside the window I could see them feeding ducks in their coats and hats, my little Californian surf girl. Don't think she'd ever known such cold. The pond looked icy, but I'd seen it icier, I'd seen it frozen over, I'd seen men walk across it, my dad included.

I could hear them both through the glass, laughing and shouting. I promised Mum I'd try to stop sleeping downstairs, it wasn't fair to Molly to have to play in silence, or have to go outside, especially in weather so cold and sharp. I needed coffee, something to get me warm, it was a house full of draughts and gaps. Floorboards and fireplaces, windows so thin they wobbled, it was a fucking igloo. I spent most of my time by the fire, watching it, or stoking it, adding coal or wood, making sure it was always at a roar or spit. Mum would curse, charging around sleeveless in a permanent state of summer, calling me a sissy, in the only American accent she had in her vocabulary.

After two days of being back, I very quickly realized that my American wardrobe wasn't suitable. I ended up wearing Dad's old sweaters till I made the trip across town to buy all things thermal. Everything was so far away here, I'd forgotten how remote and isolated we were. I was used to life being on my doorstep, here it involved petrol, it involved forward planning, buying in bulk.

I heard giggles through the glass, Molly looked so happy out there and so settled. She'd taken to village life and the drop in temperature better than I ever thought possible. This was her little adventure, her winter vacation. Air travel was an experience, she wasn't fond of take-off, same with landing, and mid-air wasn't much better. She cried or slept or ate, the pattern for most of the thirteen-hour journey from one front door to another.

Three years I'd been away, didn't know why I should have expected change, might have made my time away seem more significant, but apart from the disappearance of a post office and a renovated church, it remained as I had left it.

It was the last time I'd seen Dad, too, three years ago, the morning he drove me to the airport. He never even got to be a grandfather. That was the one good thing to come out of all this. At least Mum could finally get the chance to be a grandmother, rather than a picture in a frame or a voice down the phone. I'd never seen Mum so happy, she hadn't let go of Molly since we landed. I'd never realized it back in LA, but they had the same eyes, strangely even similar mannerisms, their bond was instant too. I watched them together, the two had become inseparable, and every task had become one done as a pair. Molly's hands in flour on the kitchen floor, digging Mum's vegetable patch, having her hair brushed in the bath. I hoped that soon, it would be me with batter, mud or hair in my hands, sat cross-legged with Molly, laughing, but for now I wasn't taking part.

Mum has been amazing in all this, took Molly everywhere she went, involved her in everything she did, baking, cleaning, washing. Me, she left me to it, gave me a hug, gave her condolences briefly. Typical of Mum, by the next morning she was ordering me about, giving me lists and chores, similar to when Dad died. I think she felt it better to be sad but busy, than to be wallowing in pity – not that I disagreed. But strangely it did help, a big ironing pile, a big bag of potatoes to peel, it took my mind off things, took me away into rooms on my own, which was all I wanted, not to have to face people, even my own mother and daughter. Mum would try, of course, make a joke, sing an old song, but they were never tasks done with a smile. I was far away from smiling or joining in, in fact I'd barely said a word since I'd come home.

I heard the door open and close, heard them pulling off boots and unwrapping scarves, I pretended to be asleep. Mum whacked me round the head with an apron, ordered me to the chopping board, said to get all my tears out with the onions.

★ ★ ★

At the table later that night, we ate dinner, sipped red wine that would have been better in the stew.

"Molly is ready to start potty training."

I nodded.

"After Christmas. Next time we drive into town, we will pick one up."

I nodded again.

"It'll need both of us to help and encourage her. Two-man job, that one. And it's just a matter of time till she figures she can get out of her cot. She will be in a bed soon. That's when the fun begins."

31

I didn't answer.

"Who was the letter from you got today? Cassie's folks?"

I nodded.

"What's it say, then?"

"Read it yourself. I know you've read all the others," pointing to the side table, as she stood up to grab it.

"What a nice letter, Tom. She seems a nice lady. Oh, how lovely," showing it to Molly. "Here's a picture of your mummy when she was a little girl like you. Shall we hang that up in your room tomorrow?"

Molly agreed.

"They keep asking when I'm coming back."

"They must miss you."

"You mean Molly."

"No. Both of you. You still haven't replied?"

"I will."

"They are hurting as much as we are, Tom. Little advice, grandparent to a grandparent. Don't leave them out of the loop and don't make them wait."

"Wish they would stop sending me cheques. Makes me feel like we are a charity."

"It's their way of showing support. Their way of coping. I'd do the same."

"Here, Mum, you have it." I passed her the cheque.

"No, keep it for Molly."

"Mum. I know food and nappies aren't cheap. You take it."

"Put it away."

"When are we going to talk about money? You keep putting it off."

She deliberately took a mouthful of food.

"Mum. I'm not contributing."

"You don't need to. This is your home."

"How tight is money? Be honest, please."

"Don't worry about things like that. I've survived worse times than this. We'll manage."

"I'll look for work."

"We both know how hard it is to find work round here. Besides, you're not in the right state of mind to be working."

"I can't expect your pension to look after the three of us."

"What would you do? Not much need for a tour guide round here, is there?"

"Anything is better than nothing."

"I could sell some more of your father's pieces."

"Sell? You said he gave them away."

Mum went quiet.

"Since when?"

"It doesn't matter, Tom."

"Since when?"

"Last month."

"Promise me, no more."

"I promise. Right little miss. Time for bath and bed." Molly looked up from her picture book like she'd only just realised we were there.

"I'll do the dishes," I said, already stacking plates.

"No, you're not. You go up."

"I'd rather do the dishes."

"I know what you'd rather. I'll do them. You're on night duty."

"She prefers you to me."

"And I wonder why that is."

I looked down at Molly, she looked excited at the prospect of bubbles with Dad.

"Not tonight, another time I will, promise. Just not tonight, Molly. I'm tired."

Mum took Molly's hand and led her upstairs. I didn't have to see either of their expressions to know I'd let down both.

★ ★ ★

It was getting late, Molly had been asleep a few hours, together me and Mum watched TV till we heard the baby monitor crackle, a scream from upstairs. I went to get up, but Mum was already halfway across the room.

"Did she need her inhaler?" I asked as Mum came back down.

"Nightmare, that's all. Do you want a brandy? I'm having one."

I pulled a face.

"No one likes it, Tom, but it feels like a night for brandy."

She poured a little into a glass and put it my hand.

"I'm not doing well, am I?" I said. "How am I going to do this?"

"It won't last forever, it will fade."

"I'm not going to forget her, Mum. You don't need to put her photos everywhere."

"They're not for you, they are for Molly. When it's your house you can bury your photos in drawers and boxes if you wish. But in my house, she will always be on my walls."

"It'll make her ask questions."

"And we will answer them. And we'll answer them honestly. Children are clever. They can deal with a hell of a lot more than we give them credit for."

"And what is the honest answer? Your daddy couldn't control his vehicle and killed your mummy."

"We both know that isn't true. The police said you weren't to blame, you told me that. Issuing blame doesn't solve anything, or change anything. Tom, do you realise how affected Molly is right now? No, because you are still too caught up in your own grief to realise that your daughter isn't coping either. Do you know how often she has nightmares? How often she screams in the night? She is grieving harder than you. She has lost more than you, though still she smiles more."

"What do you want me to do?"

"More than you are doing now," sitting herself down, turning the TV off with the remote.

"I'm trying."

"Not enough, you're not. Just take each day as it comes. Get through it the best way you can."

"I'm doing that. Tomorrow feels no different. She keeps asking for Cassie. What do I say?"

"Tell her the truth."

"The truth will scare her."

"Not if you say it in the right way. Anyway, she knows, she may not understand it, but she knows. I've told her, you've told her."

"Then why does she keep asking for her?"

"Because she is two years old, Tom. She may know a little about death, and heaven and angels, but it doesn't mean she grasps the fact that her mother has gone."

"Where are you taking her tomorrow?" I asked. "The weather is a little warmer, looking at the forecast. Maybe you could take her swimming, something active, get rid of all of that energy? Get her out of the house."

"What, so you can wallow alone? Besides, you don't have a choice. I'm out tomorrow."

"What?"

"I'm out. I've got plans," taking her nail clippers out of a drawer.

"What do you mean 'out'? Where?"

"A woman doesn't have to disclose where she chooses to go off to," inspecting her toenails.

"So, I'm left with Molly all day so you can have a blowdry."

"Not all day. A few hours. Take her swimming, like you just said."

"You are joking?"

"I'm not joking."

"What am I supposed to do with her?"

"Take her swimming, you said it yourself that you'd like her to go. Play with her. Take her out. You know those village fields

35

better than I do, there'll be plenty of tractors and fields to keep her occupied. There's some Shetland ponies too, she always enjoys seeing them."

"Mum, this seems a bit soon. I'm not in a condition to look after her."

"Tom, you're fit and able. You can muster a smile, pretend to be happy, just sit with her, watch a film. Oh, the fish man is coming tomorrow too, around midday normally. I've ordered a bag of haddock, there's some money in the fruit bowl in an envelope. We'll have it for dinner when I get home."

"Molly won't eat fish."

"Well it's going to be a day of big changes for both of you by the sound of it. I'm not having you sat around in this constant malaise."

"Malaise? My wife died, Mum. I'm not under the weather. If you think this whole 'throw me in the deep end' is going to work then you're wrong. You said take each day as it comes."

"Yes, and this is how tomorrow is coming. So, you better get to bed, as Molly will probably be up at seven and she'll want her porridge."

"She doesn't like porridge."

"She likes lots of things now. Off you go then. I've got some soaps to watch."

She turned away, aimed the remote control back at the TV.

"What if tomorrow doesn't work?"

"Then we try the next day."

"I can't rush this, Mum. Rushing could do more damage than good."

"Time is a luxury you don't have. You have a confused and scared little daughter upstairs. You need to mourn, but you need to mourn on your time, not hers. She needs a father right now, not a ghost."

★ ★ ★

Getting into bed, I wasn't even tired. Felt like all I'd done was lie down and it wasn't because of my body – my injuries hadn't taken long to heal, even by the funeral I was back walking without the need for crutches, just bruises and aches. The only pain still left was my back – sometimes it still hurt when I sat for too long, so the flight home wasn't the greatest. I was told I should see a specialist, lie down with an osteopath and let them rub and bend me. I was in no hurry, my back could wait, there were other things that needed healing first.

I'd seen a Doctor a few times actually, he didn't do much, asked lots of questions, some I answered, some I didn't, gave me drugs and leaflets, medication and information. I didn't swallow either, put the pills in the cupboard and the pamphlets in the bin. What was wrong with me wouldn't be solved by talking feelings or by pumping my bloodstream full of chemicals – what I needed was time, to feel sorry for myself, to be angry. I wished Dad was still around, he was always a calming influence on me, we were very alike, he knew how to deal with me, what to say and when to say it. I had Mum, but her idea of mourning wasn't the same as mine. She thought that it should be done loud and fast, painful but over quickly. I was the reverse of that opinion, not that I hadn't tried her method. I'd attempted normality, tagged along with Mum and Molly, supermarkets, the park, pretended I was cured. But I might as well have not been there, I was a passenger. Despite my best intentions I couldn't get out of the hole I was in, regardless of how much I tried to climb out of it. I knew I wasn't being strong enough and I knew I wasn't being the parent I needed to be. I was losing Molly and in all honesty I couldn't understand why she hadn't given up on me already. I'd done nothing to win her back, still she gave me nothing but love and affection, even when I fought it off. I had to be angry at something or someone, Mum and Molly were the only thing I could aim it at. I found looking at my daughter difficult – she was the mirror of her mother, in every which way, which meant Cassie was always in my head, always in view. I didn't know what to say to her, how much to tell, what to keep back. A relationship between a father and his child shouldn't be awkward and it was pathetic that I felt the need to take myself away from whatever room she was in. Though things had always been awkward for me and Molly – well, on my part anyway.

Fatherhood must come naturally to a lot of men, men that flourish in the role, work alongside the mother, the dream tag team, the guy with his child in a sling, the one who never gave them sugar, one boob away from breastfeeding himself. Mine had been a harder transition, and no matter what I tried, I always felt like a third wheel, like Cassie was in charge and I was there just to back her up. Maybe it was my own fault – I let Cassie do everything, when I should have taken on more responsibility. Embarrassing really, but I'd only had Molly on my own a handful of times and even then, I spent most of it running down the clock, just making sure she avoided injury or worse till Cassie came home. I was still a good dad, did the little things, cuddled her, watched cartoons with her on my lap, let her play with my phone, just not the things that win Father of the Year. I mean, Cassie didn't help, always looked disappointed. If I attempted discipline I was being too mean, if I gave in then I was too soft – which kind of meant I was damned either way, forced to apologize, regardless of my methods. And now I had no one to answer for. Without Cassie, I could parent Molly however I wished and that was absolutely petrifying, knowing I was in sole charge of fucking up without anyone to tell me otherwise.

I hated being weak and defeated, but that was who I was. I just hoped I wouldn't be for too long. I needed something to happen, and quickly. I hoped tomorrow would be it.

3

October became November. Seasons didn't change like in the movies, leaves didn't fall from trees, green didn't turn to white. Days and weeks were identical. Ups didn't feel high enough, my downs far too low. I thought a lot, about the future, how unclear it looked. I thought about the past more, how I had left America so abruptly, deserted the house in the same mess me and Cassie had left it in. I took only the essentials, anything sentimental I left behind, stuffed everything of Molly's in a suitcase. Anything of Cassie's, her clothes, her books, I sent to her parents. The rest – the furniture, paperwork, fridge full of food, my cell phone – I left for the landlord to sort out.

I regretted that now. I wished I'd taken my time, sorted out the finances, the legalities, packed away everything neatly labelled, made sure all necessary boxes were ticked. But I didn't, I just grabbed things and ran, shut the door on the place and the people inside it. Said some unkind things to Cassie's parents, things I didn't mean, told them they were never there for us, that they chose sunshine and Disney castles over her. That was a mean thing to do to someone and I wasn't a mean person.

I smacked Molly too, only once, not that it made it right. I smacked her hard across her leg, for nothing more than trying to get my attention. I regretted it instantly and I could see the disappointment in my mum's face as she took Molly off to another room. I didn't even know why I did it. That was the turning point. I realised my way wasn't working and it was time to let someone else have a go. So, I went back to the doctor; he recommended medication again so I took what he prescribed; he recommended counselling, so I sat in front of strangers and poured my heart out. Still, nothing worked.

The only thing that helped was running. Every morning, and sometimes again later, I would run for hours across ploughed fields and pathless roads for miles, in rain, wind and sun. It was a physical therapy, simple and cheap, the only thing it cost was my own blood and sweat.

Another thing: I got a job, too. Mum thought it was too soon, the doctor agreed. But what could I do? I hadn't a choice, I literally had no money and I couldn't keep taking it from Mum, she didn't have it to give. I asked my bank for a loan to tide me over till I could get back on my feet, but I didn't even make it to the credit check. Jobless and out of the country for three years, I could hardly blame them. I wouldn't have lent me money either.

I searched for jobs but there weren't many, not ones I was qualified for. Ended up as a machinist, working in a dirty grey factory, pressing buttons and pulling levers. Long shifts, four on, four off, it was tough. When people say they would do any job to support their family, this was the job they were talking about. Windowless buildings, womanless, air thick with dust, angry men and thick boys, pissed off about everything they had or didn't have. My hands hurt, my back hurt those first few weeks, but what hurt the most wasn't my muscles and bones. They may have paid me six pounds an hour but they took away a lot more.

But it worked, the running, the job, getting out of the house. Edges became smoother and small steps became strides. I didn't think I would ever be truly fixed but I wasn't broken any more. My sky was looking bluer, paler than yours, but blue nonetheless.

November became December.

I was still waiting for something and I knew this wasn't it. Not yet.

4

"Wow."

"What do you think?" I took off my dust mask.

"I think she'll love it."

Coughing. "It's not finished obviously, but the hard part is done."

"Can't wait to see her open it."

"If I get it done in time." More coughing.

"You will. Here," Mum said, passing me a mug of tea. "Warm up those hands." Drinking, we stood in our coats staring at the carcass of a shed. "I should have had a girl. I would've been better suited to this sort of parenting, dainty things, pretty things. You always had me climbing bloody trees or building army forts."

"Why didn't you?"

"Didn't we tell you? We must have," Mum said, sitting on her wall.

"No, you never did. I don't think I ever asked."

"I miscarried."

"I never knew that. Sorry."

"It happened when you were about five," said Mum, checking her rose bushes.

"Did you not try again? I thought they were quite common."

"I had three in total, some easier to take than others, the last was especially hard. By that point I was broken and tired, the moment was lost. Still, we were blessed, one little miracle in a lifetime is enough."

"And now you have Molly, too. Where is Molly?" realizing I was missing a child.

"Don't worry. Next door has taken her to the farm. She won't know a thing. I can't believe it's the same shed."

"Don't think Dad would mind, do you?"

"He hasn't got much choice, has he? Besides, it was a waste, all of his tools and machines just sitting there, left to rust and perish." Mum sipped her drink. "I'm guessing pink will be the colour."

"You'd be right."

"I've got an old bone china tea set she could have. It's a bit worse for wear, but it will suit your theme. What are you doing with all this?" she said, inspecting the pile of crap and debris piled on her lawn.

"With the wood, I'll try and knock something up. An oven maybe, or a little dinner table, something for Molly to use when she hosts her first afternoon tea."

"And what about the heavy stuff? Sell it on eBay?"

"It would cost a fortune to post. Better off putting an advertisement in the shop, or just giving it away."

"It must be worth a fortune. I know the amount of money your father used to plough into that bloody workshop. I tell who might take it off your hands, your dad's old friend Martin. I haven't seen him around in a while, from what I've heard he isn't too well. But I know he'd get some use out of all this junk. He only lives up the road."

"I don't want to bother him if he's unwell."

"He's been unwell for years. His lungs and heart have taken a fair battering over the years. I'll give him a ring for you if you'd like. I'm sure he'd bite your arm off."

"What was his name again?"

"Martin Baxter. Taught in the same school as your dad."

"Baxter. Sounds familiar. Was he there when I was at school?"

"Most probably."

"Smelt like an ashtray. Looked like Geoff Capes."

"I don't know who Geoff Capes is, but yes he was never too far away from a cigarette, or a Scotch for that matter."

"Here you go, Mum," I passed her my empty mug, "I better get this finished off, get all the panels cleaned down. I want this ready for painting tomorrow."

"Let me know if you need anything," she said, walking back down the garden. "I'll ring Martin and then I'll start thinking about dinner. You've put a lot of work into this, Tom. I'm really proud."

"It's only a shed, Mum."

"Not to me, it isn't. And it certainly won't be just a shed to Molly." She ripped off a handful of thyme and headed into the kitchen as I returned my attention back to wood and splinters. My mind filled with something other than dead wives and twisted metal.

★ ★ ★

"Is that a Sureweld 103 arc welder?"

I'd been at Mr Baxter's house for less than ten minutes. He wasn't how I'd imagined, nor was the house. I don't know what I expected of a former teacher, but it wasn't this.

"This is a treasure chest, young man. Pillar drill, bench grinder. You sure you don't want more for these? There is a lot of money in these boxes. I mean some of it is ancient, but fantastic pieces of kit."

"I'll have to take your word for it. I haven't a clue," I said, moving a stack of old curled newspapers from the chair so I could sit down.

I looked around his kitchen – it was old and unloved. It looked like breakfast hadn't been washed up yet, nor dinner the night previous. I'd be surprised if he had running water.

"What did you teach before you retired?"

"Officially, myself and your father taught everything on the art curriculum. Unofficially, I was your fine arts guy, life drawings, watercolours. Your father was a wood and metal man. Damn good artist though, mind. A better artist than me, the things he could do with ink and graphite. Blew me away."

"I never knew he drew."

"Well he didn't. Found it limiting and predictable. He preferred all the 'isms', cubism, neo-expressionism – he was a little pretentious like that. Me, I just liked to draw women's tits, that or trees. Strange to be aroused by such polar opposites."

"Is that one of yours?" I pointed over his shoulder to a picture hung up at an angle in a doorway.

"It is, yes."

"From round here?"

"No. Badby Woods. Where I used to live. Spent many a summer in those woods, I can tell you. A certain Joseph Merrick used to be rather fond of it, too. I don't suppose that name would be familiar to you?"

"I'm a huge David Lynch fan, so yes. Is that Badby too?" both of us looked at the similar picture underneath.

He laughed and coughed. "That is Fangorn Forest. A bit further afield. Trees are great subjects. I find them less prone to breaking a pose."

Mr Baxter attempted to lift another box from the floor to the table. It looked an effort. He wasn't in a good place physically, looked like his legs and back weren't playing to the same tune. He was a large man, still his clothes hung off him like they were meant for someone larger.

"When was the last time you saw Dad?"

"In the hospital," he said, taking a seat, breathing out like it was a relief. "I'd seen your mother completely by coincidence, she said he'd had a funny turn, offered to take me to see him."

"How was he?"

"We mostly played cards. I don't think he thought he was dying. He was already planning his next exhibition. Talked a lot about you, in fact."

"What did he say?"

"Lots of things. Think he just missed you. I got the impression you had been away quite a while."

"He wasn't in pain, was he?"

"Not when I saw him. He looked on top form. I miss him, he was a damn good friend."

A cat came through the back-door flap and tiptoed around its food bowl. It purred at my feet like it was about to spray its territory. It looked in worse shape than its owner.

"Last time I saw your mother she said you were living in America?"

"I was. But I decided to come home."

"For good?"

"I'm not sure. At least for the short term. Need to find a job – well, I have a job, what I need is a career."

"Good luck in finding one round here. Unless you don't mind driving a tractor or a forklift."

"I may have to move. Find a city."

"Not going back to America, then?"

"No, I don't think so."

"Missed home, hey?"

"No, my wife died."

"I'm sorry to hear that."

We looked down at our feet. Men's natural reaction.

"How are you holding up?"

"Better than I was. Trying not to forget her. Trying my hardest not to remember."

"Loss is a funny beast. I have never been one to cope well with such an emotion."

"Your wife died too?"

"She might as well have." He laughed, then coughed, like one always followed the other. "No, she left me about ten years ago. Just walked out the door one morning and didn't come back."

"Why?"

"I'm a difficult man to live with. There are reasons artists are solitary creatures. We struggle in the company of others. She was a good woman. Treated me far better than I deserved."

45

"You didn't meet anyone new?"

"Does it look like I've met someone new?" he laughed loud, coughed louder. "Take a look around. Take a look at me. I'm a Neanderthal. I'm from a different age. I'm good with my hands, but not a lot else."

"You still love her?"

"I'm afraid I do, Tom. That's the problem."

★ ★ ★

At the door we said our farewells, he thanked me for the donation of Dad's old junk, said I'd made an old man very happy, gave me an analogy about not looking back, closing doors, not leaving them ajar.

"You know I think I may even be your unofficial godfather?" he said. "Though your dad was a bit drunk at the time he gave me the title."

"Seems like a lot of things were unofficial back then."

"Well it was the seventies. We did things at a different speed back then."

"Thank you, Martin. I hope things turn out well for you."

"I'm sure they won't. But there's still hope for you."

"Let's hope so," I said, stepping into the fresh air, breathing out, like I'd been holding it in.

As I drove home, I couldn't help but smile. I'd been set up. Mum swore I hadn't been, laughed it off when I brought it up, but I knew my own mother. This was an intervention, a warning of what might happen. I'd met the Ghost of Christmas Yet to Come. I genuinely think Mum thought seeing my morbid future up close would be enough of a threat. God bless her for trying.

★ ★ ★

"What would you like from Santa, then?"

"Chickens." Molly was still looking at me funny.

"Chickens?"

46

"Yep, a girl and a boy one. Girls lay the eggs. Boys make the cock-a-doodle-do noise."

"It's a big responsibility looking after animals. You have to make sure they are fed, kept clean, kept safe from naughty foxes."

"I know. I have a book about chickens. Ouch, Daddy!"

"Sorry," I said, as Molly returned to staring at my genitals and I detangled her hair.

Baths used to be a mum-and-daughter thing. They sat in the tub whilst I sorted out downstairs, got dinner on, ironed things. Now the job of shampooing and detangling had fallen to me. Molly still looked a little uncomfortable with my naked self, intrigued and grossed out, just like her mother used to be.

"Anything else you gonna ask for from Santa? Something easier for the elves to wrap?" I asked, helping her with her pyjama top.

"No, just chickens please. I have enough toys."

"Are you sure there isn't anything else?"

"I'd like some mummy cuddles."

I kissed the back of her head. "What colour chickens do you like?"

Downstairs Mum was in her dressing gown, staring at the tray of chocolates on her lap, brushing her hair, always brushing her hair.

"She go down OK?" she said, mid-toffee.

"Out like a light," I said as I fell into the sofa. "Mum, have you watched *Bambi* with her recently?"

Mum looked confused. "Few days ago, I bought her a stack of old VHS tapes from the charity shop. Why?"

"She was asking me questions about it. You think it's appropriate?"

"Why wouldn't I?"

"The last thing she needs right now is tragedy and a dead mother."

"Don't be so silly. It's a bloody cartoon."

"Just be mindful of what you let her watch or read."

Mum didn't answer. She ate another chocolate. "Her chest wasn't great today, Tom."

"How bad? Worse than last week?"

"No, not that bad. She wasn't in pain, just doing that grunting thing again. Might be worth us booking her in to see the doctor again just to be on the safe side." She winced as she knelt down to grab her book off the floor.

"I'll ring them first thing. You OK, Mum?"

"I'm just old. No cure for that, I'm afraid. I wish you didn't have to go to work tomorrow. The weekends go so quick. I don't envy you spending your whole week in that horrible factory. Just remember it isn't forever, Tom. Just get your head down. Save up and then you and Molly can start planning for your future, whatever or wherever that might be."

"Feels like it will take forever. I need to earn more. Or work more."

"I can always help. I've nothing in regard to savings. I could borrow on the house, I've plenty of equity."

"No, Mum. That's your money."

"I'd like to help."

"You've helped enough."

"Please take these off me, Tom, before I eat the whole box. I shouldn't be eating so much sugar this close to bedtime." She passed me the tray of chocolates.

"Molly said she wanted chickens for Christmas by the way. Is this your doing?"

"No, that's all her, I'm afraid. I think it's a good idea. Better than wasting money on something she'll be bored of by the new year. Not to mention the prospect of fresh eggs. You had a missed call by the way. Completely went out of my mind. Rang whilst you were at Martin's."

"Who was it? I don't know anyone who has my number, unless it was work."

"Said his name was Vince. He was a bit rude actually."

"Vince?"

"That's what he said."

"Was he American?"

Mum nodded. "I thought he was a wrong number at first. Thought I was about to be sold a time share again. You all right, Tom?"

"No, I'm fine, honest. Just a surprise. What did he say?"

"Just gave me a number and where he was. I wrote it down, it's over by the phone. He said to ring him as soon as you can."

"I wonder how he got this number."

"Me too. I'm supposed to be ex-directory." Mum got up out of her chair. "You coming to bed, or staying up?"

"I think I'll stay down a bit longer. I'm not that tired."

"I'll say night then, Tom. Going to read my book and have an early one. I've loaded the fire, so it shouldn't need any more coal. Make sure you ring this Vince. He sounded pretty hurried."

"We are about eight hours ahead. I don't want to wake him."

"Oh, he said he was in London."

"London. What's he doing there?"

Mum shrugged. "You'll have to ask him." Mum lent over and kissed my head. "Night, Tom".

It was inevitable I'd revert to an old habit. I grabbed mum's car keys off the side and headed for the front door.

★ ★ ★

I drove, not far, my aim wasn't distance. My village was small, it took less than a mile for kerbs and tarmac to turn to mud and sludge, street lights to complete darkness. I parked the car on a long stretch of deserted road, fields either side, engine on, my lights illuminating the first few yards in front.

A helicopter buzzed overhead, loud and then quiet as it sped over the horizon towards a nearby airport. In the distance, I saw the Iron Man over the chalk quarry. To look at those lights as an adult I could still see how it would be easy to believe. Sons believed their fathers and I believed mine every time he told the story, even if I always knew it wasn't a metal giant, it wasn't two eyes, it wasn't my friend that I used to wave to. In the cold light of day, it was just a tower, looked nothing like an Iron Giant with eyes and a smile. Dad always made life a fantasy. Men in suits were spies. The school doctor, a good witch. His appendix scar, a bullet wound. Dad was a great father, they both were great parents and it was a shame they were robbed of having more.

I forgot how magical childhood was living here. So many things to explore, endless hills and fields, woods to be climbed and conquered, an Iron Man. I took the village for granted, focussed on what it didn't give me, rather than what it had, spent most of my teenage years plotting my escape. And now I was back, plotting a similar escape again, even though I'd chosen to return. I wanted to love my village, I wished I could be happy living there, it just wasn't where I wanted to be, where I thought I'd end up. America had always been the goal, America was the only place I'd ever wanted to live.

My fascination with all things Americana was gradual and constant. It wasn't an intentional love affair, but it was a love affair. One that started young: a cartoon beagle that talked in balloons, a Butthead and a Beavis. There was the food and drink too, stuff that fizzed or fattened, the stuff I'd spend my pocket money on, the stuff I'd eat behind Mum's back. It didn't stop when I grew up either, the music gave me the same type of hit, grunge, punk, hip hop. I couldn't get enough, everything there was faster and better, the weather, the women. It was of no surprise when I studied it for two years and I loved studying it too, it was never a chore, never felt like a forced subject. And I read everything, Columbus, Custer, Clinton, the Constitution, I wanted to know it all. But I still didn't know enough, books and lectures and essays weren't enough education. I had to smell and taste it. Had to see it for myself.

I knew one day I would go there and once I did it did not disappoint, I fell in love with it even more, for reasons I predicted, but for a lot of reasons I never would've seen coming. I had no intention of coming back. I was there for good. There wasn't an alternative dream. America was the dream. England was the punishment.

Mum asked me a while back to try and explain why I loved LA so much but I couldn't, not in the way I wanted. I could have told her about the glamour of it all, the history, the buzz, the culture. But all I said was, I missed the sunshine, which was true, but selling the place rather short. Here in the village I was always safe and content, but yesterdays and tomorrows felt very much the same. Hollywood was all about the 'just around the corners'.

I knew all about that first hand, the curve balls the city could throw at you. The excitement that your day and your life could change in an instant. Being in the right place at the right time, or the opposite. That was the gamble, that is what I missed, the uncertainty of it all.

Coming back, I realized how much I needed that uncertainty. The constant looming threat of a low but also the constant chase for the highs. And even though LA was hard on me I always felt things were about to change. That city gave me the grandest of ideas, some realistic, not even plausible. But honestly, I felt anything could happen. There was possibility. The endless kind.

I never had that here. This was a place for the very young or very old. It had always felt too small to me, and all one colour, all one volume. But somehow, I needed to find a way of making a life here, both financially and emotionally, where I would wake up inspired, rather than lethargic. Being safe and content wasn't always a good thing. Every single decision I'd made, travelling across the world on my own, moving in with Cassie two weeks after meeting her, taking a job as a tour guide. They had never been the safe option, and putting all my cards on the table, I'd always gone out of my way to live life a little recklessly. Later, it was different, Cassie and Molly came first in every decision, now just Molly. But I still had to think about me, too, I had to find way of living here, not just surviving but prospering.

I didn't realise how low I'd gotten when I first arrived back. Didn't matter what I did, or who I spoke to, nothing helped. I was drowning and all anyone could do was describe the water. Every day felt like a slog, like I had to get through it, that was no way for a father to live, to wish away his time, celebrating midnights, when it should have been mornings, or middays with Molly.

One night I took the car over the Humber Bridge. I'd be lying if I said I didn't briefly think about the 100ft jump as I drove across it, how easy it would've been to fling myself over into that black water, I wouldn't have been the first who had done it and I wouldn't be the last. The finality of it all was a tempting alternative, and an easy way out. I may not have stopped the car that night or even jumped, but I thought about it and that was close enough to reality to make me want to change.

I hadn't thought of LA in a long time, that was done purposely and for a good reason, and it had been working. I had been in a good place, I was on the right path. I may not have been happy all the time, I may have known I hadn't the perfect life or job or situation, but I was on the right path, I was moving on. One phone call and it felt like I was back to square one all over again. Vince ringing me was like America calling.

I could just not ring him, I thought. I had no moral obligation to contact Vince. Our friendship was brief, we hadn't spoken in over a year, maybe even longer. For God's sake, he didn't even call when Cassie died, or even attend her funeral. I had no loyalty towards him. But it didn't mean I wasn't curious about why he had rung.

This was more than a phone call. There would be repercussions if I called Vince back. Butterfly wings, dominoes, ripples, it would start a chain of events. This wouldn't be a chat, it would be an offer, a proposal, a favour. The easiest thing to do was to forget he'd ever rung me at all.

Two days later, I was on a train bound for London and snow.

5

The journey home from London was a long one, angry commuters and festive cheer, a day of being on trains both under and over ground. I was glad of the time to think and digest Vince's offer, but it also felt good to finally get a hot shower, wash London off and take a breath.

"Is this job legal?" Mum asked after I'd told her what Vince was offering, or at least the version I told her.

"Course it's legal." Even though I wasn't quite sure myself.

"Will it keep you busy?" she said, slicing bread.

"For a while at least. It isn't permanent."

"Will it make you happy?"

"I don't know. Happy isn't the right word. Excited."

"It's not going to harm anyone?"

"Not intentionally. Not me, you or Molly."

"But someone will get hurt."

"What is it you think I'm going to do?"

"I don't know. It all sounds very ominous," she said, spreading butter.

"No one will get hurt. No guns or drugs or violence, I promise."

"When do you have to start?"

"Soon, was all he said. I will be away a lot, could be for weeks and months. Means I have to leave you and Molly for longer than I'd like."

"Is it worth it?"

"Yes. I think so. Financially, yes."

"And for you? Will it get you back on your feet?"

"I think I need this."

"Then it looks like you've made your decision."

She got up and kissed my head. She was about to go to bed.

"Mum, do you still have your old library card?"

"What for?" she yawned.

"Books, funnily enough."

"OK, I walked into that one. What sort of books?"

"Just books. There is stuff I might not be able to view online."

"Is this how it's going to be from now on? Secrets and lies."

"I'll tell you in more detail tomorrow. I'm pretty tired. Long day."

"There's a casserole in the oven. Even 007 needs to eat from time to time." She was about to go upstairs. I was already scribbling notes. I had lists and ideas I needed to get down on paper.

"I will. Just got a few things to do."

"Those things can wait for now. You get some rest. Your new life can wait till morning."

★ ★ ★

I didn't hear from Vince after that first meeting at Christmas. I waited, then waited some more, did my best to keep occupied, prepared what Vince asked me to have ready. Studied like an exam, read every article, watched every clip. My bedroom became my office, clippings and cut-outs, maps and pins. Wall-to-wall investigation, solving a crime, or about to commit one.

Still I waited, kept busy, kept preparing, factory in the day, researcher at night, even managed to turn a year older, twenty-six became twenty-seven. I nearly started to give up. I was tempted just to throw all the reams of paper and piles of jotted notes away, screw them up, fling them into Mum's fire, watch all my work turn to orange.

Till finally on a normal Tuesday at the end of February, out of the blue, I got the call, the green light.

"She is coming, Tommy. She is coming," he kept saying.

★ ★ ★

Cassie had never been on a train. She'd always wanted to, had visions of individual wooden cabins, china plates and cutlery, limitless indulgence – she'd read far too much about the Orient Express. Probably best she never did see the reality, it was no 1935, that's for sure.

Even though I'd done the exact same journey only two months before, I was equally as dumbfounded second time around with the price of my ticket – a trip to London wasn't too far removed from what I had paid to cross the Atlantic. Fuck, I needed the money, with the small amount I had left in my account I knew those trips were going to leave a dent that would be hard to fill.

I'd come better prepared than on my first visit back in December. A packed lunch, a flask of tea, a heavy book, and of course all the things I'd need to discuss it over with Vince. I'd be lying if I said I hadn't been excited by it all, it had given me a new energy and purpose. Don't get me wrong, I was nervous, and no matter how much of my book I read, how many pages I turned, all I could think of was how absurd this all was. But at that very moment there wasn't another option and absurd was better than sensible. I'd refused to be the grieving widower any more and I had to force the change.

I rested my head against the window of the train, looked at the blur of green. If she was coming as Vince said she was, then we both had to be ready. And I felt readier than ever.

★ ★ ★

She offered me another tap water. I wasn't sure how long she would let me sit there without paying for something that made her boss a profit. I felt for some coins in my pocket, it didn't feel enough to even buy a coffee, instead I continued to fold napkins, watched people eat spaghetti. He'd chosen the same place as last time, the closest restaurant to Euston station, playing every Dean Martin song with an Italian chorus. The waitress brought over a bowl of olives, said she felt sorry for me with my water. I thanked her – she was pretty, foreign, not Italian, but foreign enough to make you feel you could be eating on the Amalfi coast.

On meeting Vince back before Christmas, despite the difference in appearance – the whiter teeth, the smaller waist, the smarter suit – everything else had remained the same. He had greeted me with long hugs and hard pats on the back. He briefly mentioned how sorry he was for my loss, ordered us both drinks, apologized for his absence, explained his whys and why nots, ordered us both lunch. I nodded and he talked, it was all heartfelt. Thankfully for us both the small talk was kept small, and quickly he moved on to the important matter of why he was here, and even more importantly, why I was here. If indeed his apology was sincere, it was a quick one – he didn't fly halfway round the world to offer condolences

"Tommy."

He grabbed my shoulders, firmly.

"Hey, Vince."

"Fucking weather. Fucking taxi drivers." He looked wet.

"Tough time?"

"Nothing an espresso won't sort out." He ordered over a waitress and demanded drinks. Menus followed.

"You look better." He said.

"Do I?"

"You've put on weight, you look better for it."

"What's with the bust-up nose, Vince? You been making new friends since I last saw you?"

"Would you believe me if I said a door did it?"

"No, I wouldn't believe that for one minute."

"Good, cos it ain't the truth. You hungry?"

"I could eat."

Food was ordered, it arrived promptly, not like the waitress had a choice.

"How's Molly?"

"She is improving. We're not there yet."

"How old now?"

"She'll be three in September."

"Early fall, hey. They grow fucking fast don't they? And your Mom?"

"She's well."

"Your dad's passed, hasn't he?"

"Few years back, yes."

"Mine too. Cancer." He put his hand inside his jacket. "You fancy a smoke? Bought two hundred in the departure lounge, that and a case of Woodford Reserve. I'll give you a few packs."

I took a cigarette.

"I'm guessing we can't smoke these in here. Fancy stepping outside? Better not still be fucking raining."

Outside the smokers were congregated around patio heaters. It wasn't raining but it was far from warm.

"How is LA?"

"Brutal. Just how I like it. You not fancy coming back?"

"One day. Not sure how it works."

"How what works?"

"Well, me and Cassie never married. I don't know how the laws work. I didn't stick around long enough to ask."

"Well, Molly is half American, that must count for something."

"I've no idea."

"Place is full of immigrants. I'm sure two more wouldn't do no harm. I'll find out if ever you're serious about coming home. I've got friends in high and low places."

"I do miss it."

"I know what you mean. When I go to New York, even here in London. They might be cities, but they ain't LA. She's an animal, Tommy."

"Who'd have thought me and you, two of the worst tour guides in Hollywood, would be smoking Camels in the centre of London, hey, Vince?"

"It's no White Horse Inn."

"No, can't imagine we'll get a free hot dog here. Can't see no jukebox either."

"I'd rather be back there than here. Jeez, this place is too fucking cold. I can't feel my hands and dare not feel down for my cock."

"So, what's the story with the nose?"

"Let's just say it will heal quicker than my pending injunction."

"You make it a habit of upsetting people don't you."

"I was just doing my job. Don't worry, her bodyguard will be getting a letter with a nice little misdemeanour charge any day now."

"Which 'her' are you talking about?"

"The same 'her' in that little folder of yours."

★ ★ ★

"Right, timescales," Vince said, feeding himself more mortadella. "She lands at Heathrow, April 2nd. Early hours."

I made notes, I could tell this gave Vince a hard-on, he liked being the boss and me his secretary. I listened as he talked, making more notes and scribbles as he fired off instructions.

"Next day, she is attending some red-carpet event. Every pap and his dog will be hosing her down. I'm inclined to not even bother with that one. It would be nice to get one of her walking off the plane though at least, ruffled, no sleep, no make-up. The uglier the better. Ugly sells."

By now we were on our third round of coffees, Vince had just ordered grappa.

"I've been informed she is travelling down to the coast on the 5th, some farmhouse out in the sticks. I'll sent you the zip code once I have it, I should get it in a couple of days. That way we can do a bit of recon work, scope out the surroundings, find some good angles. Filming is due to start a week later, so there is a good seven days where she will be out and about. How are you for these dates so far?"

I read back my notes. "So, London on the 2nd for a few days, then Devon the 5th."

"We'll head down to Devon on the 4th, give us a day to find our feet. You can sort out transport and logistics. Don't worry about money," he said, throwing a roll of notes across the table. "I'll give you more as we go along. We are going to need a car. Something inconspicuous, something like a sedan. In grey. Something you wouldn't look twice at. But make sure it's reliable."

"They're all farmers down there, Vince, the roads aren't even roads, they are mud tracks – it's not Melrose. A sedan is out of the ordinary. A Jeep is most likely to blend in."

Vince agreed. "OK, make it bottle-green. In very good condition, with a big tank. Please tell me you still have a UK licence."

I nodded.

"How much will a Jeep cost in this neck of the woods?" he said, chewing olive stones.

"Not worth buying. I'll check prices on a rental. You not having any bread?" I said, pointing at the bread basket.

"Oh, me and bread are no longer friends. Makes me fat and gives me heartburn."

We picked at our food again.

"I always thought paps worked in teams?"

"Fuck teams, Tommy. The more involved, the lower the cut."

"You do realise two is classed as a team?"

"I know, I'm breaking my own rule on this one. Anyway, I can't get too close. I need to keep my distance till my legal team fight it out over this fucking injunction. Tell me about the castle."

"Security will be heavy on set."

"No matter. No one's too fussed about location shots. The big focus is when she is at her base, the farmhouse. She will be there two months, three tops, gives us plenty of time. What do you reckon to the target?"

"What, the farmhouse?"

"The girl, you moron."

"I can see why she has so much media attention, put it that way."

"That's why it is so important we can get in there first. That's why you are so important to the operation. The English paps aren't too interested in her, but she is all they are talking about across the pond. You'll give us the upper hand, you know your way around these places. Hey, what do you think of her boyfriend?"

"He sounds horrendous."

"Fuck, yes. Our price doubles if he tags along, but I've heard nothing to suggest he's coming."

"Look, Vince, I need to go, it's getting late. It's a long journey back home."

"Hey, feel free to stop at my hotel. It's big enough."

"No, Molly will wonder where I am. I promised I'd be home."

"Tommy, we have got a lot to get through. I'm sure she will be fine."

"No, I must go."

"I'll give you another hundred if you stay."

I looked at him. I couldn't tell if he was being serious.

"You stay one night, I'll make it two hundred for the trouble. I can't say fairer than that."

"OK, Vince. But I'm leaving first thing."

"Good man." He ushered over the waitress. "More grappa please, doll."

"I'll need to ring my mum. Tell her the situation."

"Fine. You check in with the Mommy."

He looked at me, a mad grin, folding more meat into his mouth, stuffing himself like a king.

"It's gonna be an interesting couple of months, Mr Tommy Smyth. You ready?"

"I'm ready."

"Good man. We need to be on point with this."

"We? Sounds like it will just be me."

"Hey, I'll be involved, don't you worry. Now let's talk some more about the target."

"I'm not calling her the target."

"LG, then. That's what she's getting called these days."

"Initials. How 21st century."

"Initials is good Tommy. Means she's getting more famous," he said, raising his glass to another salute.

★ ★ ★

Fast-forward a few hours and I was on a fold-out sofa. Vince was spreadeagled in nothing but socks, at least I still had on my clothes, wished I had a toothbrush to get rid of the liquor taste.

Tonight was pointless. We didn't even talk much about the girl, we briefly talked long camera lenses, but it was too technical for such a late hour, so millimetre discussions would spill over to tomorrow. For the most part, Vince turned to flirting with married waitresses, and like me they played along, long enough to keep him entertained. It was harmless, both parties knew this. They were nice girls, my age I expected, younger actually, they joked about my accent, sometimes I forgot how it must sound, the mix of Yorkshire and California. Vince was snoring. Beside his bed he had photos of his two children, and a wife I never even knew he had either.

"I won't fall in love again, Tommy, that's for sure. My wallet couldn't take it," he'd said before as he stumbled out of our black cab. "She's the one for me. We drive each other insane, but she's the one. You Tommy?"

"Me what?"

"Another woman?"

I didn't answer, he was already stumbling towards his hotel.

I'd rung home hours before. Mum sounded angry, said Molly was upset. I'd hoped to catch her before bedtime, but I'd rung too late. I should have gone home but I was in a predicament where I couldn't turn down money, especially not the amount Vince was throwing at me. Vince was promising a lot that night. Apparently, I'd be getting a cell phone, apparently a laptop too. I didn't know how much these photos would make, but the way Vince was spending it, I had to assume it was lucrative.

I never understood the fascination of celebrity. I had been a tour guide so I knew its pull, but it was a different fascination now. People wanted their stars to be accessible, they wanted to see them off screen more than on. We now lived in a 'Look at me' or 'Look at her' generation and the celebrities were worse than their audience. Self-promotion and documentation to prove they existed and not just existing but leaving legacies and dynasties. Hey, I'd bought the magazines myself, not out of interest, but I still bought them, funded the organization that profits from others' misfortune, it was part and parcel, part of the role of celebrity. She wouldn't even be coming here if it weren't for the media attention, she needed us as much as we needed her. She was just another creature of our time. Still, didn't make it feel right, it was spying and my new profession was to be the spy.

I felt sick from the grappa. I walked over to the windows, blanket wrapped round my shoulders as I slid open the doors. The fresh air hit me, as did the sunrise. The balcony was high up, an impressive view of bridges and spires, a horizon of grandeur. It was hard to appreciate with such a hangover.

I thought of Cassie, asked her if I was doing the right thing, asked her questions I knew would not be answered. I went back to bed, closed my eyes, but it was too bright and too close to morning to go back to sleep. Instead I decided to go home, run away whilst Vince was still sleeping off last night. Left him a note, thanked him for the opportunity, but it wasn't for me, that there were different ways to make a fortune.

* * *

He rang constantly the next few days, but I didn't answer his calls. Vince even sent money but I still didn't take the bait. He messaged me, I messaged back, him offering the world, me declining all the riches he threw at me.

Days went by as I tried to get back to normality, cleared my bedroom of anything to with Vince, stashed all the paperwork and notes in a box and stuffed it in my wardrobe. Took Molly on long walks, took her clothes shopping, tried to work out my next move.

Then one night there was a knock at the front door. I already knew who it was before Mum got up to answer it. I was just surprised it took him a week, I'd been expecting him since my escape.

6

"Did I oversleep or something?" I asked, surprised by the set table, the tablecloth, the matching teapot.

"No, but I think a certain little girl may have under-slept. Didn't you Molly?"

Molly smiled, she was on Vince's lap as Mum poured him another filter coffee, as Vince took the last slice of toast.

"You should be very honoured, Vince," I said, looking for any remaining breakfast. "These plates and cups are normally reserved for royalty," I added, resorting to a box of cereal.

"She is an excellent host. Thank you, Mrs S." Vince raised his cup.

"Is your back OK, Vincent?"

"My back is hunky-dory. I thought I would have gotten here earlier. I didn't think I'd be turning up as late as I did. And there was me thinking a train would be on time."

"I thought Tom would have at least given you his bed?"

"Honestly, it's fine."

"Vincent was nice enough to grab us all eggs and bacon." Mum looked at him like she suddenly had a new son. "It will be ready in five minutes."

"Up early was you, Vince?" I smirked. "Unusual for you?"

"Early worm, Tommy." He smiled. "I could get used to this rural living. Met me a couple of farm girls. Talked to some broad with two Great Danes. Some old chap with a fishing line cornered me. Kept calling me Joe."

"Don't mind him, his head's still stuck in World War II," Mum said. "Probably thinks you're trying to steal all the women

64

with promises of tights and chewing gum. You'll be the talk of the village. They don't see too many new faces round here."

"What's the plan, then?" Vince stretched, a yawn and a smile. "What are we doing with the rest of the day?"

"I thought you'd be heading back to London?"

"Tom, don't be rude. I'm sure Vince wouldn't mind staying a little longer."

"Yes, Tommy listen to your mom. It would be a shame for me to travel so far and not be shown around."

"Let's all go lambing." Mum said, looking pleased with herself.

"Lambing, as in lambs?" Vince said, taking a bite of toast.

"Yes, Vincent. Baby sheep."

Molly started clapping. It sounded like she agreed with the idea.

"Vince, you don't have to come," I said. "If you've come to talk, we can stay back, say what needs to be said. Then you can go. That's what you are here for, isn't it?"

"Tom. What has gotten into you this morning? I'm sorry, Vincent, for my son's rude behaviour."

"That's OK, Mrs S. Tommy is right. It was wrong for me to turn up unannounced."

"Rubbish, Vincent. We are going lambing and you are coming – you're invited too. That is final."

"If you say so. You OK with that, Tommy? Me tagging along?" knowing I could hardly decline.

"The more the merrier," I said, as Mum ushered me into the kitchen, towards the smell of bacon fat and the threat of a telling off.

★ ★ ★

"I like Vince," Molly said through her dummy under the glow of her night light. "He's a funny man."

"He certainly is."

"He pulls funny faces." She laughed. "And he sounds like Mommy."

"You remember how Mommy talks?"

"Yes. Mommy calls me 'Moo'."

"What else?"

Molly suddenly went shy, her voice a whisper. "She was very pretty."

"That is very true."

"She sings me lots of songs. And combs my hair like a princess."

"You remember a lot, don't you?"

"Daddy, Vince's face went green at the farm?"

"I don't think he liked lambing very much."

Molly found this hilarious. I was lying beside her, curled up in her bed, my spine bent and my knees tucked in, surrounded by stuffed animals and dolls, a position I found myself in most nights. Painful but perfect.

"Vince can sleep in my room."

"No, he's going home tomorrow. Early I expect."

"Where Mommy lives?"

"Yes, going back home."

"Heaven?"

"Come on, Molly, you need to close your eyes for me," I said, kissing her head goodnight.

I found Vince and Mum downstairs drinking bourbon, laughing at the funniest joke they had ever heard or told.

"You're not getting my Mum drunk are you, Vince?" I said.

"I might be." He touched her leg, as she swooned. "Just telling your Mom about the Hills."

"It sounds amazing, Tom. So, you've seen the Shangri-La studio then, Vincent?"

"Yes, Mam, many times. We both have."

"My husband was a big Dylan fan. He would've loved it there. Have you been to the Getty Museum? You must have been," she said, fiddling with her hair in a way I'd never seen.

"I've never been. Art isn't really my thing. Unless I was selling it."

"Art is for everyone. When you fly back, Vincent, you must start educate yourself in the arts. It's very liberating."

"But I'm living here with you. I'm never leaving."

"Fine by me," she said, as I noticed my mother's plunging neckline and jewellery. "We'll have to get bunk beds for you and Tom. What do you reckon? You fancy bunking up with Vincent?"

"You took your wedding ring off, Mum?"

She pulled her tongue out, she sensed this wasn't a night for three, found a way to excuse herself, wished us both goodnight. We waited for her to go upstairs, sat and waited till we had the room to ourselves.

"You've got a nice set-up here. Molly's a great girl, your Mom's a star," said Vince, pouring himself a drink from a bottle that wasn't his.

"Things are working out OK. I don't really want much to change."

"That's not what you said in London."

"That was London. I hadn't drunk like that in a long time."

"Look, I know you're not too happy with me turning up here, that is fucking obvious. But what was I supposed to do? You weren't answering any of my calls."

"I agree that was wrong, Vince. I should have given you the common courtesy of telling you to your face."

"What will it take for you to change your mind. Money?"

"It's not the money, it's just not me, Vince. I haven't got that ruthless bone in me. I don't want be one of those vultures swarming around an SUV. A dozen men leaning over the bonnet, a dozen camera shots of some poor girl just trying to fill her car with fuel. I'm not a leech, I've seen them in Hollywood, they swarm about like a plague. It isn't natural. It isn't human."

"It's humanity in its purest form, Tommy. Celebrities have been around for fucking centuries. Fuck me, Cleopatra, Julius Caesar, Princess Diana. People are interested in people, especially the rich and powerful ones. That'll never change Tommy."

"I know it exists, Vince. I just don't want to be part of it."

"This will be different. You won't be a swarm. I don't want you following others. No one knows about this little cottage retreat. It'll be just you. This will be under the radar, a secret mission. Colonel Kurtz style. Come on, Tommy, you were one of the best tour guides I knew."

"That's hardly a compliment. Besides, I don't even think that is relevant. I'm not guiding anyone. I'm chasing. There is a difference."

"It is relevant, Tommy. You were the best cos you were smart. You get inside celebrities' heads, you know their next move. I still don't know why the Boss sacked you, she never knew talent when she saw it, never knew how to get the best out of people."

"She sacked me cos she knew deep down I hated it."

"You didn't hate it."

"I did, Vince. Every day I hated it. Showing people around a city, famous landmarks I was comfortable with that, that I actually enjoyed. I was never fine with what it turned into."

"But admit you was good at it."

"I did OK."

"Fuck that, Tommy, you were better than me then."

I said nothing. Vince wandered the room, exploring the walls, the art, the photos of a dead father and a dead wife. He turned back to me, away from Cassie, knowing she would not approve of this conversation.

"This girl's a cash cow, we get the right photo, we are talking a lot of dollars."

"No, Vince."

"What's the alternative? I mean seriously. Cutting sheet metal for the rest of your life? Pulling lambs out of arseholes like today? You have no money, Tommy, your Mom has no money, she told me so. I'm giving you a way out. Do you even have an alternative?"

"I haven't got one, is that what you want me to say? Is that why you are here? To make me feel like a failure?"

"I'm not a bad man, Tommy. We aren't bad men. We aren't harming the girl."

"It doesn't feel that way."

"One job and you are set. Hell, you probably won't need to work for six months after that. A year. Two years even."

"Seriously. That's how much I could earn?"

"If we do it right."

We stopped talking. Vince was walking around the room again. I had my head in my hands.

"Just once, Vince. One job and that is it. One job. Promise. You come home with your treasure chest. The big hero."

"We're breaking the law, aren't we? I've done my research. Trespassing on private property, intrusion. If we get caught."

"We won't get caught. You worry too much." Vince lent in, his hand on my knee. Hey, I love you, Tommy. I'm not out to get you. I'm here to help you. This is good for us."

"Good for our wallets, bad for the soul, hey."

He laughed. "Story of my life. You in?" He poured me another drink I never asked for. "I'll treat you to a Miceli's when you finally decide to come back home."

"Veal Scaloppini and a bit of old blue eyes."

"As always, Tommy." He smiled. His big perfect white teeth.

"OK, I'm in."

"Good man. Right then, lots to talk through." He sat beside me on the arm of the chair. "Talk me through it, step by step, what we know. LG arrives in a month…"

A week later Vince gave me a month's money. I quit my job. It felt good, better than good.

It felt like a fire had been lit.

7

The day had come. After all the planning it had finally arrived, it was happening, April 2nd was here. The airport terminal was as crazy as Vince said it would be, the plane was already an hour late. The mood was turning more and more unfriendly and impatient the longer the arrival was delayed. Paparazzi liked to earn their money fast, not having to be made to wait, it was a numbers game, and the more minutes they stared at the runway, the less they were being paid for their hourly rate. There was shouting and jostling for best positions, elbows and bad language, a controlled madness about to spill into chaos. There were little groups and packs, friendships and enemies. I heard accents too, French, German, people had come a long way for this.

I'd underestimated the press interest. I knew LG would get attention, even when I lived in LA she was causing ripples but I didn't expect the waves to have made their way this far overseas. If she was a girl to be rationed then there wasn't enough for everyone, she would be fought over, people here were in it for their own personal glory, best angles, best view. The better the photo and the quicker it was wired to some office somewhere, for men in ties to haggle and fight over, then the bigger their split.

But I wasn't in the rabble, I was away from the shouting and jostling, hanging back on the periphery, watching the melee unfold, as I stood alone in relative calm. To any person in the profession it must've looked a ridiculous position to have stood and it was obvious the rest of the rabble agreed, giving us sneers and smirks. But there was a reason for my location, a reason why I'd chosen the worst angle with potentially the least chance of a big pay cheque.

The night previous, Vince took a phone call, it was long and loud, he came off hysterical.

"We have hit the jackpot buddy!" he said, jumping off the couch.

"Really?"

"This shit just got interesting."

"What, is he coming with her? The boyfriend?"

"No, better than that."

"Well, what?"

He was pacing the floor.

"He's only gone and hit her."

"He hit her?"

"Some party last night. Left a mark, too."

"He hit her. What, like a punch?"

"Slap. Punch. Who gives a fuck anyways?"

"That guy is a prick. Someone saw him do it at the party, surely?"

"Apparently not, no one saw, it was over really quick, or if they did they are keeping it quiet. But it won't stay quiet for long."

"Is she OK?"

"It's a bruise, Tommy, course she's fucking OK. This changes tomorrow. We have to rethink. This is a game changer."

"It's domestic violence, that's what it is."

"She'll be fine. This could be big money for us."

"They'll find a way to cover it. Make-up. Sunglasses. It will be hidden."

"Still doesn't make it invisible. Right, we need to change lens, get us right in close. Let's hope to God this shit doesn't go viral before she arrives."

"The paps will catch wind of it? If you know I'm sure someone else does too."

"They don't have the same source as me. No one knows about this."

"Still a gamble."

"That bruise could make us a lot of zeros, Tommy boy, a gamble is necessary. We need to be smart. It's her left eye, so we have to think about our position." He grabbed the camera, fiddling with its buttons. "I can't stress enough how important it is you get a picture of that bruise."

So here I was, camera poised, Vince's voice in my ear, barking directions from wherever he was in the airport, asking me to describe my view, describe my tactics.

Suddenly the place went wild, a circle of bodyguards protecting a cargo I couldn't see, using their muscle to fend off the frenzy. Somewhere in the middle she was there. Men shouted her name, bulbs flashed. I couldn't get a visual on her, not even the top of her head. I quickly jumped on top of my chair.

"Right, Tommy, it's now or never. Now!" Vince voice cackled through my earphones.

I aimed my camera, stretched my arm as high as possible, tried to get inside the circle.

Click, click, click, click.

It was over so quick.

She disappeared down a corridor, led away to safety, the mob disbanded, rushed to their laptops and phones. Hours of quiet, for a minute of panic.

"Quick, the laptop," Vince shouted. "I hope to fucking God we got that left eye. Did you get the shot?"

"I don't know, Vince," I said, taking the things out of my bag frantically, plugging wires from camera to laptop.

"Come on, Tommy. We need this quick. This is a fucking race."

"It's downloading. Give me a few secs."

"You better not have let me down, Tommy."

Waiting for the pictures to upload. Waiting to see how much money we'd made or lost.

★ ★ ★

The next day. Newspapers and magazines scattered over our hotel bed, headlines and front covers. Big money had been made, it was all there to see, the eye and the bruise. Someone got the photo, someone was smiling this morning, having a champagne breakfast or smoking a big fat cigar, but it wasn't us.

There was no smiling, no champagne or cigar, as me and Vince sat at the end of our hotel bed. Vince with his head in his hands, me looking at the photo, feeling sorry for LG but not for ourselves like I should have been.

8

I got off the phone to Molly, more chicken updates and the wait for our first eggs continued. Molly sounded concerned, her chicks were her babies and the role of Mother Hen was one she was taking seriously, quite cute really, I wished I was there. She was growing up fast, changing every day, so the more days I missed, the more I resented my time away.

The day I left for London, as soon as she saw a suitcase she started to get upset, playing up, clinging onto my leg. Mum had to take her upstairs, it wasn't pleasant, Molly hysterical, Mum trying to settle her, the taxi beeping its horn. I wanted to hug her, give her a big kiss. Instead I waved up at her bedroom window, as she waved back, red cheeks and a frown that made me feel like throwing up. I left her the biggest chocolate egg I could find, so she had something to open come Easter Sunday, but it would be no replacement for her father leaving.

I'd rung her every day since, of course, made sure she didn't feel abandoned, reassured her she had nothing to fear, that I was coming back, but months are hard to explain to a child, their minds only grasp day and nights, their minds only work on short term, waking up and going to bed. I told her sixty sleeps till I was back, but to her I might as well have said a year.

★ ★ ★

I was in our hotel room, internet on my lap. Every couple of days I'd check in on LG, see what she had written on the web on her various social media profiles, what photos she'd uploaded, where she'd been. It had become a routine, I told myself it was for research, to find out clues and vantage points, give us the edge, as Vince would say. Maybe at the start that's what I was checking for, not any more, now I just checked because I liked her, found her actually quite witty and clever.

I always assumed celebrities got someone else to update their web pages and fan sites, but she seemed to prefer to do it herself. Let the world in on her little bubble – quite refreshing really, can't imagine a lot would, the rich and successful tended to be closed books, least they tried to be. They never stayed closed for long.

I didn't think LG did it for popularity or for fame, I think her intentions were far simpler, she just liked to speak her mind. Some would say it was career suicide, others would just say freedom of speech. Either way it was a dangerous game to play, one that left her quite vulnerable, and an easy target to shoot down.

Certainly, made her more accessible though, the openness and frankness, all her little remarks, photos of her breakfast, photos of her hotel suite, her rants at presidents, her views on climate, might be why she was so popular, or so unpopular, perhaps that was the key to being famous and staying famous. Love or hate, neither mattered as long as she was being talked about, as long as she was dividing opinion.

I logged in, opened up her profile page, I wasn't expecting what I found. Jesus Christ, it was horrific, I scrolled down at the comments, there were hundreds, pages and pages. The internet hadn't reacted well to LG's recent update, a close-up photo of her bruise, her comment posted underneath. "I probably deserved it. LOL"

Then the hate started, and there was a lot of it.

Glorifying abuse. Great work Lilly.
Wish he'd hit you harder bitch.
Only way you can get on a front cover these days.
Cry for help. How original.

It went on.

I agreed LG's comment was ill-advised and I'm sure in hindsight she probably regretted posting it, and I'm sure her little team wouldn't be best pleased either. But I didn't agree with the abuse that followed, people had turned brave behind their keyboards, bullies who typed as well as punched.

I hoped LG hadn't read it herself, it wouldn't be nice to see that volume of abuse in one swipe. But I bet she had.

★ ★ ★

Vince was still out, meetings, people to see he said, I didn't ask. I'd actually enjoyed my day alone, took a walk through Covent Garden, had a little to eat outside, till the clouds opened. In an attempt to stay dry, I managed to find shelter in Shaftesbury Avenue movie theatre.

It was empty, London's midday possibilities were endless, but I chose to catch a film instead. Apart from me there was a young couple a few rows ahead. We were the only audience, the three of us, sat in the dark, me eating popcorn, them giggling and kissing. I did my best not to stare, felt like a private moment.

Coincidentally, the film I chose was one of LG's recent works, not sure why I chose it, there were plenty of others to pick from. Think I just wanted to see her up on the big screen, not on laptop screens, not in inches, I wanted to see her in high definition, her voice in surround-sound, how a movie star should be watched.

Regretfully, it wasn't great – weak plot, too much CGI, lots of needless explosions, a box office flop and it was easy to see why, it felt like a movie chosen for its pay cheque rather than its credibility. I'm sure LG had her reasons, but it was suddenly a step down from her previous work. Anyway, the film looked pretty, as did she, killed a few hours too and better than getting wet.

I made my way back towards the tube station. By then the rain had cleared, the city left fresh and damp. I kept laughing to myself, thinking about that young couple kissing in front of me.

I missed fondling in cinemas, took me back to a Sunday evening under the sun, a million other deck chairs, me and Cassie sipping warm Buds over a horizon of heads and palms, it was our first date. We barely watched the film, made out for most of it. I remember quite vividly she wore a stripy wife-beater vest and her hair in tails. She said she wouldn't have sex with me till the fourth date. She was true to her word, it took me three visits to Hollywood Forever till she let me into her bed, after that I never left.

The last time we went to the cinema we didn't kiss, I can't remember the movie, but I remember arguing in whispers. She told me I wasn't doing enough with Molly. Told me that I needed to do more with her, create a bond, that I was always too busy with work, always tired. I disagreed, of course, so we watched the rest of the film in silence, and the drive home was in silence too.

We argued too much, some things got resolved, some never did and they never would have, alive or dead. So many things left unfinished and unresolved. I couldn't stop thinking about it as I made my way back to my hotel. What we said we'd do, our plans together, things I'd promised her. I couldn't resolve everything but some things I still could.

★ ★ ★

I closed the laptop. I'd seen enough abuse and Vince would be back at any minute. I knew he was keen to leave so I knew it would be best if I was prepared to vacate at the drop of his hat.

His moods were getting worse. The previous night had been a no-show, three hours in the rain, nothing. Turned out LG must've stayed home, that or she was at some other red-carpet event or party or exclusive dinner, though nothing I'd seen online suggested she had. More than likely she was cooped up in some hotel room attempting to recover from jet lag, or for her bruise to go down. The red carpet was hardly the best place to hide yourself, she probably wanted to stay below radar, let the press attention subside, but it hadn't, in fact it had multiplied. The big conversation on every other blog, broadsheet and tabloid was still that first photo of her bruise, the photo we, or I, had failed to take. Vince was still sulking and was even more determined to put our mistake right.

I heard keys rattle. He tossed me a paper bag.

"Didn't know if you'd eaten."

"Cheers, Vince. You want one?" offering him a pastry.

"No, not hungry," as he emptied out his pockets on the table. He looked tired. "Just got off the phone with Jen and the kids."

"How are they?"

"It's the twins' birthday. They made me sing 'Happy Birthday'. Quicker I get home the better. Is the Jeep ready?"

"Yep. Just gotta finish packing."

"How long is the trip again?"

"Hard to say, most of the time will be getting out of London. 'Bout four and a half hours, let's say six hours, just in case we stop somewhere."

His face wasn't impressed

"Least you get to see the country."

"It's hardly Route 66."

"So how did your meeting go? As bad as you thought?"

"Worse. We are spending more than we are bringing in. Bosses aren't too keen on that maths."

"We still get paid though, right? No matter what, Vince, at the end of this, we get paid?"

Vince laughed.

"What's so funny?"

"You don't get it, do you, Tommy?"

"I'm not stupid, Vince. I understand we have to deliver to get paid. But surely we get paid something, even if it's small?"

"This is the world of self-employment. Long and short of it. No photos, no money. We both go home with nothing."

"Nothing?"

"Nada."

"That can't happen, Vince. I need the money."

"And I don't. We both have the same interests. We've all got mouths to feed. Your little mistake at the airport cost us six figures."

"You serious?"

"That bruise was a money shot. Someone got rich out of that. It was supposed to be us."

"What do we need to do?"

"We need to leave."

"Now?"

"No, I've got some people to see before we leave, try and convince them I can make good on what I promised them. Get a decent night's sleep, but we start early. 5am we are getting out of dodge."

He went into the bathroom and started to run a shower, as I went over to my bags and cases to check I had everything packed. I noticed my new reflection in the mirror for the first time, my newest additions.

Still couldn't believe I did it. The jeweller was very patient, his shop wasn't busy, asked me lots of questions. I didn't tell him about Cassie, I wanted the moment to feel genuine and celebratory, not mournful and dreary. Once I had chosen a pair of rings for me and Cassie he asked if I knew her size. I told him a six, he brought out an L, said she can come in and get it altered, I said that wouldn't be necessary. He even checked I knew which finger she had to wear it on, third finger, left hand, just like the song, he said. Still I played along and smiled. In the end, I walked out of the shop with a ring for Cassie, a ring for me and a chain so I could wear them around my neck. It cost a lot, money I didn't have, money I hadn't technically earned yet. But it was something that had to be done, I knew all the things me and Cassie talked and argued about couldn't be resolved, but getting her that ring I always promised her and making her my wife would not be one of them.

I slipped on a T-shirt and started to get my belongings into some order, started to prepare for departure. Tried to tell myself that buying those rings was the right thing to do, as everything Vince had just said told me it wasn't, not when I knew how much my family needed money, rather than the platinum sentiment around my neck.

The journey felt hard work and longer than I or the GPS had predicted, a combination of bad weather and rubbernecking. There was a nasty accident, a lorry and a caravan, a mangle of iron and glass, ambulances and police, a line of traffic curious to see why they had been made to wait and queue. Brought back horrible memories seeing that crash, ones I'd thought I'd forgotten. Vince offered to take over, I lied and said I'd be fine to carry on, changed the subject quickly. We talked about home, talked about our fathers, I loved mine, he feared his. Talked about old Hollywood, Pantages, the Max Factor Building. Our favourite leading ladies, Lombard, Ryder, Harlow, Sheedy. We talked about LG too, a subject I knew far too much about, Vince too, to his credit.

We didn't agree on her acting ability, Vince said she wouldn't last long, but we agreed on one thing though, we both liked her. She was different than the others, hard to pin down, hard to read, conflicted, just how we liked our film stars. She had only been in a handful of films, but it was her first that caught all the excitement of Tinseltown. Mesmerizing, intense. Oscars and Baftas, plaudits for her and her director boyfriend.

LG wasn't the polished, media-trained A-lister that Hollywood had come to expect, those who did as they were told. She was the opposite side of that coin. She was refreshingly shy, always truthful, awkward in her skin, uncomfortable with the position she had been thrust into so suddenly. She was the perfect description of what we expected from a modern-day celebrity – troubled youth, difficult to work with if rumours be true, turbulent relationships, spoke her mind, prone to nudity if the part demanded it, said the wrong thing – and she looked the part. I couldn't put into words the way she looked. Vince had all manner of phrases and I'd heard all of them over the course of my employment.

"If you were a rock star, she is what you'd expect to be riding your lap," he told me once. "Girls wanna kiss her, boys wanna kiss her. Dads just wanna fuck her," he'd said that numerous times. "She'd look good wrapped around a pole," was his new favourite. Vince enjoyed finding new demonic ways to insult or compliment LG, depending on your own opinion. Truthfully, despite his vulgarity, he was right in his assessment, not that I told him that. Rightly or wrongly, she was the girl everyone could fantasize over and she fitted a broad demographic. Beauty was beauty, and she had enough sides to hers for everyone to fall in love with.

Not that she was everyone's cup of tea. LG caused debate, that was for sure, and I liked that about her. Some said she acted the way she did to make a statement, to rile people, but from what I'd read and seen, my view was she was just being herself, there didn't seem to be an ulterior motive, she was just being who she was. There wasn't enough of that in Hollywood – being yourself was frowned upon, being yourself was a sure-fire way of being derailed. I hoped she would never change, but I was sure over time, moguls and execs would grind her down to fit the appropriate mould. Eventually she would probably become the same as every other actress. The same smile, the same answers, the same films, but for the time being she was just being LG, which at that moment was tabloid gold. No wonder Vince and all the others were salivating, she would be around for a long time as long as she didn't self-destruct. It always seems only a matter of time until fame turns people loco and it was easy to see why. LG fitted the bill when it came to predicting her future timeline. Awards and adulation, a lifetime of limelight, perfume commercials, clothes ranges, hounded by paps every waking hour, front-page wedding, awful offspring, cosmetic surgery, drugs perhaps, early death, another legend, another cemented handprint. I couldn't work out if I felt sorry for the girl. I think I did. The more I found out about her, the more I felt a pang of sympathy. For all the glitz and glamour, I couldn't help but feel anything else. The wolves were circling, all out for a little piece of her, fighting over scraps and fortunes. Me being one of them.

Much to Vince's distaste, wanting to beat the GPS, I decided to pull into a service station about two hours into the drive, for petrol, coffee and toilet stop. Vince decided to buy the whole of Marks and Sparks, magazines, chocolate, music, even showed me how to lose at fruit machines. For all his flaws Vince has always made me laugh, and despite his mood the night before, he was secretly enjoying discovering an England that Americans rarely got to see.

Back in the Jeep spirits were high as we made up lost ground, told dirty jokes, recited *Dumb and Dumber* quotes, debated breasts and arses, doing what men do when in each other's company. There was plenty of singing too, courtesy of Vince's brand new power ballad compilation and no surprise that Vince loved the sound of his own voice – both spoken and in song – and his renditions of one-hit wonders made up the soundtrack of the journey. It felt like a road trip, felt like I was going on holiday, for those few hours with me and Vince in the car, laughing and joking and singing, I completely forgot what I was driving towards and the person I would have to become to succeed.

I parked the Jeep a short walk away from the house. Vince agreed he should have worn more appropriate footwear and he cursed every puddle and bog, as if I was singularly to blame for the terrain and weather conditions. But he was adamant that before we checked into our hotel he wanted a quick look at the farmhouse before LG's planned arrival the following day; said he didn't want any nasty surprises, wanted to make sure he was happy with the set-up before he let me loose on my own.

The house looked as impressive as I remembered, even more so. I'd seen pictures and visited the property several times as part of my research, but on seeing it up close again it reconfirmed its purpose of making its guest feel safe and comfortable and, above all, undetected. Inside would be low wooden ceiling beams, an

Aga, open fires, a roll-top slipper bath. It was old fashioned and must've been over a century old, but there was enough modern luxury to make an actress feel at home

In the driveway, it was heaving with bodies as furniture, flowers and food were being transported from the back of vans to inside the house, it looked an organized outfit. LG would be there in less than twenty-four hours and you could sense the urgency around the place, men with clipboards shouting down their phones. It had to be perfect, it was not every day a world-famous actress came to stay.

Me and Vince walked closer towards the house through the trees and bushes, whoever had found this property had done an excellent job. Sat at the bottom of a big hill, sheep and trees made up the horizon, it looked like any other country farmhouse, so it was easy to miss, hard to get to and perfect for someone wanting to avoid the gaze of the public. God knows how Vince found out she was staying here. I asked him but all I got was a wink, he obviously had his sources and thank God, he did, otherwise finding LG's house amongst a million holiday homes would have been damn near impossible.

The garden itself had changed dramatically since my last visit in early March. Fresh turf, sculptured bushes, extra security alarms, a whole corner of patio had been removed and in its place a floor of white flowers, in fact white flowers were everywhere, and a bench sat in the heart of the garden. The whole rear side of the house was the kitchen and was predominantly glass, which led straight out onto grass and trickling ponds. According to the floor plan, her bedroom was right above the kitchen. I guessed that was where we would see most of our action – the kitchen, the bedroom, the garden.

Together, me and Vince climbed over the brambles towards the place I'd unofficially declared our base. Luckily it had not been pruned or altered since I last saw it and was still as erratic and unkempt as it had been previously. It was the perfect hideout, my little hole under a tree.

"This is out of my comfort zone, Tommy boy. You're pretty exposed out here. Be careful in the daytime, keep low and quiet. You can't be getting burnt out early in the game."

Vince talked some more, tactics and advice, but even he could see its potential. As Vince discussed camera angles I could already see dollar signs in his eyes – he knew we would make money here. He very nearly gave me a compliment, but it never came. We didn't stay much longer, just enough time for Vince to whet his appetite. We headed back.

★ ★ ★

We arrived at the guest house just as it was getting dark. The owners, Alfred and Dot, were there to greet us both, with warm smiles and welcoming arms. They had been very kind to me before, especially Dot who fed me and looked after me like I was her own. Their huge dog was sat by reception in the same coma-like state that I'd last seen him in. I stroked him but he didn't recognize me, nor did he move from his slump. We ate our dinner quickly and without much conversation – we were all talked out and just wanted our beds.

"That dog Tripod you liked so much. Could be…"

"His name isn't Tripod."

"Dogs have saved me on many occasions. Oh, sorry officer I'm just out with my dog. I didn't know this was private property."

"A dog accomplice?"

"Yes," he said, finishing the last of his steak.

"It's not even our dog."

"Why does that matter? Look, we are doing the dog a favour. Looking at it, I doubt it gets walked much. That's even if it can walk, seeing as it's missing a front leg."

"No, Vince."

"Just saying, that's all."

As our plates of leftovers were taken away we agreed a time to meet at reception and both went our separate ways to our separate rooms. I rang Mum, it didn't sound a well house, Mum felt under the weather, kept blowing her nose down the phone and apparently Molly wasn't much better, blocked nose and an awful cough. Mum said Molly had gotten a little upset at bedtime, kept asking for me and Cassie. I felt helpless, Mum shouldn't have to do that all on her own and I told her that, too. I thanked her for the present I'd found when emptying out my suitcase. She had written a message inside, Molly had scribbled one alongside it too, I assumed she wished me the same luck as Mum. It was nice of them both, completely unexpected, very thoughtful. I promised I would make a conscious effort to write in it every day, my trials and tribulations, the memoirs of a paparazzo.

In bed, my phone beeped, it was a message from Vince, complaining about English television and the lack of adult pay-per-view. I messaged him back, he messaged me, and so on and so on till we both agreed to call it a night – we had an early start, we needed our rest. I sometimes thought it was the only reason I was there, to keep Vince entertained. Apparently, I was vital, so Vince told me, but it didn't feel that way. I was there to keep Vince company and all my research and planning didn't seem to add any value to the job at hand. I wasn't qualified to be on this job. Yes, I'd been a tour guide, but it was hardly the same thing. I had no experience, limited camera work, above all I wasn't cut-throat enough. All I could say was I was knowledgeable. I had to laugh at myself, three months of work, what a farce.

All I knew was LG – an expert on one person, three months of learning about someone inside and out, lies and half-truths, a hundred contradictions, I couldn't see how it made me any more equipped or qualified to take photos of her than if I didn't know anything at all. And what did I know exactly that was of any value? That she had a peanut allergy, that she loved Walt Whitman, that she smoked a little pot, that her sister married a vet. None of it mattered, the outcome would be the same. Photos, photos, photos. Of her hair, her clothes, her body, her bruises, whatever sold.

I wasn't this person. I wasn't this job. I'd avoided both, battled with it long and hard, changed what I'd become into more desirable titles, stuck up for it to make it feel less sadistic. But my job title didn't matter anymore, I needed money. I had a sick daughter, a sick mother, a dead wife and no way of supporting any of them.

Perhaps that's what Vince saw in me, I mean really saw in me – a man on his knees, vulnerable, with nothing to lose. But I didn't resent Vince for it. I was old enough to take responsibility for my actions, I was the one who agreed to do it and this was what needed to be done. I looked at the clock, she would be here in less than eight hours, and soon Vince would go back to LA, leave me to do what needed to be done.

Better go to sleep, I thought. That's when the madness would begin. Day one. First page of my journal. I'm sure she doesn't deserve any of what is coming her way. She mustn't take it personally, I hope she understands this is business, I hope what happens, good or bad, won't do her any harm, it's just photos after all, yesterday's news, tomorrow's chip paper, it will just be spying, an infringement of her privacy, all part of the cycle, she will have her role to play and I would have mine.

Tomorrow she would arrive in a little corner of England that no one's ever heard of, including her.

And tomorrow I would become a paparazzo.

And from tomorrow, until she flies back to Hollywood, my job would be to follow her day in, day out, no matter where she goes or how far.

Lilly Goodridge, I'm sorry in advance, I really am, but not sorry enough to stop.

PART TWO

LILLY

The bridge/April /shot 36

9

Wish he'd hit you harder bitch.

I hope you get raped.

Whoever punched you, must've just seen your last movie.

What a waste of $7!

I scrolled down my cell, screen after screen. The funny thing was, I wasn't even being ironic when I posted the photo the night before. I did deserve it, I wasn't being witty or vulgar or trying to get sympathy, I 100% deserved it, I would have hit me too. I suppose I should have been more offended than I was. Frank called them cowards, Sally had another word for them, starting with the same letter. Me, I just called it freedom of speech. And for some twisted reason the worse the abuse was, the more it felt like comedy. Sally says I should take it more seriously, but it's hard to feel threatened by someone you can't see. It's hard to be threatened by someone typing at a keyboard.

Despite Sally telling me not to, the temptation to add more fuel to the fire was hard to resist, but somehow, I didn't retaliate. Not that I knew what I would've written, something to fuel the fire, or just one word in capitals, both would have given Sally a heart attack.

Sally was still in a mood with me, told me I had to consult her before I opened my big mouth online. I told her I could open my big mouth whenever I wanted, with or without her authority. It didn't go down well, she called me a time bomb, said she was the one who always had to pick up the fallout. Not to worry, she'll simmer down eventually, she always does.

I felt a tug on my bangs. Two women were working on my head, possibly three, moving around my chair, arms flailing madly, brushing and clipping and painting. It was my third transformation of the day, application and removal, application and removal, the more elaborate and time-consuming, the prettier I looked at the end.

Bored at looking at cyber trolls I turned my cell off, picked at the sliced mango on the side – breakfast was fruit, lunch was fruit, my drink was fruit, my diet was juiced or about to juiced.

Jeez, I was hungry, I could eat everything right now, my stomach rumbled, though my dress felt tight against my bladder, made me feel hungry, made me want to go for a pee. A young girl came over and offered me a drink. I declined, I didn't fancy attempting a toilet break in my current ensemble. Instead, I dreamt of room service.

I caught a quick glimpse of myself in the mirror. There was a brief talk about playing up the whole bruise thing, making me even more bloodied up, boxing gloves and gumshields, but the powers that be agreed that it might send out the wrong message. Three said Yes, four said No, that was how my life worked – democracy, just not my democracy. My hand wasn't part of the vote and why would it be?

Hey, I couldn't complain, it hadn't been a bad shoot, I'd been on worse. The photographer was a sweet old dude, spoke with whispers and his hands. Survived the day with no real direction, just smiles and thumbs up. He gave me flowers, I thanked him, put them with the rest, the corner of my dressing room was starting to look like a grave. I wasn't in the mood for smiles today, which was lucky seeing the mood of the shoot was quite sombre and serious. Meant I could get away with looking distant. I often got asked why I looked so sad all the time and I never knew quite how to respond, or what response they expected. I was tempted once to say it was because I wanted to kill myself, see how they took it, see if they took it like the joke it was intended to be – I'm guessing not. It was easier to give them the answer they expected, or the answer that caused the mildest reaction. I had gotten called lots of things in my short life as an actress – antagonist, spirited, one hack called me ingénue. I quite liked being abused in words I didn't understand, meant I could take it neither as cruel nor complimentary. People always get me wrong, perhaps it was better that way, let them write around me rather than inside it was better they didn't get me exactly, no matter how hard they tried. My agent said not to worry, just to keep doing whatever it was I was doing, apparently whatever it was, it was paying the bills and then some.

I felt cold, I thought of how many sweaters and scarves I'd packed and how most photo shoots always involved me showing skin. I'd been more naked than I was today, but still my arms and legs were out and not all the green tea in the world was going to change that. It didn't help the dressing room being open and closed constantly, people coming in and out, constant draughts. I hoped this wasn't how cold I would always be in England, the next two months trying to keep warm. Sally assured me the farmhouse would be heated, two open fires apparently, it would be fun working that one out. I assumed I'd just light a match, wasn't that how fires were started, I assumed it would be that simple? If cavemen could work it out I was confident I could too.

This was my first time in England, and all I'd seen so far was an airport terminal and a studio, and of course my hotel. Didn't matter what city I was in or what continent, all I ever saw was the first five yards, from kerbside to indoors, but somehow those fuckers still managed to get their shots of me. Luckily my hotel room was top floor, too high up for paparazzi, though I wouldn't put it past some to attempt the climb.

Sally came in, face like thunder, told me I had a radio interview in two hours, told me not to mention the bruise, or Max, or the shit storm online. I jokingly asked what I could say, she said why don't I try talking about why I was here and let her in on it, too. As you can tell, she wasn't best pleased to be back on home soil.

I felt my cell vibrate on my lap – it was Max. I typed a reply, short and prompt. I felt obligated to respond, I could hardly ignore his messages after what happened at the party. I must have been his only friend, seeing as to the rest of the world he was still public enemy number one. Though I wasn't sure how long I wanted this daily communication between us to carry on, made life more difficult and our break-up harder to get over. I needed to get a new cell, get Sally to sort me out a new number and quick, not that that had ever worked before.

I heard my name being called. It looked like it was show time, action stations, time to pout and look thin. Frank came through the door, handed me a sub. Told me I needed to eat, as it looked like it was going to be a long one. This was what I liked to call a 'shit ton day'.

* * *

Four hours later I was on a plane. It was only a short flight, still, I slept through most of it. Just what I needed, more jet lag. The drive was insane, I asked the driver if we were driving off-road, he said no. By the time we arrived the sky had gone from dark to black, Frank cursed every pot plant till he found the elusive door key as we did our best to transfer us and our luggage from car to house without getting wet. Finally, we'd made it.

My new home. Our new home.

Shame I was too tired, went straight from car to bed, the grand tour would have to wait till tomorrow.

* * *

Apparently next door was given away free eggs, a 'bumper lay' the neighbour told Frank, whatever that meant. Not that I was complaining, I hadn't eaten properly in two days. Sally made sure I had no bread, of course, though Frank passed me toast from under the table, I ate it quickly, like contraband.

"Did you get hold of your dad?" Frank asked sorting through a box of travel plugs.

"No, he wasn't there. Spoke to Mom though."

"So, did he like it?"

"I think so. She didn't really say. It was all a bit weird actually."

"I bet he loved it. Probably out taking it for a spin as we speak."

"I'll try him again later, wish him happy birthday probably." I walked over to the kitchen doors. "Are we expecting a great flood?" pointing at the sandbags piled up outside the door.

"Think it's just a precaution. I'm guessing our little stream may burst its banks from time to time."

"What stream?"

"Over there," Frank said, pointing through the glass towards a stream I still couldn't see.

"How much rain they expecting?"

"I'm guessing quite a bit," Frank said, taking my socks off the Aga.

"That's why I need today off, Sally. Have a look round, find out where everything is."

"And you will," she said, typing at her cell. "Just not today."

"Can't we just have today off? I think I deserve it."

"Not a fat chance."

"Go on then, hit me with it. How bad is it?"

"Wardrobe at twelve. Voice coach around two, actually I need to check if their train left on time."

"OK. That's not too bad."

"Oh, and Jon too."

"Jon as in Director Jon?"

"He said he wanted to touch base with you. Though I don't know when."

"I have some hours free then?"

"Well, not free, Lilly."

"You said wardrobe aren't getting here till after lunch. It's seven am."

"That is correct. But it doesn't mean you can slack off."

"I'm not planning on slacking, Sally."

"What are you planning?"

"A long bath."

"That sounds like slacking off."

"You haven't let me finish. A long bath, whilst reading my lines."

"Better."

"Then we explore?"

"Explore what?"

"This place. The village. I read last night that we are close to the sea."

"Lilly. I'm not having you roam the village. You'll stick out like a sore thumb."

"Fine. Exploring the house then."

"Later. I want your nose in your script for a good few hours. Promise."

"OK, Mom, deal," I said as I ruffled her hair. "Right, who's for more coffee? I'll make it." I walked over to the Aga and grabbed the kettle. "And we'll drink it outside, have a wander round the garden."

"Not me, not in that weather."

"Come on, Sally, the sun is out. I'm guessing in this country it doesn't come out that often."

I started to fill the kettle with water. "Frank. You up for a coffee outside?"

"Let's concentrate on the coffee first before we think of where we are going to drink it."

"How do I know when it's boiled?" I said staring at the kettle and the Aga.

"Don't worry, you'll know," Frank smirked.

"Isn't this place awesome? C'mon, Frank, it's pretty fucking cool."

"I haven't made up my mind yet. Ask me in a couple of days once I've had a chance to find my feet."

"Admit it's a nice change, though. I knew I made the right choice. I knew it."

"It's her that needs convincing, not me," Frank said, looking over at Sally, still staring deeply at her cell.

"Her and everyone else," I said, startled by the kettle, whistling like a fire had broken out.

★ ★ ★

After my bath Sally backcombed my hair, as Frank tried to make sense of the house's internal workings. We left him to it, Frank never could settle until he'd located the supply of water and electrics and know how to turn it off and on. Before she left I gave Sally a hug and thanked her for making me look like Jackie Kennedy and I was left to potter and wander, we'd made up on the journey down here, four hours forced to sit beside each other with nowhere else to go, it was inevitable we'd sort our shit out.

The house itself was lovely, just the right side of nautical, any more themed and it would be Jimmy Buffets. Every room was huge, only one TV though, so I'd have to invest in one for my bedroom. I kept finding umbrellas everywhere and old books, a Dan Brown, an Agatha Christie, a book about birds, great tits, blue tits, bearded tits, lots of tits. Frank had started the fire, too. I added a few logs but it seemed to have a bad effect so Frank had to do his best to turn smoke and grey back into flames.

I felt tired, last night's sleep was not the greatest – new bed, new draughts, the sound of birds, too many birds. I made a note to buy earplugs, I was living in an aviary, it sounded like one might be trapped in a chimney, or the attic. Not to mention the sheep – I wasn't used to so much wildlife on my doorstep.

As I walked downstairs I met Frank, stood by the front door like a dog with a lead.

"Sally won't like us venturing too far."

"What she won't know, won't hurt her."

"I wanna check the lawnmower situation. Find out where the coal is kept."

"I'll need to get dressed."

"Be quick then. I don't think Sally is going out for long."

Ten minutes later I was ready. Frank looked at me and as per usual, his eyes rolled.

"Well, what do you think?" looking down at myself, wellington boots, mac, headscarf, sunglasses, scarf, the only skin on show was my nose. "Still Jackie Onassis?"

"Bin Laden, more like."

"You don't think anyone is out there do you, y'know, paparazzi?"

"If they are, I'll be impressed."

"We could use this as an experiment, Frank?"

"Could be an expensive one if it goes wrong."

"But if they aren't, then I've got a free pass."

"You ready girl?"

"I think so, no wait a minute." I grabbed a walking stick from next to the door. "I always wanted to use one of these."

We opened the door, in front of us a long road that disappeared over a hill. Although it looked daunting, we both had the biggest smiles on our faces. Well, I did, it was always hard to tell if Frank was smiling or not.

★ ★ ★

Next morning, I checked every tabloid, blog and forum for photos of me and Frank rambling over fields and gates, I expected the worst, expected the two of us to have been caught. I checked the next morning too, still nothing.

Success, I thought, but deep down I knew they would eventually find me. Paparazzi always did eventually, being in the middle of nowhere just meant it would take them longer.

But still, I regarded it as a mini triumph, my day of freedom, I was going to make the most of it till the cavalry turned up.

10

England had rendered me disabled – my waist hurt, my back hurt, my breasts hurt, though despite my new disability, my first seven days' filming had gone surprisingly well. The cast were lovely, a small gang, which only made it feel tighter knit. Jon had done a great job of creating a warm family atmosphere, set out his stall early on, made us all stand in a circle on day one, say what we all expected from each other, that we left our previous work behind us and our egos too. We all took our turns to speak, the highest paid to the lowest, those in front of and behind the camera – it was all very theatre, which should have been obvious seeing as that was Jon's background. Though it all felt a little tranquil for me – I was used to more chaotic forms of direction. Yes, Jon had made us a family, created a calm environment, I just wasn't quite sure at what point calm became lethargic.

Shame about one particular co-star. My initial predictions of my fellow patriot Chris Rogan were accurate – he was a dick, and most of his tasks and comments were made very much with his dick in mind. But I would have to get used to him – to be fair, he was handsome, a part of me thought he would be nice to have some fun with. It would be interesting in the next few months to see what side of my moral conscience won that particular battle.

It had been quite refreshing not having so many Americans around, to be in the minority, although the accents around me sounded nothing like I'd been practising, they all sounded so different, which I found peculiar seeing as it turned out they lived within a couple of hours' drive of each other. The crew found that comment hilarious – apparently everywhere in England was a couple of hours away. But I appreciated the warmth they gave me, I wasn't used to it, especially from the girls. Me and girls have never tended to get on. With a decade of dance education, I'd seen most types and the majority of them I tended to avoid, so most of my friends were either boys, boyish or tomboys, so I didn't expect to meet a bunch of girls that I would now consider to be close and comfortable with.

Talking of comfort, the painful process of getting me in and out of a corset was one I dreaded most mornings. I'm guessing a guy invented it, a guy who liked small waists and big tits. I hoped it hadn't damaged me internally, I remember reading something on the plane about it moving organs out of place. I had visions of my intestines getting lodged in my chest, my lungs near my pelvis. This week showed me one thing, though, I'm starting to finally see the transition from Hollywood starlet to an English lady, at least physically. I made all the girls laugh as I waddled in front of them chanting 'The rain in Spain stays mainly on the plain.'

Jon agreed my accent still needed a little work, but not to worry myself too much, he assured me I would grow into the part. I was determined to nail it, spent days and nights going over and over each page, spent a week with a voice coach, becoming best friends with my tongue. It was tedious and repetitive, but necessary if I stood any real chance of not looking a fool, not being another American who failed at being un-American. Besides, it wasn't like I could deviate from it, it wasn't one of those movies, no room for ad-libbing. But I was used to rehearsing, Max drilled that into me, said spontaneity only comes from practice and planning, so ever since I always made sure I knew more than just a character's lines, trying to find that "magical accident", as Max called them. That is why I'd spend the bulk of my days pronouncing my Hs and not rolling my Rs, lots of "How now, brown cow," looking inside my character's head, working out what she was about to gain or lose. Making her human, making her more than words on a page.

I heard the sound of my doorbell.

I was neither dressed nor expecting guests, I nearly didn't answer it. I shouldn't have worried, it was only a courier, another box. I was getting a couple of boxes every couple of days, mostly clothes, sometimes make-up and jewellery, occasionally a new camera or a new pair of shoes, God knows where they came from.

What's worse is, I never opened most of them. Just because they were free, didn't mean I particularly wanted to wear them, didn't mean I liked all of them, even if they were designer. Not that I was being ungrateful, it's just I had so much of my life already planned out for me, I thought choosing my own clothes would not be one of them. It was strange, this constant box after box of gifts, I should have thanked them. But I didn't think for one minute the gesture was meant for me, it was not for my gain. I knew why I was being lavished with such things – if I wore it, if I endorsed it, better still if I was photographed in it, then every girl in the world would want one too and some man behind a desk would make his millions, and his company would go from small change to global. Perhaps I'm over-exaggerating, a tad cynical, but perhaps I wasn't. Not to matter, Sally normally stole a few garments anyway, I always let her rifle through, take what she wanted, some lipstick or eye shadow. I could take some home with me when I go back to LA, I thought, let Mom choose what she liked, perhaps send a big box to my sister, we were about the same size. Worst case, I could donate them, give them to some flea market, just what the starving and homeless needed, accessories and red-carpet heels.

I walked back to the front room quickly. I avoided the hallway, gave me the creeps at night, big and full of echoes. I wasn't used to such a big house; my apartment back home was the size of the kitchen. Frank and Sally always offered to stay, and sometimes they did, but I insisted I wanted this to be my house, that I didn't need babysitting, even though I was still a little scared of the dark.

On the rug, as I returned to the task of buffing my nails, a pile of nail clippings about to be thrown on the open fire. My new bad habit: pistachio shells, dirty tissues, anything that could sizzle in the coals. This time it was toenail clippings, gross I know, hardly demure, in fact I was just doing it to pass the time, clock-watching. Tonight, I had plans.

Jon thought it a good idea to all go out for a bite to eat, a nice way to get to know one another, said he'd take us to his new favourite restaurant in the world. So I'd spent the last hour getting myself ready, tending to my eyebrows, listening to hip hop. The only thing I hadn't done was decide on what to wear, it was a dilemma I faced every morning and night. I'd underestimated the cold here, it was a temperature that didn't make sense. How can such a blue sky be so cold at the same time? All I knew was, I would be in layers. I went upstairs, lights on of course to seek out appropriate attire, when what I'd most like to have worn was a fucking duvet.

Luckily Devon wasn't Melrose Avenue, and Jon assured me the Oyster Shack was the sort of place you could turn up barefoot and still be greeted with a smile and a bucket of crab claws. Frank told me there was quite a big surf scene around here, lots of little beaches and coves, seen lots of board shops around the place, said he was itching to hunt them down. I could get it arranged, I thought, I'd be a little rusty, hire out some beach. No, scratch that, sounded like far too much planning and knowing my luck I'd turn up and there would be no surf, probably upset the locals, and probably stir up too much media attention. Better to leave the quiet paradises untouched, I didn't want to be the one to bring the whole of Hollywood's scum life to their shores. I looked inside my suitcases. I still hadn't unpacked, I didn't think I ever would, tried to find something understated and above all warm.

Frank messaged me asking if he needed to wear a suit. I very nearly told him yes, so he'd be the only one in a tux. Sally was coming tonight too, not that she'd be great company, I'm not even sure why I invited her. My radio interviews hadn't gone down well, admittedly I wasn't in the best of moods at the time. I suppose in hindsight I regretted some of the things I said but, hey, it had been a long day, I'd just done a six-hour photo shoot, and the guy interviewing was an absolute arsehole, it was obvious his only intention was to create a headline. He asked me some dumb questions about sexuality in celebrity, said I was more concerned with the current Nigerian military coup. Even asked me about the legalisation of cannabis and I really had to bite my tongue not to shout "Hell, yeah." What else? He asked me about Obama; by that point I was bored of staying quiet, told him I'd wasted my vote, that it wasn't progress, just blind hope, that I'd vote Republican next time. As you could probably tell, I wasn't the interview they expected, and was certainly not the interview Sally had requested either. Someone blogged that I sounded stoned. Arseholes. Try jet-lagged, overworked, sleep-deprived.

Now, after my telling-off by all in the Goodridge camp, Sally would be watching my every move – no white wine for me. I might try and get her drunk, I thought, sit her next to Frank, see what might happen. Actually, Sally would be doing me a favour, I'm not a particularly good drunk, some people flourish under the influence, me, I revert into myself, don't think before I speak, get aggressive and even more opinionated – I was better without it. Now pot on the other hand, well that I did miss, a friend I knew in Brentwood grew the best hydroponic weed around, that I could quite happily sit and smoke all day.

Fucking hell, my third movie, some God-awful saga set in space, months of set work and green screen. Me and a couple of co-stars, I won't mention names, well we smoked a hell of a lot when we made that movie. I only ever saw the film once, thank God, it was embarrassing, my eyes in a permanent glaze. Critics blamed the script, but I think some of it rested on the actors too. Still, it made everyone lots of money, even though it was awful. There was actually talk of a sequel, which worryingly I may still have to do as I am contractually obliged. Worst case, if it happened, I'd speak to my agent, try and worm my way out of that one, ask if I could be killed off in the first scene – an impressive death, explosions and laser guns. I'd never died in a movie yet, so perhaps it could be my first, I'd have to practise my gasps and chokes. All I got from that movie was bad memories and a big pay cheque, which shouldn't be anyone's motivation, least not at the start of your career. Least it paid for Frank's medical bills. I hoped this movie would be different, the money was certainly less. I felt happy here though, content. "No hiccups," I overheard someone say the other day, sounded a good way of putting things. Tonight, tomorrow, the next few months, my aim was just "No hiccups." A simpler life, like it used to be, before Lilly Goodridge, when I was just Lilly, Lilly from Silver Lakes. Before Max.

Reporters and journos, no matter if instructed not to, still asked me about him on every single interview, directly and indirectly, and I could see why people would be interested, and I didn't expect that to stop soon, not so soon after all the turbulence. But even though I had no cause to be loyal, whenever questioned about Max and my relationship with Max I always did my best to talk of the good in him. And there was a lot of good in Max Salter, not many saw it, but I had, and I didn't feel it would make anything better by making him an enemy, that was one thing I would not want to be. I'd known him three years and one thing I knew was, life was easier with him on my side, and that wasn't fear talking – being loved by him was as complicated as being hated, the trick was somewhere in the middle, where he liked me enough to let me go, a clean break, without the need to haunt or hound me.

God, how did things get so difficult?

I was twenty when I met him, things were going well at that point, not in the career sense, but life was busy enough. My big sis had just got married and was expecting a little boy, Dad had gotten a bit part on some new daytime pilot on NBC. Me, I was doing OK, I'd gotten a new job over at the Dream Centre, felt good to help, I liked helping people, and the people there needed a lot of it, that and I was keeping up with my classes a couple of times a week.

Dancing in a professional capacity was a world no longer available, it was now just a hobby, something I did after work, I was OK with that. It was Mom who had the issue with it, how much of a waste it was, both in time and money. Me, I was genuinely content with dancing for enjoyment rather than a pay cheque, not being up in front of all those stage lights suited me just fine.

Now no one in Hollywood would have heard of Mr Maxwell Salter at that time, but in the circles I was in, everyone had heard mutterings of his arrival way before he turned up at our little dance school. And I was the only one who wasn't caught up in all the hysteria.

I'm going to be honest now – as much as I have tried since I was a little girl, all the hours spent practising, the years studying it at College, all the wanting in the world, I have never been a particularly good performer. Technical, but never natural; passionate, but quite ordinary. I wasn't a natural exhibitionist, I hated the focus being on me, if only there'd been a way I could have danced alone with no one watching, then I would have been fine. But it was an art form meant to be observed and critiqued, live shows, auditions. It wasn't for me, not the performance side at least. Came to reason that when rumour spread that a well-known theatre director was scouting dance schools for a lead actress in his first film, I was not in the least bit enthusiastic.

All the girls in my classes were caught up in it, they'd whisper about his potential arrival, and the longer it went on the more absurd were the stories of this nameless visitor. He trained at La Scala, one of them said, he'd met with ballet mistresses in New York, apparently – it was all complete lies. The truth was, Max later told me, he was on his last legs. His last two productions had bombed, he'd parted company with his theatre house, and all he had was a self-penned screenplay that a small film company had agreed to make on the smallest of budgets. But to any dancer in the know, Max Salter was the ticket to the big screen, even if at the time he hadn't even a ticket for himself.

The day, or should I say night, he turned up at our dance school I was the only one there. The last class had just finished, I'd stayed back with one of the younger ones as their Mom had gotten stuck in traffic, so I waited with them till they turned up. It wasn't a big deal, some nights I closed shop, the manager was an old friend, so occasionally I locked up, switched on the alarms. By the time Max showed, I was just about to turn off the lights and start the security checks.

"Excuse me, miss. I take it I'm too late to see the show?" he said, stood at the doorway.

"Just me, I'm afraid. Hardly much of a show."

"That's a shame. I'll come back another time."

Despite the rumours of a mystery man's arrival, no one actually had a clue what he would look like or even his name, me included. To look at Max he did not carry himself in such a way that would make one feel he could control a room, or direct an actor or actress. At the time, I would've guessed he was late forties but I later found out he was a good decade younger.

"Do you want me to leave a message?" I asked him.

"No, you're fine little darlin'. I was just passing on the off chance."

I picked up my things, walking towards him, the clock above him told me it wasn't long till I had to start my late shift. That was me back then, dancer by day, counsellor at night.

"Do you mind telling me where the nearest dance school is from here?"

"There are quite a few. Probably best you try tomorrow though. Not many will be open now. Sorry."

"Don't apologize. I had some time spare and I don't tend to get much of that. Thought it was worth a punt, see if anywhere was still open, stupid really. Why would a dance school be open at this time?"

"Are you looking to enquire for your daughter?" He found that funny. "Or son perhaps?"

"No," he laughed again, "I'm enquiring about dancers, actually. Well, a dancer, to be precise."

"Oh, you're him. The director."

"Him? I didn't know I was a him. I prefer the latter. Sounds far more influential," he said as he walked into the middle of the studio.

"Sorry, that sounded rude."

"That's all right. You are right, at least anatomically."

"Are you looking to hold auditions?"

"Eventually, I expect. Would you be interested in trying out?"

"No, I don't think so."

"That sounds rather defeatist."

"There are better dancers here than me. I'd rather not waste your time."

"You don't even know the part yet!"

"You haven't seen me dance."

We both laughed, talked for a little longer, I told about my new job at the Dream Centre, he said it sounded like a cult, I assured him it wasn't, he told me about his movie, till finally we got around to exchanging names.

"Look, Lilly, I can see you are busy and we can't proceed to talk in doorways like vagabonds. Here is my card, please give me a call. I think this role could be perfect for you and I would like to see you dance with my own eyes. That way, I can judge for myself."

"Sorry, I appreciate the offer, Mr Salter. But you can find other girls here with better ability than myself. I can give you a few girls' names who I know would love to speak to you. Girls that can really dance."

"That is the problem, Lilly. I have too many girls that can really dance. I'm actually sick to death of girls that can really dance. I'm not looking for perfect, the complete opposite. Believe it or not, this role requires an actress who is unable to dance."

"Sorry, Mr Salter. I'm confused. Why visit dance schools if

that is your aim? It doesn't make any sense. Look I really need to go now. I've got to be somewhere."

"Apologies, I'm not portraying myself in the right light here. I didn't mean to offend you. I mean I'm looking for an actress who dances to – how can I put this? – to a tolerable level. One with flaws and inconsistencies, imperfections. Look, you've got my card, ring me. I'm here till next week and I'd love to meet up with you. I'm not some strange perverted old man, promise, least not perverted anyway. Bring your parents, or a friend with you." He started to walk off.

"I can't act either." I followed him onto the street.

"Good," he shouted from his car door. "That's means you'll be cheap, clueless and malleable." He closed the door, smiling as he drove off.

It's hard to explain what happened next. I couldn't tell you how or why, luck mostly, suddenly I became an actress, reluctantly and without any intention. The critics went wild. I've kept all the paper clippings.

Goodridge's powerful portrayal of a young dancer crippled by grief is both nuanced and real.

Raw, maddening, a bravura performance, virtuous.

Unsurprisingly, some noticed my inexperience in front of camera, rabbit caught in the headlights; monkey in silk – had to ask Max want it meant, he asked me what I thought it meant, he said I wasn't far off. All I knew was my life would never be the same – agents followed, scripts next, money, condos, paparazzi.

By that time, me and Max were inseparable, from filming in LA to promoting overseas, from red carpets to awards ceremonies, Max and I would eventually become lovers. Officially, according to internet rumours, I had been sleeping with Max since before the film was even made, viral trolls suggesting I slept my way into the role like a lot of women were forced to. But in all honesty, it wasn't till the night of the Oscars that anything physical happened between us, and even more the revelation, it was myself that initiated the encounter.

I loved Max in every way possible at the beginning. Normally, it was the other way around, least with all my previous boyfriends, so it was strange that I felt nothing physically towards Max, that came much later. But my initial attraction to Max happened pretty much instantaneously, from that very first night at the dance school. Watching Max, being directed by Max, observing how he got the best out of people, I found a powerful form of seduction. He had a way about him, a quiet unassuming position, but one that was very persuasive, to make you believe that what he told you, no matter how far-fetched or ridiculous, was always with the intention of making things greater. Hey, he convinced me, and even my dad for that matter, that I should go half-naked in my first feature film, that took some doing. He was a master at his craft and knew the power he had over people and me for that matter.

Despite our differences, Max was great at what he did – I didn't realise it till I worked on other sets. Max did this thing on our first day, made us shoot a really intense scene off the bat, and after it was done he shouted "Cut." That was that, no second or third takes, just "Cut." I thought nothing of it, I was a virgin in all this, but I could sense it wasn't the norm, judging by everybody else's reaction. After I watched the movie for the first time I asked Max what happened to that scene. Max told me he never intended to use it. I asked why, of course. He just laughed, said it was a tight schedule, but I could tell by his wink there was a method to it, playing with people's motivations, making everyone up their game, behind and in front of the camera. Max's movies were made with more than entertainment in mind, he wanted to take it a step further, for those making it and watching.

I did find it attractive, his complexity, his intensity. I knew what it must've looked like, young girl of twenty in the arms of a middle-aged man. Like secretaries who fall for their boss, or pupils that lust for a teacher – predictably and regrettably, I fell for Max, and the world fell for us, too. Max hated it, of course. He wanted adulation and fame, yes, but based on merit, not the girl on his arm. But he changed his tune over time. As much as he hated celebrity, he knew how important it was, and in turn he knew how to use it for his own gain. I never knew if it was his intention, or some master plan, but he suddenly became known as a bastard, and not in a bad way.

Whether it was planned or not, it made him a superstar. Some said it was down to me, but I didn't take any credit. Men like Max were born for Hollywood, he would have got there with or without me. Funnily enough, despite his many female conquests, there were rumours he was gay and I could see why people would think that. A man working in dance the obvious one, but he had a certain demure, a way of carrying himself. But I never believed it, still don't, he loved women far too much. Night of the Oscar ceremony, after too much celebration, too much Tequila Patron, I asked Max if he was gay. He laughed. Later he walked me to my hotel room, me in my dress, him in his tux, bow tie loose, Oscar in one hand and cigar in the other. Jeez, he loved cigars, he'd even got me smoking them that night, even though I'd always hated the smell. I asked him again if he was gay, this time he didn't laugh, that was when I kissed him. First, I kissed him in the corridor, the hotel room, then my bed, the rest, well the rest has been well documented. We became Lilly and Max, never just Lilly, never just Max, always Lilly and Max.

There were nice times, he made me laugh a lot, he was and still is a kind man. I've only ever seen him lose his temper twice, the first was enough to make me worry, the second was enough to make me leave. Fame changes people, I knew it had changed me, certainly it changed Max, I didn't know if it made us better, it made us something different.

We split up in June of last year, the day after Michael Jackson died, for once we weren't headline news. August, I found out I was pregnant. Max would say it was a joint decision – as I said, he was a master at his craft, made me believe it was my choice. It was never my choice, I signed the forms, spoke to doctors, sat in hospitals. Sally would have known, might have agreed with Max that it was a necessary outcome. Frank would not have seen it that way. Regardless of how logical it may have sounded, my age, the point in my career, the point in Max's career, Frank would have stopped me. How could he not? He told me himself, he was an illegitimate child, he would have treated it as murder and he would have been right. Forget the fancy words 'termination,' 'removal,' 'expulsion' – in the cold light of day, it was murder. I never even got to see a scan. I don't think I could have done it once I'd seen a scan, once it became real, an outline, a baby. I read later it would've been around 6cm, the size of my little finger, thirteen weeks old. Even now I find it hard to look at myself, mirrors are difficult, I find it hard to smile sometimes, though I try. I have never regretted anything so much in my life. If Max hadn't been there, holding my hand, reassuring me it was the right choice, I wouldn't have gone through with it. Without a doubt I would have not done it, but I did go through with it.

I tossed my toenails into the fire and watched them crackle and glow, I would need a glass of wine tonight, Max had that effect. You know, he sent me a message the first day I arrived in England. 'Hope the shoot goes favourably,' it said, 'remember not to over-think it, just be you, Lilly G.' I deleted it with no reply, I'd seen him twice in the last six months, first time I hit him, the second he hit me, made us even, though I think he came off worse.

Upstairs I pondered the inside of my wardrobe. Eventually, a pile of rejected alternatives carpeted the floor. In the mirror was the finished product – I looked pretty, simple tee, expensive shoes. The door knocked, thoughts changed to oysters and wine. One glass of wine wouldn't hurt, I thought. Sally says I am always one drink away from a tabloid front page. It was her little mantra. Surely one wouldn't hurt? It would numb the senses, make me forget. Didn't make me stop thinking of Max, though. Max the Director, directing me from afar.

11

I didn't remember much, there was singing, loud singing, far too many scallops. I remember me and Sally hugging, Frank may or may not have given me a piggy back at some point, I remember making a toast, there was a possibility I made a move on Chris Rogan, or was it the other way around? I have no recollection of getting a cab, but somehow I was home, standing in the glow of the fridge, drinking milk straight from the carton. I briefly thought about udders and purchasing my own cow. I'm guessing it must have been around that time I threw up. I couldn't quite work out why I had muddy feet, but I do have a vague memory of being in my garden, shouting abuse at someone or something that wasn't there, there were curse words, but there may have been an invitation, too.

I closed my eyes again. It was too early for piecing things together, all I knew was, wherever I had chosen to sleep was neither my bedroom nor a bed. Regardless, I felt myself drift back into a broken sleep, as drunk became hung-over and dreams and memories and nightmares became intertwined.

★ ★ ★

The day before I flew out to England, a producer friend of mine had thrown another one of his crazy-ass pool parties up in Malibu, where hundreds descended from every far corner of the entertainment business to gossip and network. The house was ridiculous, I was obviously on the wrong side of the camera – marbled floors, spiral staircases, it was built for parties, grandeur that deserved a grand occasion. The theme was the same every year, a strict dress code to match the décor of the house, ball players in white linen suits, singers in small white dresses, tiny sluts in tiny white bikinis. It was everything you'd expect a millionaire's party to be, but for all the attendees it was lonely place too, full of fakes – fake friendships, fake boobs – the only way to endure it all was drugs, which this party had on tap and not even discreetly.

Unsurprisingly, Frank had begged me not to go and I struck a promise that I'd be plane-worthy, said I wouldn't drink, and to be fair I didn't, I had a line of coke, but only because I was being courteous. For the most part I was being good, sat at the bar, kept myself to myself. The barman was nice, kept me company, kept filling my glass with Virgin Coladas, told me about his career aspirations. I wasn't listening, my mind was already in England. Frank told me to let him know when I'd had enough, he and Sally weren't far away with our suitcases and our passports. I was about to message him, I'd shown my face, I was ready for the airport, mentally preparing for the long flight, plotting how I'd slip away from the party unnoticed. That's when I saw Max making his way toward me through the crowd of cocktails, his eyes on me, my eyes on him, I couldn't move, couldn't escape.

"You didn't get the memo then, Max," I said, eyeing his clothes. He looked impeccable, but he wasn't dressed to theme.

"It takes a big man to pull off a white suit and I'm not quite that man."

"Are you sure it's not just your way of being the minority, standing out? The man in black."

"If you say so, Lilly. It's been too long since I last saw you. When was it, New Year's?"

"I'm impressed you remembered."

"How could I not? You slap pretty hard."

"You deserved it, after the shit you pulled that night."

"Sweetheart, you added two and two and got five. I was only talking to the girl."

"It's never just talk with you, though, is it, Max?"

"You look beautiful."

"I'm just leaving."

"Please don't, not on my part."

"I think it's best I go."

"We can be civil, surely?"

"Plane to catch, I'm afraid."

"I read about that." Smiling, like he'd remembered a joke.

"And why's that funny?"

"I've heard of Jon, haven't seen his pictures, but I've heard only admirable things. I think it will be good for you to get away, clear your head. I'd like to meet with you soon, I don't like the way things ended. I don't like to think I made you run away."

"Is that what you think I'm doing? Running away?"

"Well, aren't you?"

I started to walk off. I'd had enough party for one night.

"Look. I'm sorry about all the unpleasant business that happened before, Lilly. It wasn't handled in the best way and I take some ownership for that."

"Unpleasant, Max. Is that what you call it?"

He went to hold my arm.

"Get the fuck off me, Max."

"Max, is everything OK?" said a voice from behind me.

I looked around, it was a woman, holding two drinks.

"Everything is fine, darling," Max said calmly. "Forgive me. This is Lilly." He took her hand. "Lilly, this is Darcey Sterling, she worked over at the American Ballet Theatre. I'm sure you'd get on like a house on fire." He turned to Darcey. "Lilly is one of us."

"How wonderful. I feel in better company when with a fellow dancer," she sipped. "And how do you know my darling Max?" she asked, passing him his drink.

I couldn't talk.

Max smiled. "Apologies, Lilly. Darcey isn't one for movies. Humphrey Bogart could say hello and she wouldn't have a clue who he was."

"I'd have to agree with Max," she said. "Dancing, yes, movies, not so much. To be honest, not doing much dancing now either, seeing as now I've got this little bundle."

And she patted her stomach, and worse, Max patted it too. Worse still, she smiled at me, not at all malicious, just a woman excited and proud. What I did next was unforgivable, it makes me sick when I think about it, I just, well I just flipped, I launched myself at her, slapped her, pulled her hair. On reflection, I'm glad Max pulled me off her, as quite honestly, I dread to think what I would have done if he hadn't been strong enough to stop me. I'd like to think I would have stopped, but in retrospect I don't think I would. I deserved to be hit and when Max slapped me across the face I was glad of it. All I knew was, I ran, ran past the bustle of the party, through the gates, rang Frank to come and save me, to take me off to a runway, fly me a trillion miles from Max as soon as possible.

Max messaged me straight after, but I didn't get to read it till I was quarter way across the Atlantic. He was full of apologies, said he had never hit a woman before and that was something he would have to live with, said no matter how mad he was, or out of control the situation, he should never have raised his hand. It wasn't the first time he'd tried to get back in contact since our split. No matter how many times I'd changed my number he'd always get the new number. Before the party I would never have messaged back, but it was different this time – I owed an apology too. I wished I could have said sorry to her directly, I really did, it was all I thought about on the plane. I nearly rang him to get her number, I so wanted to, so I could explain. Not that my explanation justified my actions, but at least she would understand. Anyways, Max assured me Darcey was OK, no harm to the woman or child, she wasn't going to press charges, not that I would've put up much fight if she had. I didn't blame her, it wasn't her fault she'd chosen to sleep with Max, he probably didn't tell her about me. I hit her because I was jealous, not of Max, but that my baby wasn't good enough for Max and hers was.

It wasn't right how Max was hung out to dry. He wasn't a violent man and I would have hit me too, I was in a rage, it was the only thing that could've stopped me, words wouldn't have worked, it took the shock of a slap to wake me out of it. It would not have been Max's intention to leave a mark or bruise, it was something done on impulse, a reaction to seeing a pregnant woman being attacked. To the big wide world, Max took the brunt of the blame, plastered on every single paper and blog, labelled the guilty one, an alcoholic, a woman-beater. For a change, the press got it wrong that time, but at least they were consistent. It's funny as if they'd asked me directly, flat out just asked me what happened at that party, you know I'd probably have told them the whole truth, all of it. -They always seem preoccupied with exposing the lie, setting me up for the public execution behind my back, when most times I'd have helped them hold the rope.

The strange by-product of what happened that night was it made me and Max talk again after four months of avoiding each other. It was effortless how easily we fell back into what we used to be, and I could see the danger in letting in continue, even if I enjoyed the flirting and the attention. I decided after I left London that would be the last message I'd read or send. It was hard and a few times I very nearly slipped back into old habits, but the key word was 'nearly,' I managed not to cave in to temptation.

How Max saw it, I didn't know. Badly, I expected, he didn't take too well to people making decisions above his head, and knowing Max as I did, he would take this as a loss and he wasn't too great at accepting those. But I suppose he had two choices, either he could concentrate on Darcey and his new baby, or more likely, continue to persist with me. He's always preferred the option he couldn't have. But hey, he might prove me wrong, though he never has before.

The mood downstairs wasn't pleasant. Frank was doing his best to be mother but he was struggling to fend for himself, let alone attempt to help anyone else. Outside in the garden we hid behind our sunglasses as we tore at croissants and sipped OJ hoping the combination of vitamin C and D would speed up the healing process, which so far it hadn't.

"The food was gorgeous, wasn't it? Such a cute little place. We'll have to go back. Maybe not drink as much next time."

"Don't talk about food. My piss smelt of crab this morning." Frank's eyes looked to the sky. "You have yourself a little garden party last night? You left the patio doors wide open."

"You would be right in your estimations, Mr NCIS. Don't make out you're all innocent either. I wasn't the one wearing a life ring and hugging the bartender."

He didn't answer.

"Is there anywhere round here that sells fluff, Frank? I could seriously go for a fluff sandwich right now."

"You've got as much chance of fluff as I have of finding a copy of *USA Today*."

"Am I filming? Please tell me today is a day off?"

"It's a Sunday. No one is working."

"Good. I'm not feeling very ladylike today. Could we go to the beach?"

"Let's get through this morning first. I can barely see five yards in front of me right now let alone scale over sand dunes. I'm gonna grab up some more coffee, I think the caffeine is wearing off." Frank picked up our cups and limped himself from grass to kitchen as I decided to get on my feet and attempt to move.

Despite the migraine across my forehead, it was a pretty view. There were sheep in the distance, I watched them clamber and chew as I took myself around the garden. I wondered who would live here when I went home. I guessed people like me, people who make it home for a little while, before the next car load do the same. A shame, such a nice big house, felt like it needed a permanent family. It wasn't perfect, don't get me wrong, the restrooms were too small and Frank was always banging his head on the ceiling beams, but it had a feel to it, it must have been there for centuries, added to obviously, but it still had all the charm and characteristics to make you feel quaint and prairie-like. I enjoyed this lifestyle more than I ever thought I would. I thought I'd miss the LA scene, the juice bars, the nightclubs, but noticing frogspawn or leaving milk out for hedgehogs got me more excited than dance floors and after-parties. It would be nice to be a kid growing up here, I thought – hills and rivers, forests and beaches, trees to climb. I'd like to come back one day, bring my folks, invite my sister, she could bring the kids, they'd run riot.

I walked downward through the tall bamboo, towards the stream, my own little Laguna, my Table Rock Cove. The other morning me and Frank made paper boats out of old newspapers, had little races, couldn't believe how fast they moved, such a strong current for such a little stream, I wondered where they might have ended up, probably in the middle of some ocean by now.

Frank returned with a fresh tray of coffee. "You better brace yourself."

"If I'm in trouble you're going down with me."

We looked over, Sally was already halfway down the garden, pointing her keys at the driveway, locking her car mid-stride.

"You never heard of knocking?" I shouted.

"It's not my fault you live in an open house, a wall would be nice, a gate, heaven forbid a lock, seeing as you're a famous actress and all." She took a cup and poured herself a coffee. "Makes me wonder who chose this house in the first off."

"I thought it was you."

"Not me, darling. My choice would have been a fortress, fucking Alcatraz."

"Who chose it then?"

"Fuck knows. Whoever did needs shooting. Security nightmare, this place. Exposed from all sides. Sitting ducks." Sally sank into a chair, her hand across her forehead. "Never let me drink cider again. Scrap that. I'm never eating apples again either."

Standing over her, I gave her a big cuddle. "Was this all worth it, Mom?"

"I need serotonin. Some clomipramine."

"Well, I had a great night," I declared. "Besides the puke."

"Lilly." Sally didn't look impressed. "Where did you puke?"

"Sinks mainly, various sinks. Stairs. I'll clean it, don't worry," I said, feeling my insides bubble again.

"You haven't even cleaned it up?"

"I will." I had no clue where I'd even find the mop and bucket.

We sat there in silence, fixed and emotionless, in our own private turmoils, must have sat there for a good fifteen minutes.

"Right, we can't sit in this state all day," I said.

"I agree," Sally said, searching for tablets in her bag. "I feel worse for sitting down."

"I don't," Frank sighed. "I'm happy as I am, thank you very much. This is me for the day and I ain't moving."

"We can tackle today in either of two ways, guys. Feeling sorry for yourselves or facing it head on."

"What do you have in mind?" Sally said, swallowing a handful of pills.

"No idea. Just not this. Just not sitting. We could go to the beach."

"Sounds a tad strenuous. I've had about four hour's sleep. And I'm supposed to be replying to emails."

"Come on, you two. The sea air will sort us out. You can send your emails later."

I could see Frank's distaste for the idea, but could see Sally's brain taking it all in, trying to work out whether the idea had wings.

"Where we would go?"

"Can't imagine it would be hard to find one."

"There'll be people there, I take it."

"I assume so, Sal, it is a beach."

"If there's too many, we come straight back. I haven't the energy to fend off fans and cameras."

"Deal. We'll keep low profile."

"OK, I'm in." Sally smiled

"For real?"

"You look surprised."

"Cos, I didn't think for one minute you'd agree."

"Well, I have agreed."

"And no cell phones. Cell phones are banned today."

"Don't push your luck, Lilly." Sally held her cell to her chest like a newborn. "I'm taking my cell."

"Fine. But only important calls, no checking emails or diaries. This is family time. Come on, guys, let's get ready, whilst the sun is out."

"Do I have a say in any of this?"

"No, Frank, you go where I go. Part of your job, I'm afraid. This is gonna be so fucking cool." We started to walk, all three of us, arm in arm, back towards the kitchen. "First, I need to pack a beach bag, towels, lotions, a book. Money just in case we fancy lunch."

"No way. First thing you're doing Miss Goodridge is cleaning up that puke."

"No problem. Will you help me find it?"

"The mop?"

"No, the puke." I said, as Sally's eyes rolled and Frank took his roasted socks off the Aga.

★ ★ ★

On arrival, the car-park was empty and not the view I'd expected – pale boys stripping out of wet suits, hanging them inside a van, about a dozen of them, smoking and laughing, looked pretty rowdy, a few of them were on the beer and it wasn't long past breakfast.

Frank handed me our bags and blankets from the trunk, he was still sulking, don't think he appreciated Sally's and my duet from the back seat, singing the only two Beach Boys' songs we knew the words to, lucky for him the drive was over in less than five minutes.

"You sure this is a good idea, you two?" he said, looking over at the group across from us. "You could get recognized."

"Frank, you serious?" I looked down at my clothes. "I'm hardly Hollywood today, am I?"

"It's your face that is famous, not your sweats. Just keep that hat on, the less skin on show the better."

"Holy fuck." Sally stood hands on hips, looking toward the sand dunes. They looked impossible. Somewhere behind them was the ocean, not that we could see it.

"You'll be fine, Sal," I lied. "Pretend it's your treadmill back home."

"Howzit guys?" A voice from behind me. A man, small, in a wet suit, an accent. "You three thinking of surfing?" His dog started to lick my hand. I assumed it was his, though it wasn't on a lead.

I didn't answer.

"I assure you, it looks pretty gnarly, but it's quite warm once you're in, worth a go, for sure."

"I'll think we'll leave it for today, friend." Frank slammed the trunk. "Got a sore head."

"Too many jars last night, hey? No better cure than Mother Nature."

"Another time."

"Well, let me know if you do ever fancy it, got plenty of sizes of boards and suits. Can do you a nice deal for the three of you. You guys look pretty cold. Got some coffee in the van. Where you from, California?"

"Los Angeles," I said. "Have you been to America before?"

"Ocean City in New Jersey. Me and my bro are thinking of going to Montauk soon. Where you staying around here?"

"A cottage," Frank answered, purposely vague, borderline rude.

"This place certainly has a lot of cottages. You like it, though?"

"It's beautiful," I said.

"Plenty to do, that's for sure. Have you been to Salcombe? North Sands?"

I shook my head.

"Full of convertibles and Botox. Try the Winking Prawn. Best Po Boy in Devon, too."

"We haven't seen much, to be honest. Been in our cottage mostly." I felt guilty for talking.

"That's a shame, guys. There is a lot to do round here, if you are willing to find it and depending how long you've got to explore. You guys just here for a long weekend?"

We didn't answer. I noticed Frank had started to lose patience, stood there in a frown, his hands full of bags, his face red from the cold, he wanted to stay under the radar, this wasn't part of his plan.

"Can you get signal here for our cell phones?" Sally asked our new friend.

"Not likely."

"What about a beer?" Frank asked. "Might do me good"

"If you look to your right there is Bigbury on Sea." He pointed, but all we could see was the sand dune. "There is a little café serving scones and crab there, you can walk across if the tide is out, if not then you'll have to drive. Other than that, there is a pub up the road, The Sloop Inn, if you fancy something warmer and indoors."

"We best be off, whilst the sun is out. Thanks for your help today." Frank offered out his hand.

"No worries. The name's Dave. You are?"

"I'm Frank, this is my wife, and this," he paused, looking at me, "this is my daughter."

I looked over at Sally, I did my best to hold in my laugh.

"Well look, guys. Maybe not today, but feel free to ring me if you fancy a surf. Here is my card, ring me the night before and we'll sort out times depending on the weather and tide. I'll be here for a couple more hours depending on how busy it gets, so if you change your mind then swing by the van."

"How busy does it get here?" Frank enquired.

"This time of year, Bantham is pretty quiet. You'll have the beach to yourselves."

"Perfect." Frank's eyes brightened up.

"Frank, do you need a hand with all that stuff, those sand dunes are killer. I can have the guys help you over to the beach. They are all hung-over, stag do. Have a guess which one is the groom? Have you got windbreaks?"

"What's a windbreak?"

"Don't worry," Dave laughed. "I've got a few spare ones. Don't want your wife here to blow away, do we?"

He whistled and soon a selection of pink men with beards and bellies were walking towards us. I handed my bags to the nearest set of hands, thanking him as I did. He said his name was Gary, and he felt obliged to apologize instantly for his appearance, his prom dress and matching Viking hat. I looked over at Sally, she was being piggybacked by Frank. I couldn't work out who looked angrier.

★ ★ ★

"Bars don't smell like this back home. Smells like my grandma's old kitchen table. Old and varnished."

No one answered, not for a long time.

"This is more my speed." Frank took a sip of beer, his feet up. "I could die for a pack of Lucky Strikes around now."

"Don't get any funny ideas," I said. "Your doctor will kill you, not to mention me and Sally."

"I've cheated death once. I ain't taking any more chances, don't worry. It's just some moments call for a smoke and this feels one of those moments."

"You enjoyed today then, Frank, after all your sulking?"

"It wasn't as bad as I thought it would be."

I laughed.

"What's so funny?"

"Max said the same thing after my first audition." I put my feet across Frank's lap. "You admit today was a success?"

Frank nodded. "Better than just sitting, I suppose."

"What about you, Sally? Had a nice time?"

"Once I warm up." Sally was leaning even closer towards the roaring fire.

I noticed Sally check her cell again.

"Still no signal?" I asked.

"How does this fucking village survive? It's the 21ˢᵗ century for God's sake."

"Just think of the all the things you are missing. There might be a world disaster going on, an asteroid has hit America, zombies have taken over Manhattan."

"Ha Ha. You shouldn't joke about stuff like that. Besides you forget one thing, Lilly darling. I haven't had no signal in about seven years, I'm literally about to have a panic attack, this is fucking psychological warfare."

"It's just a phone, Sally."

"It's my fucking right arm. This shit will set me back five years." Sally looked over my shoulder. "Oh great, another dog." The owner apologized as it licked her hand.

"It's like going back in time," I grinned. "Look at us, no phones, no TV, no distractions. Just a fireplace and good company."

The bartender came over, lighting the candle on our table.

"You folks warm enough?" he asked Frank, assuming he was in charge of keeping it roaring. "Give it a stoke every half hour, lob a log on it if it needs it. Can I get you folks any more drinks? Something to eat? Some cheeses perhaps? Some port?"

"That sounds great," I replied quickly. Frank and Sally looked at me from over their glasses, as the barman walked back to the bar.

"Cheese and port? Whenever have you ever had cheese and port?"

"Lots of times."

"When? Name a time."

"Thanksgiving."

"That's a lie. What do you reckon, Sally?" Frank asked. "This cheese and port business."

"Let her eat what she wants," Sally sniffed, turning another page of whatever magazine she was reading. "Just as long as she can still get into that corset tomorrow." The three of us returned to silence again, sipping drinks, reading things, it was all very civil, all very British.

I enjoyed the beach, everything about it, start to finish. Dave and his dog, Gary, all those lads we met. I liked Gary, I'd never seen someone so sunburnt in a place so cold, he didn't stop talking either, about his last few nights, sounded pretty wild, told me about his upcoming wedding, his poorly fiancé, his shoestring budget. Jeez, I nearly paid for his honeymoon there and then, I've always been a sucker for a sob story, but I didn't of course. I was supposed to be just a normal girl after all, not the celebrity version of myself, I couldn't just give strangers thousands of dollars without a real reason.

Felt nice to be talked to, though, to be an ear rather than a mouth. You'd be surprised how little that happens, fame brings out the worst in people, it is hard to find genuine honesty. Gary invited me to play drinking games on the beach and I agreed. It was fun, sat in a circle, me the only girl, all of us clapping and shouting, took me a while to grasp the rules, they were hardly complex, win or lose, the outcome was always vodka. As you could probably guess, I lost more than I won, not that I told Frank or Sally that.

Dave was right, too, we did have the beach pretty much to ourselves, except for a few dog walkers. "Only mad dogs and Englishmen, hey?" one said, Frank laughed but I didn't understand why. Sally, who has been in a permanent state of loss all day, asked if they had the time. They said between lunch and dinner which again they found hilarious, as did Frank. I didn't know if they were joking, but this place was genuinely unaffected by clocks and time and felt very much dictated by weather and stomachs.

The sea was so cold, colder than it looked, which was a miracle seeing how uninviting those first few yards of tide were. Frank and Sally stayed on shore, said I was crazy, but it wouldn't have felt right to visit a beach and not let your feet feel the water. Today was a first, though, I'd never seen people wear coats on a beach. Only in England – this country was not what I expected. Actually, I got the impression Devon wasn't a representation of England at all, and somewhere quite special on its own merit, a grey Utopia which, though not as blue as back home, was still a place I was starting to prefer.

"Here is your cheese, miss." The bartender handed me a plate. "Eat it left to right. Mild to mature."

"Thank you."

"Anything else, folks?"

"There is one thing," I said. "When I was at the beach I saw a big white house on an island."

"Burgh Island," he smiled. "It's a hotel, actually."

"How do you get to it? Boat?"

He laughed. "Sea tractor. You can walk to it if you catch the tide at the right time, but when the high tide comes in then it's either sea tractor or swim. Best thing is to check the tide times the day before."

"You have been, I take it?"

"No. I've seen pictures, like stepping back in time I've heard. I promised the wife I'd take her there for our twentieth anniversary. She likes all the glamour, the ballgowns and whatnot. Cost me an arm and a leg."

"Sounds awesome."

"Agatha Christie thought so too. I best leave with your cheeses. Is there anything else you require?"

"No, that's us finished, thank you," Sally added.

The bartender went behind his bar returning moments later with our bill and a gift.

"Here you go. You can have this if you like." He handed me a book. "Apologies for the title of it, I assure you she wasn't a racist."

"Are you sure you don't mind me having this? I've never read an Agatha Christie book before."

"I'm sure. Every house in East Devon comes with a free copy of it," he laughed.

"Thank you so much. I will read it and return it I promise.

He smiled. "You keep it. I've another half a dozen somewhere," he said, walking off again.

"Can't believe he just did that, so kind. That's it, we've got to visit that hotel, all three of us."

"What, now?" Sally closed her magazine.

"Not now. I mean, at some point whilst we are here."

"Lilly. So far today you've told me you are going to eat a Po Boy, whatever that is, go coasteering in Newquay, and zorbing, which sounds equally horrific and I doubt we are insured for, and now you want to go to a hotel via a sea tractor. If two words should not mix they are 'sea' and 'tractor'."

"And?"

"It seems you want to live your life in a state of reckless spontaneity. You do realize that my whole purpose in this team is to be the exact opposite of recklessness and spontaneity."

"Sally, we are here for a long time. I don't mean I want to do all those things now. I just mean eventually, as in this year, or in the future."

"What, you mean you may come back?"

I nodded. "I know you find it hard to believe, but I really like it here. I may even buy a place one day."

"Frank, are you hearing this?"

Frank took a chunk of cheese off my plate. "Sal, it's her choice where she lives."

"No, it isn't. It's a collective decision. It affects all three of us. Where she lives, we have to live too."

"I could live here." Frank with his two cents.

"Jeez, Frank. You could live anywhere that has a fire and beer. Lilly, admit it would be career suicide."

"I don't mean now. I mean like, in the future, somewhere I can visit, somewhere quiet, somewhere people leave me alone, where I can be just plain old Lilly. Surely you've noticed a difference in me? Surely you've noticed how happy I am here?"

"Only because you've run away from everything."

"That's unfair."

"I don't mean to sound unfair, I'm just telling it to you as it is. You are happy here because you have taken a vacation. When you go home you will have to face to reality again."

"Great. Back to depression and anxiety. Can't wait."

"There are women out there who would kill for the opportunities you have. Literally kill."

"Well, I'm not that woman."

"Maybe not, Lilly."

"I'm too exposed, Sally. There is no respite back home. I don't want to be famous all the time."

"That is the price of fame I'm afraid."

"Things have to change when we get home, Sally, otherwise I'll burn out or worse."

"I won't let that happen."

"Couldn't I just make one blockbuster and then retire? I don't care how awful it is. Some franchise. What about if I go nude?"

"You're being silly now." Sally looked away.

"Look," Frank stoked the fire, the embers orange again. "I don't care how many millions you make, but I don't think you should give up and become a recluse just yet."

Sally put her hand on my knee. "Right, let's wrap this up as I'm getting cold and tired. After we have made this car crash of a movie and we fly back home I'll hold a meeting with the team, and we'll sit down and talk strategy and all agree on a way forward. Try and find a way to slow things down a little, look at how we can make you less exposed."

"The team just see me as a money machine. A boardroom doesn't care about my emotional stability."

"There is always room for change, Lilly. And you are wrong. As long as I'm in our team the only thing that matters is that you are happy."

I smiled and she smiled back.

"And no talk of emigrating, at least for a while."

"You're just pissed cos you can't use your cell. Here have some of this." I handed her a slice of cheese that stank even worse than it looked.

"Get it away. It's worse than your roasted socks. Can we go now? Frank, stop sipping that port, otherwise you'll be unfit to chauffeur. And can someone come and claim this animal. I'm starting to smell all dog, too."

* * *

I could hear Frank in the front seat, arguing with the dark, disagreeing with the GPS, me and Sally in the back.

"Lilly, I'm sorry if you feel like we are always at each other's throats. You didn't mean it, did you?"

"Mean what?"

"That you wanted to quit. Stop being an actress." She pulled a blanket over her and then me.

"Sometimes, yes. Not that I'll ever do it. It's just every now and again I get this feeling of being trapped."

"Trapped in what way?"

"Every way. I feel everything is out of my control, my career, my life, the press. Sometimes I just want to start over. You know, quit while I'm ahead. Quit before I'm fucked up beyond repair."

"But you aren't ahead. The world out there has only seen a glimpse of Lilly Goodridge. There is so much more."

"What, me being battered and bruised, failed relationships?"

"Lilly, that is in your control. You choose who to fall in love with, not the public. You need to be more careful with your choices. Who you socialize with? Some of your friends are poisonous, damaged individuals. You need to pick them more wisely."

"Everyone is damaged."

"Are they even friends? Seems likes they are just using you."

"What do you want me to say? That you and Frank are the only friends I got?"

"We care so much about you. You know that."

"Sally. I need friends my own age."

She didn't answer. The car stopped.

"We lost, Frank?"

"Apparently we've reached our destination."

"I can't see the house."

"I'm fully aware of that, Sally." Frank sounded pissed. We left him and the GPS to fight it out.

"Would you feel more comfortable if I employed some extra security?"

"No. Frank is all I need. No big apes in suits. I feel like the President's wife enough already."

"I can't stop you being famous, Lilly. It's my job to keep it that way, you understand."

"I know. Thanks for being supportive. I must be a nightmare to work with."

"I've worked with worse. And you are right, perhaps I need to loosen up a bit. Try to chill out, stop running your life like a military operation. I didn't realise how affected you are by it all. You need to speak to me more. I don't know if you don't tell me these things."

"I will, promise."

"And I will promise to find solutions. I can't guarantee I can fix everything but I will certainly try and make things better."

"My Sally Bethany Alquist. You have changed."

She laughed. "I know. The sea air must have gone to my head."

"You're not even wearing make-up."

"No one here to impress, is there?"

"It's nice, isn't it? Not having to impress anyone."

"I must look sixty years older. I dread to think what my hair looks like after today."

The car started again. Sally's cell buzzed. She took it out of her coat pocket, then put it back.

"You got signal finally, then?"

She nodded.

"I know how much you've wanted to check all day. I don't mind, honest. You have been well behaved. I will allow it."

"Is that so? Well, maybe I don't want to look at it."

"Sally, stop fooling around and just read your goddamn messages before I change my mind."

She smiled, taking out her cell again.

"Holy fuck. My inbox has gone crazy."

"Probably all junk."

I looked at Sally, her expression had changed.

"What's wrong? Asteroids? UFO landings?"

"It's nothing."

"Sally. What is it?"

"I'm not sure."

"What do you mean?"

"Let me read them and I'll tell you."

I waited a few seconds.

"So?"

"The paps have been busy."

"Where? The beach? Today?"

"No, last night."

"How bad?"

"I won't know the full extent till tomorrow. I haven't seen the photos, just a pre-warning from the office. I've had nineteen missed calls. Fuck!"

We went quiet.

"Hey, don't cry, let's not let it ruin the day." She rubbed my knee. "We'll assess the damage in the morning. Besides, you got a full day of filming so I need you 100% focused on that. I'll deal with all this shit. Smooth it out. Everything is fixable."

"It's not that, Sal. I just thought this place was far away enough to be left alone. I thought I'd avoid all this shit. The paparazzi are here, aren't they?"

"Looks that way, yes."

The car went silent. We both stared out of different windows at the same type of darkness.

12

After half an hour trying to work out how to empty the vacuum cleaner, exhausted, I threw myself on the couch. So far, I'd polished and dusted, sprayed things and scrubbed, the house smelt floral, it smelt disinfected, it felt presentable.

I met Kate on my first feature, she was the costume standby, we hit it off, stayed in touch ever since. We bumped into each other just before I flew out, said she would be in England on business too, Wales she said, some medieval shoot, armour and swords, we said we'd try and catch up at some point, though I never believed we actually would. It was quite the surprise when she messaged me out of the blue checking the best time to visit. I don't think I'd ever do it, a three-hour drive was a hell of a long way to go for a chat. I messaged her a few days ago, said we could just meet back in LA if the journey was too much trouble, but she insisted, said she was fed up of blood and battlefields.

I'd just sent Frank out for groceries to stock up on all things slumber party. Frank wasn't best pleased, not the shopping list but in the company I would be entertaining. Frank wasn't Kate's biggest fan and had always associated her with a younger more dangerous version of myself. I'd reassured him that Kate, like myself, had changed too, but Frank as usual would not change his opinion or facial expression whenever her name was brought up. Of course, I ignored his warnings – yes, Kate had a past, we all had pasts. She was a little wild, but she was a good person, with a good heart and deserved not to be written off by men like Frank and others like him.

I'd ordered Frank to take Sally out for the night, booked them into a tapas restaurant in Kingsbridge. Me and few cast members had lunch there a while ago and thought it a nice place, very them, quiet and quaint, little boats and market stalls. I hoped seafood and sangria might cheer him up, as he's had to earn his money these last few weeks. Frank was adamant it was just dinner, just friends, not a date, but I knew first hand that Sally was dressing up as if it was.

I checked my to-do list, I'd washed the wine glasses, the shot glasses, filled a bucket of coal, brought in firewood, I wanted everything perfect for when Kate arrived, show off my house, even though it wasn't my house to show. She couldn't have picked a better time to visit, for lots of different reasons, the place had changed so much since when I'd first arrived back in April. I'd bonded with it. Before, everything felt uncomfortable, beds lumpy and sofas too soft, everything in the wrong place, wrong height, wrong temperature, but not now, what used to be flaws were now just quirks.

May had changed the garden entirely, too, blasts of colour everywhere, purples and pinks and yellows, too many flowers and not enough vases to put them in. Our little pond had ducklings now, I fed them, carbohydrates mostly, crusts and crumbs, someone in this house should have carbs, sad the wildlife got more sustenance than I did. With such good weather, I'd spent most of my time outside, sat on my little wicker bench or laid on a blanket, reading on my belly, sucking orange wedges, paddling. Even started baking, found a few bags of cored apples and pears in the bottom of the freezer so most of it ended up as a pie or a crisp. I mean, I was no Julia Childs, but the Aga was kept busy, better than warming underwear that was for sure.

I'd become used to this house arrest. Hollywood must have thought me dead, I read lots now, the owners whoever they were left behind a ton of books, every room had a shelf or stack. Travel guides and reference books mostly, *Lonely Planets* all dog-eared, spines bent and cracked, like the book had seen its country. I read them on the toilet or in the bath mostly, read about cities I'd never visit and histories I'd never understand.

I was addicted to British soaps, too, which was embarrassing. I wondered if I'd be able to watch them back in LA, probably be on some channel I'd never heard of, or on at some ridiculous time of the day. Never know, that might be me one day, I thought. If all else failed on the big screen, one day you might see me on the small screen, *Days of Our Lives* or *All of My Children*, even *Walford* or *Weatherfield*. I wouldn't mind, performing was performing no matter what stage it was on, or size of the screen. Work is work, like my dad always said.

Filming had been going really well. Still don't think I'd mastered the accent and I was certainly no natural at living in a different century. I was afraid of asking Jon how I was doing, scared he'd be honest and say I was awful, that he'd made a wrong decision casting me. I would have to take his silence as a positive, get my head down, get the job done. In all honesty I was quite bored, the script wasn't great and so far, I'd found it difficult to connect with the story or my character. For all its beauty, this movie was forgettable, and although everyone on set was having a good time, it came across to me that no one was taking it as seriously as they should, including me.

I didn't actually have that many lines, which made it worse – certainly didn't help my confidence either. From watching the dailies, I pondered and pouted a lot, perhaps they'd finally realized I couldn't act. At the end of every day's shoot when Jon handed me my call sheet, half joking I asked for more lines and he would always say some witty remark about the best actors not needing lines. And though I should have taken it at face value, instead I took it that there was another reason why my lines were so few.

I got upset the other day. I'd spent a good couple of evenings rehearsing a scene, decided to give it my all, lots of coffee, lots of reading over and over, getting into the head of my character – I didn't have many big scenes so I wanted to come prepared. But on the day of filming, after a dozen takes, Jon decided to throw in the towel. There were reasons, I expected, he said there was too much movie in the scene, too much acting, said he wanted the audience to respond not react, whatever that meant. I didn't argue why, stormed off back to my room into the arms of my on-screen father. He told me not to take it personally, come rigorously prepared but don't be afraid to let it all go, he said.

My feelings for Chris Rogan hadn't altered either, he was still an arsehole, annoyingly he was still adorable to look at though. He was quite persistent, too, and had been quite honest in his intentions, feeling inclined to offer his physical services after most takes. I had to kiss him the other day, it took a hell of a lot of takes, think Rogan was screwing up on purpose, but it was hardly erotic, a dozen camera angles, though I'd be lying if I said I didn't enjoy it. I knew Rogan did, that was for sure, told me he had a boner both before and after. He's so fucking childish, it was actually quite an attractive feature. I didn't know how old he was, I'm guessing mid-twenties, but he acted like he was about twelve. He was over the moon actually, his agent had got him a lead role in some comic franchise, endorsements, spin offs, so he was counting down the days till he could fly back home and be the bronzed poster boy. To be fair it was only a matter of time till he got his break, he was one of those fuckers who's always had life a little easy. I wouldn't be surprised if he used to play college ball, fucked cheerleaders, probably aced his SATs, probably Valedictorian, bet his dad looked like fucking Paul Newman. Not that I was jealous, well just a little, I mean I would have liked to have known what my next movie would be. Sally and my agent were in talks, I was told I shouldn't worry, which always made me worry more.

The paparazzi were still hard at work, for all my hiding and scurrying, becoming the recluse, somehow, they'd managed to find me. To be honest there weren't many, it was always the same half dozen guys I'd see, definitely not the swarm I was used to back home, but still enough to cause damage and distress, still enough to have to keep us all on guard. I didn't delve myself but I was told that so far the damage was minimal, just me getting into a car, me getting out of a car, spent most of my time driving to location, or being driven back. I wasn't sure why people would find that interesting to read or watch but for the most part these endless photos of my legs and sunglasses getting out of a car weren't doing much harm and Sally and Frank remained calm and contented with the exposure levels.

I hoped that might have meant Sally could take a breath. Things did go a bit weird initially after that first photo leaked, Sally accepting sole blame, said she had been silly and naive to let me get so out of hand and in such a public location. Even worse, she and Frank got as out of control too. I told her that it was just one of those things, that I invited them not the other way around. Didn't change her opinion of the situation, she took the role of responsibility more seriously than our friendship. The message was we were all getting too familiar and too comfortable with each other, from now on our relationships would be strictly professional. Let's see how long that lasted, I thought, me and Frank had a bet it would be a matter of days till Sally was back letting me give her a French pedicure and watching old *Friends* episodes as she plaited my hair. But the last few weeks she has stuck to her guns, which wasn't great news for Frank having been banned from touching a drop until informed otherwise. Also meant I was kept on a short leash, not allowed to venture too far unless with good reason, or if agreed by higher up first. I did feel a little caged, not as free as I would like, least the paparazzi didn't know where I lived, as long as I had my little retreat I didn't mind my temporary confinement. They could have anything they wanted outside, but my home was mine, I gave them enough of me, I deserved one thing just for myself.

I actually didn't mind the paparazzi, I just didn't agree with me having to alter my life around them. I couldn't care less if they snapped me dancing, or drinking, or singing, or whatever it was I was caught doing. I didn't even care about the money they made, sometimes the clever ways they'd hide and stalk probably deserved a decent payout, purely based on effort and desire alone. Frank disagreed, detested their very being, Sally on the other hand understood they were a necessity, didn't mean she didn't have words for them. Sally often spelt out her curses, thought it reduced its severity, and had spelt out all curses imaginable to describe the profession that was stalking and snapping.

Meant I did as I was told, kept my head down, kept my head up, tried not to give the paparazzi ammunition, and instead me and the photographers continued with our stalemate, probably as bored of me as I was of them, and the cycle continued. Me getting into a car, me getting out of a car, me getting into a car again. They may even give up and go home, turn their attention to a celebrity far more interesting, though I guessed that would not be the case.

I heard my cell ring from the other room.

★ ★ ★

I thought I would've cried, though the day was young.

Mom sounded calm, too calm, if anything she sounded quite upbeat. Dad was moving out in a couple of days, a mutual decision apparently, said it was for the best they put some space between themselves. My instinct told me it was something Dad had done wrong, asked her what he'd done this time, but she pleaded his innocence, it was just a case of two people growing apart.

I rang Dad straight after, but he barely said a word, he was more concerned about the dog. I rang my sister too, she was all tears and sobbing, but rather than join her I spent most of the conversation persuading her it was for the best, even though I hadn't persuaded myself yet.

Finally, when all phone calls had been made, that was when I cried, not loud or even for that long, just a few tears on my own, a few minutes of anger and frustration before I was back getting myself ready. It never crossed my mind to cancel tonight,

Kate would already be halfway down a motorway, besides tonight I needed a drink and Kate wouldn't need that much influencing to turn the night wild.

★ ★ ★

"I wish you had the *Grease* soundtrack." Kate was knelt down by the stereo, concentrating at my iPod.

"I thought I had it."

"Travolta was hot."

"Kenicke was hotter. You want a top-up?"

"Load it up."

"Double?"

"Only if you are."

"I'm game."

"Right, you do realize what happens when you drink bourbon, Miss Goodridge?"

"I'm fully aware."

"You are crossing a line here. I was there at our wrap party. I witnessed your downfall personally."

"Yes, but tonight I don't have a stripper's pole."

"That is both a shame and a relief." Kate sat back down on her stool. I passed her a drink. "What shall we drink to?" She raised her glass.

"England?"

"Fuck England. It's wet and cold."

"To Danny Zuko?"

"Much better. To Danny Zuko."

We downed our drinks, which were quickly refilled.

"So, gossip. Fill me in?"

"Kate, I've been in the middle of nowhere. What gossip do you think I might have?"

"Must be something? Come on I've spent a month surrounded by brutes and heretics."

"Doesn't sound that bad."

138

"Oh, the novelty wears off pretty darn quick. If I see another beard again I'll fucking scream. Come on, you must have hooked up with someone, Prince Harry, Harry Potter. I need some gossip."

"Sorry, pretty uneventful. I could show you some ducklings."

Kate looked unimpressed. "What else?"

"I think this house may be haunted. I read the guest book. There have been multiple sightings."

"Excellent. Glad I'm not staying over. What else?"

"Frank found lots of footprints by our garden fence."

"What, in the garden?"

"No, just outside."

"Farmer? Dog walker? Ghost of Christmas Past?"

"Could be. My guess is the paps."

"You reckon they are outside now?" She went over to the kitchen doors.

"Might be. You should wave."

"I can't see shit, too dark. Shall we invite them in? Liven things up."

"Let's do it."

"We could flash our tits."

"Best not. I think the pizza's ready soon. Looks pretty stormy out there."

"What the fuck is that noise?" Kate put her nose to the glass of the double doors.

"Hailstones."

"What the fuck is a hailstone?"

I laughed.

"What's so funny?"

"I asked Frank the same thing."

"Glad I'm in here and not out there. Sounds like the end of days," she said as she slumped on the couch in the corner of the kitchen.

When Kate first arrived she was dressed immaculately, J Brand jeans, camisole top. And likewise, I was equally as glamorous in a floral maxi dress, but our outfits didn't last long, they were soon ditched for all things baggy and elasticated, it wasn't a night for fashion. She had been in here for an hour and what started as quite a cultured evening of sophisticated conversation over cheese and jazz had transcended into doing nails and getting drunk, which I thought would happen anyway, and kind of counted on too.

"The house is pretty. Reminds me of the Hamptons," she said, chewing ice.

"I wouldn't know, I have never been."

"Daddy throws one of his soirées there every spring break."

"He sounds like Puffy."

"I assure you, it's pretty tame. Just old dudes masturbating over each other's profit shares, and the women cleaning up after them."

"Still, must be nice to get away from it all. Have a little retreat."

"I guess. You'll have to come. You can keep me company. Help me get through it all, keep my mom from the gin. How long till you go home?"

"Another month. Wish I could go home and see my folks though."

"Must be pretty shitty for you. Divorce is a bastard. You don't think they'd let you go back?"

"I doubt it."

"What about after? Another movie I guess?"

"Gonna take some time off. You?"

"A week here, then back home. We are in pre-production at the moment, storyboarding."

"With Max, again."

Kate paused. "I wasn't going to mention him. Didn't want to put you off your pizza."

"That's OK. I don't mind talking about Max. I'm fine with it now. How is he?"

"He's good. Busy as normal."

"Getting prepared for fatherhood?"

"Fatherhood?"

"Him and Darcey." I sat myself next to Kate.

"What, Darcey as in Darcey Sterling?"

"Yes."

"Darcey Sterling had her baby last month. Girl I think."

"That's a relief."

"A relief?"

"Sorry, I mean it's always a relief isn't it when babies are born healthy? I bet Max is pleased."

"He is, yes. They made him godfather. Darcey's husband's an old friend of Max's. Used to go to college together."

"So Darcey is with this Jeff? Max is not with Darcey?"

Kate laughed. "Max isn't with anyone. He hasn't been with anyone since you two broke up."

"Oh."

"You OK, Lill?"

"I'm fine. Another drink?"

"Fill her up."

"Double again, I assume?"

"Of course. Is that burning?"

"Oh, fuck, the pizza." I ran towards the Aga, grabbed a towel, pulled the tray from the smoke.

"How bad is it?" Kate came over to inspect the damage.

"Edible. Just about."

"You sure you're all right, Lilly?"

"I'm fine. Haven't gotten used to the Aga yet."

"No, I meant about Max. You seem a bit startled."

"Sorry, just crossed wires that's all."

"Did you think Max and Darcey were together?" she smiled. "You thought her baby was Max's?"

"My mistake."

"You couldn't be further from the truth, Lilly. Max is still besotted with you. Still hopes one day you two might get back together."

"Does he now?"

"Talks about you all the time. In fact, he mentioned you for his new project."

"That isn't the reason you're here, is it? He didn't send you to butter me up, did he?"

"Lilly, I assure you I'm not Max's errand boy. Max can look after himself."

I put the pizza on the table, and passed her a few slices, the least burnt ones.

"Would you ever get back with him?"

"No."

"You don't think it's worth another go?"

"Too much has gone on. Friends, but nothing more."

"Do you still love him?"

"I don't think I ever loved him. It was more infatuation."

"You made a good couple."

"We didn't. We clashed about most things."

"My mom always said marriages that last longest are the ones that learn how to argue properly. Trust me, she should know."

"Clashing and arguing are different things."

We both picked at our pizza, peeled off the toppings, left the rest.

"Any other potential boyfriend options?"

"Nope. Depressing isn't it? My life is sexless."

"How is it working with Chris Rogan? I've heard he's a pest."

"He's harmless."

"He has amazing shoulders."

"This is true."

"Is it wrong to love a man based purely on his shoulders?"

"I've got his number. I could ring him for you. Tell him to come around."

"No way. We could so do that."

"Probably best not to. It would ruin our working relationship."

"Fuck that. I'm thinking a threesome. You can just watch if you want."

"I'm not sure your fiancé would approve, Kate."

We both laughed hysterically.

"Sorry about a minute ago, it got too deep.?"

"It did a bit. It's the Max effect."

"Shall we do some dancing?"

"Yes, let's dance. You choose."

"Any requests? Just don't judge me. I'm drunk and you're a professional at this."

"Kate, I haven't danced in a long time. We'll be as bad as each other."

"Hey," Kate was looking around in her handbag, "look what I've brought with me."

"It's not a crimping iron, is it?"

"No, better," she held out a bag of coke in her hand. "I've not done any in ages. Come on, it will be fun."

"No, it wouldn't, Kate. Put it away."

"If you aren't having any, then I am."

"Can you not?"

"I'll only have a little, don't worry. I'm not going to OD on your couch."

"No, Kate. I mean it. Please."

"OK, OK, I'll put it away."

"I thought you'd stopped all that?"

"No, I did, I have. Just on special occasions. I thought tonight was a special occasion. Obviously, I was wrong."

"Don't be like that. You know why I can't."

"OK, let's forget about it. Can we dance now?" Kate went back over to the stereo. "A bit of N-Sync?" Kate grinned as she pressed play and the kitchen was filled with my childhood.

"Kate, you know I can't refuse N-Sync. I might be a bit rusty."

"I'll lead the way, don't worry."

"I don't think I'm drunk enough for this."

"Well down some more bourbon. I'm going to the ladies room. When I come back it's Justin and JC time."

＊ ＊ ＊

Not long after, I called Kate a cab. She literally crawled into it. I gave the cab driver extra, just in case there was any puke, he didn't look amused. I said she could stay at mine, but she preferred a hotel, so I left her to it.

Despite the empty bottles, popped corks, shot glasses, I wasn't actually that drunk, even more surprisingly I made a start tidying the kitchen, poured myself the last of the wine, put on something chilled in the background, loaded the dishwasher, cleaned down the sides. I could've really gone for some pot, alcohol always made me want pot, one drug to another, though one was far less accessible round here. I wouldn't know where to get pot even if I wanted to.

It must've been around 2am, still I wasn't tired. I grabbed a jacket, opened the kitchen door and stepped barefoot into the garden. It was no night to be out, the rain had stopped but the wind hadn't, it whistled as I made way across the lawn. I'd started to really appreciate the calmness of this place, very Zen-like, how I'd imagined rehab, nothing to do, nothing of temptation, just time to think and a view to talk to. I didn't stay out there long, till my fingers went numb and my teeth chattered.

"Night everyone," I shouted at the wind and anyone else that might have been out there, sheep, ducks, paps, it was lights out for everyone. I locked the kitchen door behind me, turned the lights off, made my way upstairs through the dark of the house, past the shadows and ghosts, too merry to care which.

I removed my eyelashes in front of the mirror, watching myself turn from beautiful to plain, before getting into a cold bed, in my big bedroom, in my big house, just me. Felt myself starting to cry, though I wasn't sure why, I had plenty of reasons to cry, my job, my parents, my ex-boyfriend, my dead baby. Got myself into a bit of state, beyond sad, an urge to be anything but alone.

Let's just say that I messaged someone, told him to get here quick, someone I worked with, dreamy eyes and big shoulders, and let's say he may have come over and at the door he didn't talk, he just took me upstairs, and we had sex, and it was great and long overdue, it wasn't romantic, but passionate and quick, quick in a good way, and quick again a second, and a third time, and let's just say on the third time we did it by the window, stood up, curtains open, the fields and trees in front of me, in full view for all to see, cameras or no cameras, paps or no paps. I couldn't have cared less, and he left and that was that, and the morning after I would be in bed thinking it over, probably a drunken mistake, but I wasn't that drunk, in fact pretty much stone-cold sober, and would it have been out of character? Probably be the most in-character thing I'd done in a long time, and that is what everyone wanted wasn't it? The real Lilly Goodridge, I knew I would feel better for it, and if there were repercussions, then I would welcome them with open arms, anything to feel different than I did at that exact moment.

Or maybe I didn't do any of those things, maybe instead of the fantasy – Rogan, the sex, sex like in the movies, up against walls, screams of passion – maybe instead I just cried a while longer, lay awake till bad thoughts turned to sleep.

I couldn't work out which was worse, or better. Neither, both were equally as tragic.

* * *

The next morning, well, the next morning was horrendous, worse than horrendous. There was an argument between me and Frank, a big one, one of the worst we'd had and we'd had a fair few, not like this one though, this was bad. 'Bad' you don't always get back up from, 'bad' that sits unresolved till someone backs down or apologizes, or never speaks to you again – all were equally as conceivable.

I decided to fly back home, packed a few things, told only those that needed to know, Sally obviously, Jon too, let them know I wasn't deserting them. I could tell neither were too happy, but I wasn't asking, I was telling, and at that exact moment I couldn't have given a fuck if either told me never to come back, I was past caring.

I just needed to be home, needed to see friends, needed to speak to my mom and dad, speak to them both, work out what happened. True to form, you could say, I'd ran away again, but I'd be running back soon, that I swore to both Sally and Jon. Just needed LA for a while, to feel that American sun again, make sense of things, a week to get my shit together, come back to England with a new focus. Sally said I'd come back worse, warned me about Max, said me being in the same city again was a bad idea, that I would do something I would regret. She was probably right, but whether I would prove her wrong or otherwise I was coming back regardless. Whether or not I'd want to was a different story, as would what I'd be coming back to.

PART THREE

TOM

My office/April/shot 91

13

There was a knock, then a rattle of keys.

"Good God," she sniffed, wafting her hands as she opened windows.

"What time is it?" came from under the covers.

"Time to get up."

"How's the hand?"

"Healing." She was already cleaning things. "Bloody chip pan."

"Don't worry about my room, it's my mess not yours."

"Yes, but it's my room."

"Dot. I'll do it. It will be spick and span, I promise. I need to do some washing today. I'll bring my clothes down later and you can show me how to work the machine."

"No, I wouldn't dream of it. We don't let paying guests go backstage, even you. Besides, it isn't a man's job to clean and wash."

"The world has changed, Dot. Equal rights. I'm a modern man."

"Not in this house, you're not."

"You look busier than normal, Dot."

"Got a bus load of Americans arriving any time soon. Rooms to clean and beds to be made."

"Americans?"

"We are being invaded, Tom."

"Do you normally have Americans?"

"Can't say we do. Must be something going on round here I'm not aware of," she said, making my bed. "A royal visit, perhaps. What you up to today? Not being idle I hope."

"Working."

"On a Sunday? How horrid. Well keep wrapped up," she said. "I want you downstairs in thirty minutes. Porridge and melon today, as requested."

"Thanks."

"You sure you don't want some fried bread? Cheer you up a bit?"

"No, porridge and melon is fine."

"Will I see you later or are you going to be back the wrong side of dinner again?"

"I'm not sure. I can't imagine it will be too late."

"Well make sure you eat. Knock on my door if you need something making up. I'll make a start on that muddy pile of yours later once all these Yanks have been fed," she said closing the door, the little tornado moving room to room, as I fell back into my bed and tried to close my eyes.

Woken up by gulls again this morning so I was in a bad mood already, I'd barely slept, last night was a late one with not much reward, as were the last few nights. I surveyed my floor – it was disgraceful, plates, camera equipment, muddy boots, clothes, they all needed washing or dusting or wiping. I'd fallen back into teenage habits, back at university all over again, surviving on fifty-pence noodles and wearing underwear for more days than I should.

On the TV, all talk was of saving the country, I guaranteed Mum would have been embroiled in all this election shit, one thing she loved was a debate, especially where she got to choose a side to hate and shout at. Me, I didn't recognize either candidate or their policies, let alone whether I'd vote red, blue or yellow. Still, the noise of men selling how good they were and how bad the other was my morning soundtrack.

I closed the windows, quickly investigated the sky. Most of my mornings started with the assessment of the weather. Today looked nice, which was good news for many reasons, meant I wouldn't get rained on, nothing worse than being damp and bored, also made getting a decent shot more probable if Lilly decided to come out and play.

Who the hell was I kidding? I hadn't gotten a decent shot since I'd got here, I'd got plenty of shots, volume wasn't a problem, just the content. I was far from front page news, Goodridge feeds duck, troubled actress makes daisy chain. I didn't have the balls to show Vince, I already knew it would make him angry, or angrier, better to give him nothing than show up with proof I was failing.

There was a pattern forming to my failure, a routine of just watching, watching her read, watching her eat, watching her be on her own, most times I'd do the same. Read when she read, ate when she ate, sharing each other's company but just on different sides of the fence. There were some days when I wouldn't even remove the lens cap, there had been a few times where I'd even fallen asleep, though to be fair Lilly was asleep too, the two of us having naps in the midday shade. Occasionally I'd get angry with myself, think of the money I wasn't making, try to act all cut-throat and Vince-like, start concocting ways to bring some scandal to her door. But I couldn't think of any, more often than not I was back to mirroring Lilly, watching her every move, trying to work out what made her tick, why she smiled when with company, but looked so sad and beaten when just by herself.

The only time my job got hard was when she was on the move. Most of her working week was pretty predictable, her hours on set may have varied, some days she'd be finished and back home for dinner in the garden, but every so often she'd leave in the dark and get home in the dark. I guessed it depended on the scene she was shooting, how many takes, how often she screwed up. Regardless, I knew pretty much her on and off days, don't ask me how but I managed to get access to the daily call sheets every now and then, turned out if you hang out in the same pubs as some of the film crew long enough, they don't mind keeping a film fan in the loop if you keep their glasses full. Good thing was, it meant I knew roughly when to expect Lilly to leave and when she might arrive back, made planning my day a little less ambiguous.

It was her days off I had to earn my money, when I knew I had to prepare myself for the question mark which was where Lilly may go off to next. Days like today, weekends when Lilly wasn't satisfied with staying at home and wanted to explore further afield than her garden wall.

That reminded me, I would need some change, learnt that lesson the hard way on that one, first week on the chase and without any coins I parked on a verge, came back three hours later with a sixty pound fine and a grinning parking attendant. I very quickly realised that any place worth visiting here involved paying for the privilege and it was a mistake I never made again.

It had been a steep learning curve becoming paparazzi, lots of trial and error. Things you don't think about, like how to charge your phone in the middle of a field, camera shutter response time, the importance of lens cleaner fluid, the life of a battery, the weight of a torch.

I mean I had a few successes. Take binoculars – Vince thought I was a mug for the amount I spent in that little shop, not to mention the thirty miles I drove to get them. But my father always taught me the importance of decent raw materials, at least that was my justification for the extravagance. 8x25, multi-coated optics, man in the shop said it was voted Compact Binocular of the Year, I must have missed that awards show. I did feel bad after I bought them, though, it was money I could've sent home to Mum and Molly, but hey, short-term loss, long-term gain, if I was going spend most of my day staring through them I had to make sure they would do the job.

But I'd made my mistakes too, I'd like to say I didn't turn up those first few days in my Converse and jeans but, yes, I was that naive. Turned out denim and canvas didn't do all that well when the clouds opened and I quickly realised there was no room for fashion in wet country, now I was head-to-toe black, head-to-toe weatherproof, too.

Another lesson – don't make friends with other paparazzi. I'd met one, Ludo, I'd seen others, half a dozen, making themselves known, in their little swarms, shouting and wrestling for better smiles and angles but Ludo was the only one I'd actually spoken to. He wasn't pleasant either, a big-mouth who couldn't be trusted, but he attempted conversation whenever our paths crossed and I had no choice but to respond and play along with our friendship. I didn't like the way he talked about Lilly, or any woman for that matter. He referred to them as "it", which at first I put down to pigeon English, but turned out was just blatant discrimination. He gave me some pot, said it helped with the late nights, I took it off him, but I hadn't touched it since, probably still in my coat or car. Thank God, he hadn't a clue where Lilly was staying, none of them did, although it felt like it was only a matter of time. Not that my upper hand made a difference, I may have known something all the others didn't, but I still had nothing to show for it and I was sure if Ludo knew where she lived there would be a hell of a lot more gossip being sold.

By now the bath had run. I'd managed to find some complimentary shortbread by the coffee sachets, biscuits in the bath, Jesus fucking Christ, I'd hit a low. I smelt of sheep shit, which should be no surprise seeing as I spend most of my time surrounded by both sheep and their faeces. They, too, had taken a mild interest in my location and when it rained they tended to congregate under my tree for shelter. They hadn't done so in a while, since the good weather, not since I'd brought the dog with me, not that he'd be anything of a threat. Bringing the dog was nothing to do with Vince, by the way, more of a favour for Dot, also gave me a little company too. He didn't do much, just sat under my feet, raising his head only when he was being handed bread crusts or sharing dog biscuits with the sheep. What a sight, me and my animals – Dr Doolittle – ironic, as that was literally what I did most days.

Under the water I inspected my belly, still not what it used to be, but better than before. I'd gained weight here, not a lot but enough, all the sitting, all the stodge and sugar. Dot's packed lunches were hardly small, had to ask her nicely to stop packing me all things butter and cream, which she did begrudgingly, sulked as scones and pasties were replaced with fruit and nuts as Dot continued to swear real men shouldn't be fed like livestock. She reminded me of my Mum, I told her that, she laughed, agreed I needed mothering. It was funny, Dot's husband Alfred warned me that there was a strong chance I would be wrapped in cotton wool by his wife, not that I'd stand in her way. Predictably, I became the boy and she became the parent. Funnily enough, though thorough in investigating my choice of coat, what time I wanted dinner, what time I got home, Dot hadn't ever questioned my daily goings-on. I'd planned for it, had some ridiculous story about being wildlife photographers which could be argued had an element of truth to it, but so far, she hadn't asked or cared – more preoccupied with the portions on my plate or the condition of my room.

I stepped out of the bath and wrapped myself in a towel quickly. Weather changed quick here, like last night, crazy, sun, then wind, then hailstones. I didn't recognize Lilly's friend, she arrived not long after me, she didn't leave till the early hours, sounded like they had a good time, she got picked up by a taxi, looked pretty tanked, shouting and giggling. I didn't stay much longer myself, watched the house till the lights went, till Lilly's bedroom went dark. Hence why I was in no real rush to get over to hers today, I guessed her hangover would last till lunch, so least I had a little bit of Sunday to myself before I turned Secret Agent.

★ ★ ★

Dot came over to take away my plate of melon skins, made some remark about my beard needing seeing to before heading off to clear another table. Then my phone rang.

"Hi, Vince, you OK?

"Oh, I'm peachy."

"Why are you whispering?"

"Cos it's one in the morning arsehole, that's why."

"Late time to call me. Something wrong?"

"You tell me, Tommy. Where are you?"

"The house."

"You're at the cottage?"

"Yep. Been here about an hour," I said, as Dot poured me another coffee.

"You are there right now?"

"Yep, up bright and early."

"What can you see?"

"Erm…" scrambling for lies. "Frank loading blankets and bags into the back of the car. I'm gonna need to shoot, Vince, looks like they are heading off somewhere."

"Interesting. LG there, too is she?"

"Yep."

"What's she doing?"

"What she doing? She's inside I guess."

"That's funny."

"What's funny?"

"Just got off the phone with a guy I know from the airline. Said she's getting picked up from her house by one of their chauffeurs in about an hour. So, unless you're seeing suitcases then you're a fucking liar."

There was silence.

"It doesn't make any sense."

"No, it doesn't. I'd ask you why but I doubt you know jack shit."

"She flying back home?"

"Yep."

"Back for good?"

"No. Return ticket, so I've been informed. Back in a week."

"Why is she leaving?"

"I should be fucking asking you that same question. That's not important. What is important is you. And what I should do with you."

"I'm sorry, Vince. I was about to head over, honest."

"Fuck you're sorry. You need to put this right."

"What, fly to LA? I'm not…"

"I'll watch her this end. I'll do this myself. Like I have a fucking choice. You are useless."

He went quiet.

"You firing me, I guess?"

"I fucking should be, Tommy."

"What do you need me to do?"

"I don't give a fuck. Go home, take a week off, try and sort your head out, Tommy. Take a long hard look at yourself in the mirror cos at the minute, Tommy, you are this fucking close. I don't like fucking liars, Tommy, especially ones that lose me money."

"I'm sorry."

"Thin fucking ice, friend. Thin fucking ice."

Then he hung up.

★ ★ ★

Dot didn't take it well, took it personally. I assured her it was just a little break, off home to see the family, she told me she'd persuade Alfred to keep my room ready for my return, stop him filling it with another potential American. In the car park, she handed me a packed lunch, warned me of the lack of fruit, even Tripod was there too, looking even more mournful than normal. I watched the two of them disappear in the rear-view mirror, watched five legs and a waving arm say their goodbyes from the tarmac, faces forlorn and friendless, as if my escape was permanent, when in fact I'd be back within a week. Unless Vince decided otherwise.

★ ★ ★

"Where have you been? The heart of darkness?" she said ruffling my hair up. "You need shearing. Quick, get inside before you catch your death."

They were both genuinely taken aback, took them a cup of tea and the biscuit tin for my arrival to sink in. I decided not to ring ahead, not sure that was a good idea in hindsight, not sure if Molly could grasp it all, she was speechless for a good while, kept staring at me, came over all shy, disappearing under Mum's arms, shaking her head whenever I tried to hold her. Mum cried actually, which I didn't expect, she wasn't one for show, she didn't look good in all honesty, pale and tired, said she had a head full of cold, so I made us all dinner, told her to get some rest, of course Mum questioned my sudden arrival after a month away, somehow, I put off my explanation till tomorrow.

Instead, I took Molly to bed, read her endless stories, endless kisses, she soon softened up. I did my best to not fall asleep beside her and by the time I'd got downstairs Mum was already excusing herself, wishing me a good night. I wasn't long off bed myself, it had been a weird day and a long drive, a weird day for all of us, confusion for Molly, high temperatures for Mum, mixed feelings for me.

14

Molly was in tears, crying into my kneecaps, I did my best to make it stop, rubbed it better, bribed her with promises of chocolate in exchange for a quieter recovery. It worked, she was soon scaling the same climbing frame she had just fallen from, laughing, making new friends. I kept my eye on her as she ran off towards a see-saw, mid-spin. I looked over at Mum, she was sat over on a bench, she was watching her too, preparing for the next potential injury.

In the car on the way over Mum talked of a nursery that Molly might soon attend a couple of days a week. Mum spoke lots of industry terms, child stimulation, tailored curriculum, emotive development, Ofsted reports, even the colour of the new uniform. Mum had spent a lot of time on it, lots, bubbling over as she explained, said she had lots of emails and printouts I'd have to read. I tried my best to sound enthusiastic and appreciative, which I was, just not that particular day. We'd been at Normanby Hall for a good hour before we all decided it was time to eat, picked a nice spot under a perfect tree, opposite a perfect view, as Mum handed us foiled parcels and flasks.

"So, you were saying, Mr Secretive?"

"It's no secret, Mum, I told you. It's literally a week off till Lilly returns. That's all."

"Just seems odd Vince has let you have a week off out of the blue. He doesn't seem the type to be so charitable."

"Vince is Vince."

"And is Vince happy with your work?" she said, flicking away a bug that had landed on my leg.

"He still thinks I'm a bumbling idiot, if that's what you mean."

"And are you?"

"He makes me feel like one, but I'm not, I just struggle with the job description, struggle to be enthusiastic. I'm doing OK, I'm not setting the world on fire, put it that way."

"At least it gives this Lilly girl a bit of respite from the constant badgering."

"Oh, she'll still be badgered, just not by me."

"How awful."

"Mum, I don't need your Princess Diana speech again. I'm fully aware I'm going to hell for this."

"Here, grumpy, have another pork pie." She offered me more Tupperware.

"Who says I'm going back anyway? I'm still undecided myself."

"What's changed your tune?"

"Lots of things."

"Like?"

"Molly for one."

"You knew what you were taking on when you accepted the job. Molly hasn't changed. The situation hasn't changed."

"I should be the one organising her schooling, not you. I'm the parent."

"I enjoy it, Tom. Gives me a purpose. What else have I got to do these days? Look, I agree that this isn't great for Molly at the moment with you away, but look at her, not a care in the world. Yes, your job isn't the ideal one, but there are worse ones out there. If I could magic money out of thin air I would tell you to stay here with us. But Tom, and it is a big 'but', we have no money."

"We?"

"Your father's pension pays enough for me to live a basic lifestyle. We made some money mistakes in our past, some bad investments that ate up most of mine and your father's savings. I do my best to live frugally, but I'd be lying if I said that you and Molly moving back hasn't stretched me slightly."

"I'm not even making money, Mum, not yet, just promises of

money. I'd rather have a normal job, with a normal pay cheque, on a normal payday."

"Yes, but where is the fun in that?"

"I'm gambling with our future, Mum. There is no fun in that."

"Sometimes we have to take risks, it's part of the appeal."

"You're hardly the ideal candidate to offer advice. You said yourself you made bad investments."

"They didn't feel bad at the time. And they still don't now. That was the chance me and your father took."

"And it backfired."

"Yes, but it might not have."

"How are you finding having Molly on your own. You coping?"

"It's tiring, Tom. She wants constant attention, but I wouldn't change it."

Mum coughed into her hands, several times, loud and intense.

"Just because you want to look after her, doesn't mean you can."

"I have a cold, that's all."

"I'm not talking now, I'm talking in general. You're nearly seventy. I'm asking too much of you."

"It was my decision, Tom, not yours. If I didn't feel capable then I wouldn't be doing it, I wouldn't have let you leave." She blew her nose. "I'm doing this because I want to, I've missed so much of her already, I've time to make up."

"Just make sure you tell me if it becomes too hard, too unbearable."

"Unbearable? Look at her." Molly was hanging from a branch. "How could she ever be unbearable?"

"That's not what I meant."

Mum poured me a coffee from the flask, and then one for herself.

"It wouldn't make you any less of a grandmother if you changed your mind. Molly would love you the same, regardless. It wouldn't be a failure if you changed your mind, decided it's too much."

"You're worrying over nothing, Tom. Giving yourself unnecessary stress."

"I can't be away knowing you are here struggling on your own. You need to keep me in the loop, keep me informed."

"I'm not the BBC. I'm not giving you daily updates. I will tell you if there is a problem, but I sure as hell don't need to have you checking in on me. A women's health is her own business."

"Mum, you're twisting my words, all I'm asking is you tell me the truth, tell me if you need help, that's all."

It went quiet, eyes out in front, a blank truce.

"I'm going to the doctor's next week if you must know."

"Nothing bad, I hope?"

"Just an MOT, checking for lumps and bumps, hope they might find something for this God-awful cold, it's driving me insane all this incessant nose-blowing and coughing."

"Well, I expect you to ring me after you've had all your checks."

"Don't worry, you'll be first to know if I'm a write-off. For now, your daughter is safe and you are free to return to spying and gambling away our futures. You need to concentrate on your job, not me."

"I'll try."

"What time is it?"

I checked my phone. "About four. We should be getting back soon if we want her bathed and in bed for normal time."

"Enough time to show Molly the gardens?"

"If we are quick."

Right on cue Molly was at our feet, lunch finished, demanding piggybacks.

"Molly darling," Mum said, kneeling down next to her. "Do you want to see a secret special garden with me and Daddy? I think Peter Rabbit lives there, a few fairies too."

"Might be an evil monster in there too, Molly," I said, as I picked up and placed her on top of my shoulders. "We'll have to keep our eyes peeled as he likes to eat little girls for supper."

"Daddy is being silly. There's no monsters." Mum picked up our belongings, as we headed towards the Victorian walled garden across the rock pools and benches and ducks. "Go on then, Thomas, I'm all ears. Tell me about this Goodridge girl. Tell me everything."

* * *

Whilst the house slept I finally took the opportunity to sort out what I'd brought home with me in such a hurry. Even though I'd be repacking in a few days' time it was a job that needed to be done, get things washed, thrown out, into some order. Most of the stuff wouldn't be making the trip back, half the clothes I'd taken hadn't been worn. My aim was to go back lighter, in every sense of the word, my possessions, my waistline, my conscience. On my duvet, I put all my toiletries, toothbrush, aftershave, razor, not that I'd shaved much throughout the whole process. Tomorrow I'd need to be de-haired, get Mum to clipper it all off like a sheep.

Mum would be impressed with my binoculars, I thought, taking them from their case. She liked to watch the birds from her kitchen stool, watch them eat the crusts and seeds from her nest boxes, with her little notepad, making her notes of number, time and species, sending it off somewhere, RSPB or some other conservation do-gooders, where it could be analysed and listed. Sweet really.

Stinking or creased I'd started to separate clothes into piles, clean and needed cleaning, but quickly realized that there were not many that didn't need the washing machine, so instead of piles I threw them all in the laundry bin. Next my Ray-bans – I took them out of their case, wiped them on my jumper, attempting to remove the specks of sand encrusted on the lens. I will take Molly to the beach this week, I thought, give Mum a day off, give her time to get well. It would not be a long drive to the seaside, the coast wasn't far away, I'd check the forecast for the rest of the week, pick the nicest day.

There was a carrier bag of books, too, that I thought I'd have time to read but I couldn't have been more wrong. I transferred the books from bag to bookshelf, they wouldn't be coming back with me second time around. Vince said books were a good foil, turned spying into reading, a criminal offence to a pastime.

Would I take back my diary, I thought, finding it wrapped in a pair of trousers. I hadn't written an entry in a while. For the first couple of weeks I'd written a fair bit, made it quite formulaic, thought I could note any patterns in her habits, keep tabs on my performance. Number, type, species.

Tuesday 6th April
  Frank/Sally arrive - 8:27
  Frank/Lilly went on walk - 10:36-13:01
  Car arrived - 14:11
  Car home - 18:19
  54 shots
  Bring thicker jumper tomorrow.
  Remember power pack!

Thursday 8th April
  Frank/Sally - 8:10
  Car arrived - 10:03
  Came home - 17:27
  Wasting too much time in the Jeep (need to think smarter!!!!)
  Shots - too dark/photos awful. Need Vince to show me how to use the camera settings again.

Monday 12th April
  Lilly first day of filming
  Garden - 7:10-9:37
  Car arrived - 11:00

Car home – 14:00
Garden – 14:36-17:48
Running out of excuses! This isn't working!
Spoke to Molly. Sang me a song down the phone.

Tuesday 13th April
Filming all day again.
*Have an idea – check it out to see if it sails.

Thursday 15th April
Lilly filming/home after lunch.
Frank mowed the lawn.
Photos of LG picking flowers in bikini (don't show these to Vince).
Molly would love it here.
How much is the place to rent? Find out.
Could Aunty Jo come with the kids?
Make it cheaper the more there are of us.
I'm bored.
Buy Gaviscon. Awful heartburn.
Miss home today.

Saturday 17th April
Big argument with Vince over dinner. Told him I was doing my best. Said he had no choice but to step in, restraining order or not. Took the Jeep and his camera.
Took Tripod for a walk to get some air.
Spoke to Mum. She didn't seem herself.

Sunday 18th April
Vince knocked at my door late last night.
Sounded over the moon. He'd snapped
Lilly stumbling out of some restaurant in
some awful state. Sounded pleased with
himself. Last thing I wanted was this,
to be proven incompetent. How long can
I keep doing this? Supposed to my day
off today. I'm gonna go and watch Lilly
anyway. See how she takes the bad news.
Thank God Vince flies home today.

Friday 23rd April
Paparazzi have arrived. I'm guessing
there'll be more to come.

Tuesday 27th April
Another morning off (Lilly filming). Helped
Alfred with guttering.
Late night. Lilly in garden till midnight.
Keeps looking towards me. May need to
change position. I swear she knows I'm
here.

After unpacking I went downstairs, tried to watch television but nothing was on, read the paper, felt unusual to have my own time, I was used to early starts and late finishes, time to myself felt foreign. I preferred not having it, it left too much room to think.

In my absence Mum had decorated the house with all things Molly, her scribbles and paintings, photo frames on every wall. Mum and her camera had been busy, Molly in the garden holding a marrow, Molly with a fishing line, Molly with a lamb.

Even I'd made the wall, photos I'd hidden away that she'd dug back up somehow. Skydiving in Auckland, elephants in Chiang

Mai, Cassie playing pitch and putt, Molly naked in the garden. Made me think of home, our little backyard with its mango tree, a string of old garden lanterns, Paulina passing us fresh *gortidas* from over the fence, Cassie chasing Molly with the hose.

I thought I'd be OK with seeing Cassie's face again, I'd avoided it for so long, but I wasn't as ready as I thought, not yet. I was sure Mum would be OK if I took them down, replaced them with something else so her walls didn't look bare.

Outside across the shine of the pond I could the see the glow from our local pub. Alcohol was the right thing to do. I grabbed my wallet and my coat, twenty yards later I was ordering my first drink.

The last pub I'd gotten drunk in was Little Tokyo on First Street, $2 a glass of Sapporo, crab cake sliders, game five on every screen, Laker fans going wild as they took home the Championship, yellow jerseys flooding the street, a wild night. Nothing like this, the opposite of this.

The Nag's Head was old and stale and even though small it still felt empty, just the three of us, including the landlord. All attempted small talk, but they didn't get any talk from me. I was surprised it had taken me this long to be drowning my sorrows, looking for answers at the bottom of my glass. If I'd had to envisage my breakdown after Cassie I'd have thought alcohol, or worse, would've sounded about right, rather than the reverse. My decline was quite a composed one, no binging or hookers or gambling or drugs, just went mute for a little while. This is when things would get interesting, I thought, where I really started to unravel, rather than a car crash and a dead wife, it just took an actress I'd never met to lead me toward addiction.

I was talking silly, too many pints doing the thinking for me.

I should have never gone to Devon – drunk or sober, I knew that much. It had never felt a good idea, even from the start, but Vince always had a way of persuading me, my evil twin, devil on the shoulder. But I couldn't blame him entirely, I was a grown man capable of making my own decisions, it wasn't his fault I was in this predicament, and if I'd actually done my job and taken the goddamn photos, then he could've sold them for vast amounts of money, just like he'd planned. We would all be happy, everyone would win, everyone would get the money, everyone would get to go home. Except Lilly, Lilly wouldn't win, though why should that matter? People like Lilly Goodridge had already won, so why should I care about how she ended up in all this? Regardless of what Vince did next, whether we succeeded or failed together, or if he went out alone, Lilly would finish her work here regardless, go back home, do another film, bigger and better probably, more photos, more intrusion, if it wasn't me or Vince it would be someone else with a camera, who was behind the damn thing was irrelevant, the ending would be the same.

The barman came over and grasped my empty glasses between his fingers.

"Last orders, fella," he said, as I left a handful of loose change, took my coat off the stool. Outside the temperature had dropped, not that it mattered much seeing as I could point out my front door. It looked nice from where I was standing, the centre of the village, the pond lit up with lamp posts, the ring of houses and their chimney smoke. It wouldn't be a bad thing if this was home, my permanent home, there were worse places I could end up, living where you grew up wasn't failure, it didn't mean I'd given up. It was the drink talking yet again, whether I'd look at that view tomorrow with a similar optimism I'd not like to say. All I knew was it'd be the same headache, different hangover, neither cured by tea or tablets.

My phone rang. I searched for it in my pocket.

"Yo, Tommy boy."

"Can we talk tomorrow, Vince? I'm not in the mood."

"Mood for what?"

"Mood to be shouted at."

"Look man, I ain't got time for whatever breakdown you're having right now. I gotta talk quick, I'm at my kid's school, waiting to be called in."

"Called in for what?"

"Boy's been throwing his weight around again. Anyways, I got news."

"I don't wanna know, Vince. Honestly, I don't care."

"She's coming back. Lilly is coming back."

"You knew that already. You told me that."

"It's not when. It's where."

"Where what?"

"London. She flies straight to London."

"Why?"

"Press stuff by the sounds of it. Trying to drum up some enthusiasm for that poor fucking movie she's trying to make. She'll be there for a few days, 100%. I need you to be my man on the ground."

"Look, I'm not going back. I ain't in the right frame of mind for this. I appreciate what you've done."

"Tommy, I haven't got time for this shit, man, I need you there cos I can't be. And I need you firing on all cylinders. We need to start earning some green on this job. Some real green."

"But Vince, I'm not going back." I started to walk back towards my house.

"You've been pussyfooting around this girl for too long. I don't want any more photos of her in her fucking garden unless she's topless and if she's not topless she better be doing something pretty fucking amazing otherwise it's useless to me."

"Vince, you're aren't listening. I don't want to do this anymore. It's over."

"Fuck you, it isn't, Tommy. I've spent a lot of money on this and on you for that matter. Do you think that comes from thin air? No, it comes out of my wallet, out of my kids' mouths. It's time to get to work. Go big or go home."

"Vince, if you want the shots, you fly over here and take them yourself."

"You do realise you owe me?"

"Yes, I appreciate the opportunities. Truly I do."

"Fuck your sentiment. You owe me money. Travel, hotels, equipment."

"I thought that came out of the money you made?"

"What money have you made me?" He paused. "You take out more than you bring in. That isn't the business I run here. If you quit now then you owe me. And I assure you, Tommy, that travel, hotels and equipment ain't cheap."

"You're fucking me over, Vince. This isn't what friends do to each other."

"Tommy, you are my friend. But this is business. And there are two things you don't fuck with. A man's family or a man's money."

"I just won't pay it, Vince. Even if I had it, which I haven't."

"Look, I don't want this turning nasty. I'm not threatening you or your family but this job needs to be done. The easy way or the hard way."

"I'll think about it." I got to my front door, rummaged around my pocket for the door key.

"Sorry, Tommy. I need an answer now. Yes or no time, buddy. Clock is ticking here."

"No, then."

"That's a damn shame. Damn shame. You are a fucking waste of time. You always were and you always will be."

The phone went dead.

An hour later, as I laid in bed, lights off, gritted teeth, head spinning, I got a message from Vince. I read it, then read it again, sat up, turned on the bedside lamp. Lilly wasn't the only one that was flying to London, a certain Max Salter would be there too.

15

I loaded the car whilst the rest of the house slept.

I'd forgotten how much two-and-a-half-year-olds needed, decided to sacrifice the buggy, mainly to free up boot space, but mainly because I couldn't figure how to collapse the damn thing. Molly would have to walk, or most likely she would have to be carried. There were a lot of things I'd forgotten which a parent should have known, nappy sizes, shoe sizes, car seats, these were always things Cassie dealt with, nappies and shoes and seats would appear without me knowing why or how. Back then my role as dad was pretty basic, cuddles and stories, making teddies talk. Being a father on my own taught me a lot, but I was still a long way away from knowing my daughter like I should, that was something that would have to change.

She didn't take well to be taken away from her grandma either, I should have expected it, in the month I'd been away Mum and Molly hadn't left each other's side, so when the time came to wave each other off from the car window it was inevitable there would be some tears and some confusion, I just didn't predict it would be as distressing as it turned out, poor girl. Luckily the sobbing and screams didn't last long, by the time I'd filled the car with petrol and filled her with chocolate, calmness resumed and she was back to giggling and singing.

★ ★ ★

Molly really enjoyed her big day out, I'd say it was a success. She loved the beach, not so much the suncream, or the donkey ride, or the paddling, or the men's urinal – those she hated – but the arcades, hot doughnuts, the little red train, those, she loved. I tried to tell her she had been to the beach before, Long Beach, Santa Monica, but she was adamant she hadn't seen ocean or sand before, must've been too young to remember.

I couldn't believe how much Molly talked either. Whenever I'd spoken to her on the phone whilst I'd been away she'd always be a little shy, one-word answers, me doing all the talking. Well, she'd certainly found her voice now, didn't shut up for the whole length of the Promenade.

"Is a donkey a horse?"

"What colour is mummy's hair? Yellow like mine?"

"Why didn't you both come to my egg hunt?"

"Mummy doesn't like spiders, does she?"

Funny how the brain worked, couldn't remember the beach but could recall her mother's phobia, kids knew more than we gave them credit for, conversations we thought they wouldn't understand, arguments we assumed they hadn't heard, or vice versa. I wondered when she'd forget Cassie, when memories would become just photographs, couldn't imagine that happening soon. Mum was doing her best to keep Cassie alive and well, found every opportunity to make Molly feel that Cassie was still close by, that heaven was just upstairs, that Cassie was always watching us. Mum tried to make death whimsical and fairy-like, but how long would that last realistically? Molly wouldn't be a child forever. Perhaps it would be easier for us all just to forget, let Cassie just be dead, let there be an ending that was hard to swallow at first but truthful at least, not made up or magical.

Till then, Molly was still all questions, questions about seagulls, about pinball, about Cassie, and I'd do my best to answer them. As we ate fish and chips on our laps, Molly's last question was whether we could go home to see Grandma, so I carried her back to the car, her hair in my face as she did her best not to fall asleep. The drive home was silent, radio at a hum, Molly conked out in the back as I sat in five o'clock traffic. I looked at all the

171

other drivers, tired and agitated, the face of the middle of the week.

Devon wasn't like this, I thought. Different time zones almost, a different speed. Devon seemed unaffected by world news, banking crises, celebrity, it was in its own little world. Dot said that would soon change, the influx of the wealthy as they trickled from the cities in search of holiday homes and guest houses, bringing their worries and stress with them, their illnesses and diseases. Dot talked of tourists like an epidemic, shops getting busier, traffic worsening, high-rise hotels. I tried to tell her it meant more customers, but she said that was the last thing she wanted, said she preferred it when they all shuffled off back home, so she could enjoy the winter in peace. For the meantime, Devon was still relatively quiet, at least where Lilly and I were staying. After the first photos leaked of Lilly I thought the town would erupt, locals transcending on her little farmhouse, the world's media flying in from every corner of the globe. But nothing much changed, things stayed the same. Yes, there were a few more paparazzi, but they still hadn't found the farmhouse, still just me hiding in the bushes, for the time being.

I'd been surprised how little Lilly had explored her new town when she first arrived, I'd expected her to be a tad reclusive, but I didn't expect her to be imprisoned in either house or film set. It made for a routine and a structure, one that was easy to read and follow, but unfortunately a life that didn't make for good viewing and certainly didn't shift any newspapers.

Strangely, what changed that was Lilly being caught out drunk and disorderly that night, though it made my life harder and meant my days were hard to predict. The one thing it did was make it exciting, like a holiday rather than a job, like Lilly's adventures were mine too, and no matter how much I tried to tell myself I was enjoying my time back home, and even though I was, in all honesty, I couldn't wait to get back down there again as soon as possible. To see Devon, to see Dot, mostly just to see Lilly again, and that made me a horrible father and a terrible husband, too.

I was sat on a kitchen chair, topless, looking outward into Mum's back garden. It had been raining since we'd all woken up, and seeing as we had no real official plans, breakfast had sort of spilled over into lunchtime, and would probably spill over into dinnertime too.

"Molly!" Mum shouted. "We're getting you dressed in five minutes, OK, darling?"

No response.

"Molly!"

No response again. Mum tutted.

"Just leave her, Mum, she's happy in there."

"She can't be in pyjamas all day, Tom. I don't like her being idle."

"Give her a bit longer. We don't always have to be doing a task or errand, Mum, you included."

"That's rich. This is hardly relaxation, is it? Look, I'm nearly finished so don't move your head or I'll have your ears off if you're not careful." She sprayed my head with more water. "You've brought back half of Mablethorpe. My floor looks like a sandpit," she said, combing with a grimace.

Mum was taking it all very seriously. Without the confidence of her clippers, which she'd not been able to find, she had to resort to scissors, which meant the process of a hair trim had become both pressured and more time-consuming than she'd first expected. Gave us a good reason to talk, though, trivial stuff mostly, about tomorrow's polling day, a prospect of a new vegetable patch, my Aunty visiting in the summer. That would be nice, Molly's family circle was small enough, so it would be nice to increase the circumference, so to speak. I'd told her about Vince, about my pending trip to London, talked a little about Dad, agreeing that we would take Molly over to Hamsterley Forest to show her where his ashes were scattered, she'd probably enjoy it, it wasn't like death was something new for her.

"Done," Mum declared, standing back to observe her work.

"It's a bit shorter than I wanted." I checked my reflection in the glass of the microwave.

"Cheeky git." Mum whacked my arm. "You can cut your own next time."

"You putting the kettle on?"

"What did your last slave die of?" she smiled, already filling the kettle with water.

I opened my laptop as I put my T-shirt back on, checked my emails, nothing. Facebook briefly, I didn't even know why I was on it, because everyone else was, I guessed. I might delete my profile, I thought, though I never would. It would be hypercritical to invade everyone else's privacy and not let people take a glimpse at mine.

I typed in Lilly's name in my search bar, curious to see how she'd spent her time back across the pond. I wasn't expecting what I saw. I'd half-expected her to lay low, imagined she'd go home, stay indoors, spend time with her family, that is what I would've expected, knowing the girl I'd watched for over a month, but she was unrecognisable. The girl who talked to sheep and watered hanging baskets wasn't the same girl propping up every rooftop bar in Hollywood. I was starting to believe fame was just millions of people getting the wrong idea of you, but Lilly was doing just what everyone expected her to do, the girl everyone pointed at, the one they whispered about, the one you couldn't take your eyes off, and for all the wrong reasons.

Though if Lilly had been busy, the paparazzi had been busier. She'd only been back a few days, but there were hundreds upon hundreds of photos, they were relentless, sunrise to sundown, there was no let-up. And it wasn't like she was even hiding away, the places she was going weren't for the social recluse, in fact they were places to go to get spotted, where paparazzi camped out knowing it would only be a matter of time before fame showed up. And I guarantee Vince would be one of them and I was even more sure that most of the photos I was seeing came from his camera lens. I knew Vince would go into overdrive on her return, with the little money we'd made he would be hell-bent on recouping his losses. And although it was a good guess not all the photos were taken by Vince, it would be a fair assumption to say the majority were his handiwork.

I closed the laptop, I'd seen enough, couldn't wait for her to be back on English soil where she was less likely to be a target. Surprised she was being allowed to fuck up so publicly, I would've though Frank and Sally would have reined her in, outside looking in I got the impression they kept her wildness on a pretty short leash – not as short as I thought.

Mum came through with a handful of post.

"Oh, that reminds me," ripping open an envelope, "Molly has a hospital appointment tomorrow."

"I'll take her."

"Good. I hoped you say that. I've booked in for a colour and cut."

"Another haircut?"

"Tom. I've had my haircut once a month for the last thirty years."

"Spending money we haven't got, by the sounds of it."

"It costs hardly anything. Lady across the road does it. Look, I even buy my own dye if that's OK with you." She pointed to the contents of her handbag.

We didn't talk, Mum reboiled the kettle, the sound of water becoming hot filled the kitchen.

"You sure you are all right with taking Molly tomorrow? I can cancel my hair if you want me to." She passed me a cup of tea.

"Sorry, I didn't meet to bite."

"And you're fine with the hospital? I know how much you hate going to those sorts of places."

"I'm cured now. Had no choice but to get over my whole white-coat syndrome, seeing I've been so often with Molly."

"It's two thirty, I think. Dr Malik."

"Do I have to take anything?"

"A couple of quid for parking. I've got a stack of notes in the other room. Better to take them and not need them, hey? Molly knows the drill now. Dr Malik is ever so nice with her. Lets her hold his stethoscope and sit in his big chair. Oh, I took Molly to McDonald's last time we went so don't be surprised if she assumes the same treat will happen again." Mum sat down, a stack of envelopes on her lap. "All I ever get is bills, that or how to save on bills. Only thing they're good for is the fire."

"Any letters from Cassie's parents since I've been gone?"

"A few, yes. In there," she pointed.

I pulled open the kitchen drawer.

"Mum, this letter has been opened."

"Sorry, I opened it my mistake. Thought it was addressed to me. Most things are."

"Mum, they are all opened, all three of them. You have read them, haven't you?"

"Well, you were away, Tom. I thought it best."

"Anything else?"

"No, why?"

"You haven't written back or anything?"

"Why would I do that?"

"Cos it's the type of thing you would do, Mum, that's why."

She didn't say anything. She walked through to the other room, started fiddling with her hair in the fireplace mirror.

"You did write back, didn't you? Why?"

"Look, Tom, I had to. Read the last letter."

I quickly scanned over it.

"Mum you should have told me about this as soon as you got it. This letter is three weeks old."

"I didn't want to bother you with it. Not when you sounded so preoccupied."

"I'm taking Molly out for a walk." I grabbed my coat.

"Don't be mad with me. I thought I was helping."

"Well you haven't, Mum."

"Do you want to know what I wrote to them?"

"Not really, Mum. It won't make a difference now."

★ ★ ★

Me and Mum barely talked the next day, purposely I'd managed to avoid her, took Molly out for most of the morning. Took her to the cinema, popcorn and Pixar, not a bad film really, kept her entertained whilst I read my phone and thought about somewhere else.

Molly seemed to enjoy the visit to the hospital as much as the cinema, cleaning her hands at every opportunity, pointing out wheelchairs, waving at every nurse that walked past. Glad someone enjoyed it as I hated every minute. Like most people I wasn't too fond of hospitals, no matter how significant or insignificant the appointment may have been, I always prepared myself for bad news. It wasn't a recent thing either, I'd hated hospitals way before the car accident, must have been some awful traumatic experience I had as a child, when I had my tonsils out perhaps, or when I was circumcised. That was pretty fucking traumatic.

You'd think I'd be used to hospitals by now with Molly spending most of her life in and out of them. We spent a good few months pretty much camped out in the care unit when she was first born, watching our little baby through the glass of an incubator, all wired up, so tiny too. The doctors said she was normal size for a baby ten weeks early, but I still thought it was only a matter of time till she didn't wake up, and every morning I geared myself up for that eventuality. God, I forget how tough those first few months were. Did a lot of crying, not in front of Cassie. I didn't want her to worry, did what most men do, crying quietly and alone, pretending we are made of stone.

Now to look at Molly it was hard to believe there was such a time when I thought she wouldn't make it past her first birthday. Dr Malik was really pleased with her progress, but as for now

Molly would still have to continue with her inhaler. I asked him how much it would all cost as he wrote a prescription for a new box of Atrovent and he smiled. I'd forgotten it didn't work that way over here, so used to writing cheques every time I saw a clipboard and a diagnosis. That's the one thing I didn't miss about America, probably the only thing. Wished Cassie could see her now, know that her little girl would be fine, that she wouldn't have to worry any more, only about the normal things parents worry about, being good at school, getting a good job, finding love, not getting their heart broken. Just normal things with normal worries.

As we ate our McDonald's, Molly continued to question me about the amputee in the car park. The human body had been a hot topic the last few days after she had found one of Dad's old reference books upstairs. Now she was fascinated, pointing out her elbow, my brain, her veins, my lungs, what happens when one stops working, or one gets chopped off, or buried?

"Is Mummy in a coffin? Did you put her favourite things in it? Does it have a torch in it so she doesn't get scared? Can I go and see it? Can we open it up? Would she just be bones now?"

It continued, milkshakes and mortality. One day I would take Molly back to America, show her where her mum was buried. I hoped someone was visiting Cassie in my absence, that when we got there it hadn't become unloved and unvisited. I doubted people would let that happen, I'd like to think her friends would have kept an eye on her whilst we were gone, replaced old flowers with new, talked to her, showed her we were all still thinking of her. Not that I believed in afterlife, not that I was religious, but hey, you never know, I think when you lose someone close you fling out science and proof. What before might have seemed ludicrous was now your only choice. What was the alternative, surely it's better to believe my wife was an angel, then be proven wrong? Perhaps that was real faith, the hope to be proven right rather than the other way around?

Funny really, what we cling onto to get us through the night.

★ ★ ★

"Happy with your decision then?" Mum asked, waving at someone on the other side of the road.

"About London?"

"No, today. Your vote."

"Oh. I guess so. I didn't have a clue, all three told a good story. I just went with the one that looked most trustworthy."

"Doubt any of them are, to be fair."

"Who'd you vote for?"

"I'm not telling. Politics naturally breeds an argument, I prefer to keep mine close to my chest to avoid confrontation."

"Then why'd you ask me?"

"I don't care who you voted for. Just wanted to check that you had. So, I take it you'll be catching the train first thing tomorrow?"

"Not train, driving this time, but yes, early tomorrow."

"I've washed your clothes, stacked them in your room ready."

"Thanks. And you're gonna be OK? Remember to keep me updated."

"I'll be fine, Tom. The doctor didn't seem that alarmed."

"Text me every day. If you ever you feel you're struggling then I'll be back straight away. I still feel bad I'm going back at all."

"I'm a strong old bird and I've got a lot friends who can help out with Molly if I get too tired. She will be in good hands."

"I want constant updates, like CNN."

We continued to walk, Molly way out in the distance, inspecting puddles, her Happy Meal balloon still wrapped around her hand like she might take off over the fields any minute. I didn't know the population of the village – five hundred, six hundred – tonight felt like we were the only three people for a couple of miles.

"When are we going to talk about Molly's grandparents?"

"Not today. I've got too much on my mind without that, too."

"It's not going to go away, Tom."

"I know."

179

"I'm hoping the letter I wrote them will help buy you some time. But it should be you writing to them, not me."

"I will, just not yet."

"You've got some choices you need to make when this whole Lilly thing blows over. If it blows over, that is."

I nodded. Molly came running up to my knees. I asked her if she was cold, her arms felt like ice. She said no, requested hot chocolate and a movie instead, the "balloon film" as she called it. I agreed to both as she ran off down the path again.

"Are you cold, Mum?"

"No, I'm fine thanks," she said, even though I'd already draped my jacket around her shoulders.

"How many times have you watched that film with her, Mum? I've only been back a week and I've watched it, like, ten times."

"I could quote every line."

"I could think of worse things to watch. Bet you wish I wasn't going tomorrow."

"Actually, no. I want you to go."

"Why?"

"Because I can see in your eyes you can't wait to get back into your little world."

"My little world?"

"Your little adventure, then."

"I have missed it. I'm not going to lie. I mean, I hate being away from you and Molly but I have missed the routine."

"You've missed her, too, haven't you?"

I didn't answer.

"You like her, don't you, Tom?"

"Who?"

"You know who."

"I've not even met her."

"That's got nothing to do with it."

"Mum, I can't even believe we are having this conversation. It's ridiculous."

"Why is it?"

"Lilly is a poster on a bedroom wall. She isn't real."

"But admit you are attracted to her."

"Yes, I admit that. But that's like me saying I'm attracted to Jessica Rabbit, it's a fantasy."

"Can you see yourself falling in love again?"

"One day, I hope. But it wouldn't be the end of the world if I didn't."

"I think it would."

"It wouldn't be for a few years anyway."

"Out of loyalty to Cassie?"

"It's not down to loyalty, Mum. It's down to being a decent human being. A decent human being doesn't fall in love six months after losing his wife."

"You can't put a timing on an emotion, Tom. It took me two years to fall in love with your father, it took two minutes for him to fall in love with me. You can't use time as an excuse. Cassie wouldn't want you to have a life of solitude in favour of devotion to her."

"I'm not saying that, Mum. I'm just saying not yet."

"You want to punish yourself a little longer for dramatic effect?

"It's not like that."

"You can't hide dark with more dark. You shouldn't feel bad for having feelings for another woman. You should remember Cassie, but not let yourself become the martyr. If I met someone tomorrow and I truly felt that there was a chance I could love them then I wouldn't use your father as a reason not to pursue it. In fact, I still cling to the hope I might fall in love again, if I'm around long enough that is."

"You'll be around forever, Mum. And even after you've gone you'll probably still haunt me."

Mum laughed.

"Why do our chats always seem to be about love and death?" I asked her.

"That's all life is. Everything else is just trivial when you think about it. That and art."

"Some days I forget about Cassie. I literally go through a whole day without her in my head, but then just when I think I'm getting over it, everything just floods back. What if I'd earned more? Perhaps I would have bought a safer car than an old hunk of a Wagoneer. Or if money hadn't been so tight, I could have concentrated on the road rather than arguing about the cost of bathroom tiles. Or maybe if I'd got my head down I wouldn't have been sacked as a tour guide and I would have been flying them to Disneyland rather than that day out to San Diego."

"That's normal. I did the same with your father. Did I spot his condition early enough? Did I love him enough when he was ill? It can eat you up but the reality is, bad things happen to good people. A cruel fact of life, I'm afraid."

"You think I'm doing the right thing going to London?"

"Do you?"

"My head is all over the place. At the moment, I think making money for my family is more important than any emotional attachments. I just don't know if I can what Vince wants me to do."

"Only you know what you are capable of doing and what line you are not willing to cross. Just know that either way you should not feel pressured by me and Molly. You just do what you need to do."

"London is what needs to be done. I've just got to grow some balls and do it."

"Sounds like you've made your decision."

"But do you agree with it, though?"

"Whether I agree or not is neither here or there."

Mum smiled. I didn't.

We sat down at the bench overlooking the pond, Molly on my lap, Mum by my side, black houses and trees, the sky still on fire.

"Shall we tie our house in balloons, Molly?" I asked her. "Sail off to Paradise Falls, just the three of us?"

Molly laughed, as did Mum.

"You've got enough adventure down here, darling, without the need for balloons." Mum put her hand on my leg. "Come on, let's get back inside, get her to bed and you packed and ready for the city, before you do something stupid like change your mind."

16

So far, London sucked. Congestion charges and city cab drivers sucked. My hotel – some no-frills, single-bed-and-sink place on Gower Street – that sucked. I wasn't expecting luxury, I didn't expect to be put up in anything remotely similar to where Lilly was staying, but at the very least I hoped I would be close by. Vince's choice of accommodation was odd, almost malicious, I was being made to suffer, Vince was getting some mild enjoyment thinking of me lugging half a ton of equipment onto the tube, or waiting in traffic jams. I thought I was supposed to be mobile, be able to follow Lilly at the drop of a hat, well anyway, that sucked. Sitting outside her hotel in my Jeep, waiting for Lilly whose plane should have arrived a good two hours before, the rumbling in my stomach, the need for a piss, the constant rain, this all sucked. Did I mention saying bye to Molly and Mum? That sucked plenty, though not as bad as the first time, left at night instead of morning, put her to bed, she knew the drill, my absence was becoming the norm, kissed her head before the long drive north to south, lorry rear ends and empty motorways.

Vince wasn't here. He did threaten to fly over, expressed more concern about my capabilities, but whether or not he ever meant to come, or if it was just to keep me on my toes, I didn't know, all I knew was he wasn't here right now. Staying in LA as some hip-hop star had created a stir apparently, some poor guy with more money than sense, police charges, a socialite girlfriend. Vince smelt blood obviously, a wounded animal was easier to take down, selfishly I didn't care, I was just happy it bought me more time.

Max Salter, that was the other hot topic, tongues would be

wagging over that one, if it was actually true. I bumped into Ludo the previous night, behind the back of Lilly's hotel, I was checking possible vantage points, getting my head round the layout. I hinted to Ludo about Max and based on his blank reaction it was clear he hadn't a clue about Max's pending arrival, unless he just knew how to lie, which I was sure he could. Ludo was a strange man, tiny and hairy, his camera worn permanently around his neck like a statement of intent. He loved this job, that was for sure, he was as much proud as I was ashamed, but Ludo was less concerned with the means, all he cared about was the end. I asked him if he had any family, attempting small talk. He told me they were back home, one day he would bring them to England, once he'd made his fortune, so me and him weren't too dissimilar in our motivations, both robbing the rich to feed the poor, trying to be the one to steal it first.

Regardless of Ludo I was still none the wiser about whether Max would actually be in London, but then again Vince was always one step ahead of the game and he'd never been wrong before, apart from recruiting me. I'd love to know where he got all his information, though it was probably best I didn't, knowing him there wouldn't be much he wouldn't do in order to get what he wanted. So far, he'd kept me in the loop, told me all he knew, but I bet he knew more, just gave me what was necessary, just enough education to perform, which turned out wasn't a lot. I knew Vince worked for an agency, that was where Vince would go for his long meetings, go off upbeat and come back pissed. Robbing scum, he called them, though I wasn't clear on how much they robbed, I'm sure Vince got his share, judging by how much he threw his money about.

The story of how Vince made his fortune was one I'd heard many times, though how much he'd choose to embellish and elaborate would change depending on how much he had drunk. From what he said Vince was just in the right place in the right time, a complete coincidence that he stumbled on the biggest story of that year. If it was true then Vince was one lucky guy, though secretly I didn't believe it was true at all, I mean what were the odds? I think Vince was in the right place at the right time quite simply because that was where he was supposed to be and where he'd planned to be. I didn't buy it, and the whole rags-to-riches story was one concocted purely to make his jump from bottom to top, a much bigger leap.

I asked Vince once how the split worked, too, the money side, who gets what and when, asked how much money we and I could make. His eyes lit up of course, one thing Vince liked to talk about was money, especially his own. Taking off expenditure such as his travel, equipment, paying off his informers he told me he earned a quarter of a million dollars last year, and that wasn't even classed as a particularly good twelve months – he said one year he made that from one photo. Vince reckoned a decent photo of Lilly and Max Salter together could fetch $100,000. All the other photos, the ones in shopping malls and red-carpet events, they were deemed as pocket change.

I guessed that was why I was here, through good luck or poor judgement my job was to get that one photo that could make us both millions. And if anyone knew how to get that $100,000 it was Vince, perhaps I should do more of what he asked me, trust him more, though he was a hard man to place confidence in. For now, I had to believe that Max would be in London, make plans for his arrival, even if I couldn't quite believe it myself, or that such money could be made just from one photo, if that was the correct value at all – could just be what Vince wanted me to believe it was worth, so my split would end up a lesser half. That was something I'd have to worry about later, negotiating my split would come once I had the photo to negotiate with, for now I just wanted to fill my pockets with something, no matter how little. For all my trying I'd made just over $700 all in, and bear in mind that was for four weeks' work, though I had an epiphany moment on the drive down, a decision to change tactics, to stop chasing the $100,000 whale and try catching what I knew could be caught day in, day out. From now it was just a numbers game, four or five of those $250 shots a day could quickly add up to a good day's takings. And if I waited long enough, persevered, followed her every move, predicted her next, then I might be that lucky bastard one day too, till luck had nothing to do with luck at all. Meant regardless I had something to show for my work and I could go to bed at night with a sense of pride and achievement, that I did have the balls to get the job done, instead of feeling like a failure every night my head touched the pillow. But no more talking about past failure, that was done, now it was time to prove my competence, to Vince and myself, that I could be that bastard, the bastard I'd spent four weeks trying to avoid being.

In the end, I sat outside Lilly's hotel for another hour, gave myself the same mental pep talk over and over, psyching myself up, imagining what success would look like. And even though, after such a long build-up, and even though Lilly's quick dash from limo to hotel lasted about thirty seconds in total, it still felt a success, managed to snap a few dozen shots. They weren't the best, but I wired them to Vince straight away so that, for one thing, he knew she had arrived and secondly, so he knew I was trying. I stuck around a while longer, few more hours window watching, but Lilly didn't come back out. I guessed the flight had tired her out, I was glad, I was pretty knackered after a long day of watching time and doing nothing.

Hey, least I got some half decent shots, it was an improvement, better to have something than nothing at all, Vince happy enough, said he could make $500 dollars, give or take. It wasn't much to shout about, and it was an amount that would have to be split accordingly based on whatever maths Vince saw fit, but who cared, it was my first pay cheque as a paparazzo, something to celebrate. And taking away the value, although small, I could still quantify it into something material, something useful, money for Molly's new uniform, food in my family's belly. Made me want to earn more, made me set my alarm earlier the next morning, made me want to search the tabloid stands the next day. Which I did, I got up at first light, ran to the nearest shop, searched each magazine page.

And there it was, my first published work, I couldn't help but grin.

I was turning wolf.

★ ★ ★

A bus stopped and what seemed like the whole top deck turned to stare through my open window. I very nearly waved. Vince could've splashed out for a room with a chair, I thought, sat upright on the bed, a pile of letters and a bag of tube station cherries on my lap. For all my worrying, the letters were actually quite pleasant, they just missed their granddaughter, that was all. Questions of when I'd be back, what my plans were for the future, how I was coping, how they missed Molly, and of course Cassie. It was strange, Rose talking to me like a son, I'd met them only twice, once for the funeral but I barely said a word, and neither did they, it wasn't a time to talk. The other time we met was a few years back, they flew over just after Molly was born, but that was a hard week too. Fresh out of the neonatal unit Molly barely slept, then there was Lou and Cassie, they had a lot to talk about, things they needed to resolve, me and Rose left them to it, washed the dishes, tidied up, talked about how she grew up, our favourite authors, stuff to fill the silence.

I wasn't expecting how they treated me that time we first met, believe me, I was prepared for an attack of sorts. I mean, I was hardly the ideal son in law, not even a US citizen, not even a career. God, I even knocked up their daughter before I'd put a ring on her finger. They should have hated me, but any hate they had toward me, I never felt or noticed. They were either decent liars or just decent people, so far, they'd given me no reason to doubt the latter.

Lou, he was retired Navy, loved telling bad jokes, enjoyed a jar or two. Rose was a sweet little thing, all wrinkles and boobs, she worked in a seaside café on the beach, one hell of a cook, her broiled grouper and her molasses bread was legendary, hopefully one day I'd get to taste it for myself. Cassie always hoped one day they would move to LA, but Florida suited their health and lifestyle so like my Mom they too became only voices on a phone or letters on a page.

Rose was the mouthpiece of the relationship. Lou was far from shy in person, but all other methods of communication were left to his wife, birthday cards, Thanksgiving phone calls, though I doubted Lou had much choice. She liked to talk did my mother-in-law, both on paper and by phone, trust me I'd seen our old bills, and her letters were no different. They went on for pages and pages and what could've been said in a few words was normally written at unnecessary length, like the stack I'd just finished reading.

I felt worse for reading them, listening to a mother pour her heart out, page after page. I had no excuse to justify why I'd ignored them for so long, I wasn't a bad person, my heart was just doing a lot of things back then, not all of it good. I took another cherry from off my lap, picked up the last letter, the most recent, the one Mum felt obliged to reply to, as soon as I saw the handwriting I understood why.

Tom,

I don't know where to start with this. I'm not one for writing and I've never been great with words. But I'm angry and you're upsetting my wife and I wouldn't be a man if I didn't step in at this point.

We understand how hard it must be since Cassie's passing, it has been hard on us all. She was my little girl, my world. If it wasn't for having to be here for my wife I would've found a way to be up there with her too I assure you. I'm not ashamed to say some days I have felt like ending it all, Tom. I may look a big man, but this had really knocked me for six. A daughter shouldn't die before

her father, and no father should have to bury his own
child.

All I have of Cassie now is Molly and yourself and that is
something neither me or Rose want to miss out on. We tried to
talk to you at the funeral but it was a tough day for us all so
instead we decided to write. I never thought you would ignore
us for so long, Tom. I expected better and you have let me
down. But that is the past now and that is a circle that can't
be squared. No point dwelling on it.

Me and the wife have been talking. We want you both to
come and live with us. Our house is big enough, the schools
are great, and it would be easy for you to find work either here
in Clearwater or even in Tampa. Maybe you could drive a
cab, there's plenty of tourists.

It doesn't have to be long term. I know the sound of
sharing a house with your in-laws may not sound ideal, but
we would try to give you all the space you need and not let our
old age impact your daily routine. Once you are settled you
could then look at getting your own place, and think about
meeting someone again, perhaps have more children one day.
You're young, Tom, there's plenty of life to be had out here.

I don't want you to feel pressured with making a decision,
but I assure you we aren't going away. We deserve to be able
to see Molly as much as anyone else and Cassie would agree.
You need to speak to us and soon, Rose is in bits, she is hardly
sleeping and I worry for her health.

A man needs to be in charge of his affairs, Tom. You need
to start taking charge. Right now, you are being a coward.
Please, from one father to another. You have to speak to us.
I don't know what we have done wrong but we don't deserve
this. I hope you contact us soon. I really do. If not, we'll have
no other option then to look at other alternatives.

I hope you understand. I'm writing this with all I have
left.

I've enclosed a photo of Cassie when she was a similar age to Molly. She was always climbing that orange tree. I'd like to think one day Molly could be climbing it too.

Yours faithfully,

Lou

I made myself a hot drink, coffee sachet and UHT milk, it wasn't nice, but bad coffee is better than no coffee at all, as I reread Lou's letter. I completely agreed with everything he'd written and it was a letter that had to be written and one that needed a reply, which is probably why Mum did what she did and wrote back.

There was one bit though. The word 'alternatives' that Lou would turn to if there was no other option. I'm sure he didn't mean it as a threat, perhaps by alternatives he just meant talk it out some more, try and meet in person, unless it was a genuine threat, that they would do all they could to take Molly away from me if things didn't go how they planned. I was sure that wasn't the case, I knew I wasn't taking it in the right context.

I grabbed my laptop and without any idea of where to start I tried to find out what 'alternatives' might look like. This was harder than expected, I searched everything though I didn't know quite where the search should start. Typed 'paternity', 'unwed parents', 'father's rights', 'wife died', 'grandparent's rights', but it was hard to make sense of. I'd have to speak to a professional, Google alone could not give me the answers I would need. Still I searched on, forums and websites, there was so much of it and so much legal jargon it was difficult to know what was relevant and what wasn't.

What if the custodial parent dies? Then the custody of the grandchild automatically goes to non-custodial parent unless he or she has been found to be unfit.

What did 'non-custodial' mean, I thought, typing the question from my head onto my keyboard. Had I done things the right way, when I ran back to England after Cassie died? Was I supposed to have notified someone of what I was doing? Did I need to sign anything? Had I broken a law I wasn't aware of?

The 'fitness' of a parent or parents is the primary issue in a third party's challenge to the parental preference doctrine. When deciding if a parent is fit, the court considers whether the parent can provide the required support and guidance for the child without state intervention. The court should consider whether the non-parent has superior ability or skills and is neither abusive, unstable nor neglectful.

Surely Lou and Rose wouldn't go down that route? Surely they didn't think Molly was at risk, that I wasn't 'fit' to be her father? I was neither abusive nor unstable. Neglectful bothered me, I'd been chasing celebrities half a continent away, left my only daughter with my elderly mother, with no money or real job. I could see a lot of courtrooms seeing that as neglect, no matter how much I didn't see it myself.

The best way to establish the father's paternity is by naming him on the baby's birth certificate. Under US Department of Health and Human Services regulations, all states must offer unwed parents an opportunity to establish paternity by voluntarily signing an acknowledgment of paternity, either at the hospital or at a later time. If the father is not present at the hospital following the birth, the father and mother will instead have to sign the voluntary declaration of paternity at a later time, and have the father's name added to the birth certificate later.

I couldn't remember ever signing a declaration of paternity. I remember the nurse waving paperwork at us at some point, but with Cassie still getting over her C-section and Molly in an incubator trying to survive, I'm guessing our minds wouldn't have been on legalities and signatures. I'd another memory of Cassie telling me we had to sign some papers just after we'd brought Molly home, but again I assumed that she'd sorted that, unless it was still stuck on top of a pile.

When paternity is established, the father has the same rights as a father of a child in a marriage. These include such rights as the ability to address custody and visitation issues with the court, and to give other input into decisions regarding the child. Though until paternity is established the father does not have the same legal rights or responsibilities as of a parent.

Oh God, I hoped that form wasn't sat at the bottom of a stack of paperwork in our old house somewhere, or worse, thrown out in the trash. I'd need to check that, make sure everything had been done the way it should, and if not, put it right. Not that I knew who to contact, or where to start, or the implications if things that should have been signed hadn't been. I'm sure it could be rectified. Form or no form, I was her father, I was the parent.

But again, I was overanalysing, this wasn't blackmail, it was Lou stating that regardless of my decision to stay in England or go back to America there would have to be an alternative option. There would have to be a way that they could see their granddaughter, that was all that Lou was saying, it wasn't intimidation.

Still meant I had an element of doubt – although the smallest of doubts it would still sit in my head and eat away at me till I had some real answers. I would have to do more research, most importantly I'd have to contact Lou and Rose, letter first, ideally, I'd speak to them, once I'd plucked up the courage and not till I knew what answer to give them.

I looked up at the clock, it was just past five, I stank of car and stale bed sheets. I closed my laptop and ran a shower in the hope the water was at least warm, which it just about was. By the time I'd come out there was a voicemail from Vince, one that made me punch the sky, call him straight back and punch the same sky again, harder than before.

The next few days were crazy, but I did as Vince asked, darted across London, underground and over ground, met tailors, posted airmail, got measured, collected tickets, found a barber, bought shoes, picked up suits, not to mention following Lilly. Luckily, she didn't stray too far, she'd spent the whole week being chauffeured from one building to the next, made for awful photos, but Vince was unconcerned, Vince was putting his eggs all in one basket. And that basket was tomorrow night's award show.

I still couldn't quite believe it was happening, that I would be the one in the warm, eating the canapés for once, sipping the champagne, I was not used to such luxury, I'd have to do my best to make sure it looked like it was a luxury I was already accustomed to, look calm and collected, like I was used to rubbing such shoulders. I was excited though, despite the nerves, the anticipation, the pressure. I'd have moments where I couldn't wait for the day to come, to walk that same red carpet, to see idols up close, but I wasn't there for a night off. Vince wasn't paying me to have a good time, me in a tailored suit and £100 shoes wasn't for my own gain, it was an expensive camouflage, to blend in unnoticed, to get up close and personal. Disguised as a gentleman when inside I was still the same scum, out to do the same horrible deeds.

Speaking of gentlemen and scum, though there was tangible proof Max would be in London there was no evidence to suggest he would be in attendance at the awards show, though Vince was adamant that Mr Salter would make an appearance and based on his history with Lilly I would have to agree the odds looked in our favour.

I wished I could say I hated Max and yes, he had done things that would justify any bad feeling I had towards him, but in all honesty the guy was a hard one to stay mad at. He oozed class in everything he did, his films were immaculate, the women he linked arms with too and there were a lot of them. Each woman more attractive than the last, each looking happier than the previous, like with Max it was always a good time and it was a good time only for the advantaged few.

It was fair to say Max Salter was the man who with one hand you'd clench your fist but with the other you'd end up shaking his hand. Some people wrote that without his money and adulation there would be no lothario reputation and I could see why. He wasn't the most handsome, he wasn't the youngest or toughest, but he was the smartest and he would be the one that would take your girl off you and if he couldn't beat you in a fight, he would try his hardest to make sure, winners and losers, all would end up bloody.

The whole Lilly fiasco had made it worse, fired up his reputation, made it difficult to say the word 'Max' and not immediately think 'Salter'. I read up a lot about Max, tried to understand what made him tick. Turned out he'd had a hard life, a successful one, but still one that left him with knocks and scars. Again, made me like him even more, us guys are a sucker for someone that kept getting back up, meant you listened when he talked, because you knew he probably had something worthwhile to say. I'd watched quite a few clips, interviews and press, he was quite brutal, very honest, but what he said I'd tend to agree with, though I'd never dare say it. That was why the press and the paparazzi liked him so much, because he was the grenade, explosions and implosions guaranteed, as long you pulled the right question.

One thing was for sure, no matter the women on his arm, it was clear he still loved Lilly, that was obvious, everything suggested that. I couldn't find a bad word said about her by Max and whenever she was brought up, which was a lot, he answered with only gushing praise and admiration for her. Even after their split he still continued to talk of her in the highest regard and it came across that it was all done intentionally, he knew that somehow, somewhere, Lilly would read about it, or hear about it and she would know that for him it wasn't over. That was why it was vital I could find something useful to help me try and figure out where he and Lilly would meet in London. They had to, there was no way Max would not take up the opportunity.

I checked if he'd visited London before, checked all the images I could find online. From what I could see it was only the once, around the time of all his accolades and awards a couple of years back. He and Lilly were inseparable, her looking beautiful, him looking enigmatic, smart suit, whisky in one hand, regulation cigar in the other. Annoyingly, despite the age gap, they looked great together as a pair, and in my time spent watching her I hadn't seen Lilly as happy as back when she was by Max's side. Still there was nothing on the internet that helped me, no clue as to where he might be staying this time around, or where he and Lilly might meet, if at all. Fingers crossed he just turned up, I mean one thing Max loved was to be on the front page, turning up on the same red carpet would certainly give him that, though deep down I knew it wouldn't be that easy. Max didn't come across as someone who made things straightforward and I was 100% certain finding Max and Lilly wasn't going to be simple, there would be a twist to all this.

I closed my laptop, pulled on some clothes. Walked out of my hotel to restaurant after restaurant, cuisine after cuisine, my stomach was spoilt for choice. Ended up in a little noodle bar, authentic and quiet, somewhere I could sit and work out how to be smarter than Max.

17

Sat in my car I took a glance at myself in the rear-view mirror. Another Bond impression, the same one I'd done in my hotel mirror. It was laughable to be honest, this fancy dress, I had fifty pounds in my pocket and an overdraft in the other, I was hardly Connery. But the transformation would do the job and was probably the best reflection I'd seen of myself since as long as I could remember.

Pat on the back to Vince in all this, I thought. I'd prepared myself to be let down, to arrive at today with nothing to wear and no way of getting in, but everything he'd promised, the places he'd told me to go, the people he'd told me to meet, had all done as Vince said they would, it was all very 'under table', nods and whispers, quiet and efficient, they played their part brilliantly. Now it was just down to me to play mine, not to mention getting inside the place, no matter how genuine my ticket looked in my hand until I was inside it was worthless.

The only thing missing was company. Vince did say it might not look customary me turning up alone, in fact he said I'd look weird and lonely, offered me a number of an agency where I could get a broad to smile and look pretty for a couple of hours. Looking over at the empty passenger seat beside me I agreed it would feel a little strange arriving at a party like this, just on my own. But I could live with weird and lonely, I couldn't live with prostitution, no matter how beautiful it could look. I imagined what Cassie would have looked like beside me now, my own little Carole Lombard, she would've loved all this, all the dressing up, all the glamour. I felt embarrassed she never had a chance to come to a place like this, if anyone deserved to sparkle tonight it should have been her, not me.

I checked my watch, it was time to go, checked my parking ticket one more time to make sure it would last me tonight and tomorrow without a fine. For the money I'd paid I should have gotten a taxi both ways, but I needed to be mobile and quick, I wished I could have parked a little closer, meant I wouldn't have to run so far if Max and Lilly decided to move fast. I got out of the car and started to make my way across the city, through streets and more streets, each busier than the last.

The nerves really hit when I first saw the Opera House, how huge it was, how impressive, the wall of paparazzi didn't help either. Felt myself take a big breath as I walked past the fans and barriers, heard cameras and saw flashes, I guessed they thought I was someone, they'd all be in for a sombre surprise when they found out I wasn't anybody at all.

I handed the lady my ticket. As she checked its authenticity, I felt like I was fifteen again, trying to convince bouncers I was old enough to drink and dance, same nerves, same euphoria as the lady smiled and ushered me towards the nearest glass of cold champagne, as I tried to take it all in, look cool and calm when I was neither.

I was instantly in the middle of a sea of people, in an ocean I couldn't quite swim in, the whole room was in a conversation I wasn't privy to, telling the funniest joke, the smartest quip, the hottest gossip, everyone knew everyone, old friends and new acquaintances. God what I wouldn't have given for the number of that agency now, someone who would just talk to me, make me feel less awkward. There were famous people everywhere, had to stop myself staring, my instinct was to grab my camera, I felt naked without it around my neck. I wasn't sure what Vince expected me to do in here, I asked him the same question a few hours before, he didn't have an answer, told me to watch Lilly and Max like a hawk, which was fucking great seeing as I couldn't find either.

I took myself to the bar, ordered something not too alcoholic, hoping someone might take me in, let me into their circle, but no one did, well one guy, but he looked even more desperate than me.

A guy called Rupert latched on to me, as posh as he was drunk, started talking about David Cameron, then the World Cup, quickly realizing I wasn't educated in football or Tory triumphs. Though I appreciated the company, albeit brief, it killed ten minutes before I was back flying solo again. But what a place to be alone, always the closet film buff, I'd be lying if I said seeing so many industry faces didn't give me a hard-on. A room full of trailblazers and heroes, experts in their field, legends and youth. This was movie people talking movie things, next projects, camera angles, name-dropping. So, when I should have been sweeping the room for Salter and Goodridge, instead I'd managed to get into a conversation about Kubrick conspiracy theories with a guy twice my age and twice as big, soon I found myself being ushered to my seat.

Wow, the Opera House looked majestic, I mean I was high up as high up could be, the amphitheatre, the upper slip, touching the ceiling, but I wasn't complaining, the view was something else even if I was in nosebleed territory. I looked once more for you know who, but the search was impossible as the voiceover introduced the presenter to the stage and room fell to a hush.

Thirty minutes later I got my first sight of Lilly, it was worth the wait.

★ ★ ★

The first time I only saw her briefly, watched her present an award before disappearing backstage again. It wasn't till afterwards, as the press took their photos of winners with their trophies and losers with their aggravated smiles, that I eventually saw her up close, watched her as she tiptoed gracefully down each spiral step of the staircase, into the crowds. My God did she look beautiful, her dress was stunning, not that what she wore mattered, clothes wore Lilly, not the other way around, they needed her more than she needed them. Whilst down below other women fought for accolades and admiration, women like Lilly, who were that beautiful, that effortless, attention came to them. I found myself laughing, a stupid grin. I'd missed Lilly, genuinely missed her, I felt such a fool.

"You thinking what I'm thinking?" I felt a nudge, Rupert was back, eyeing up Lilly with a snort, I didn't reply, left him clutching his cock and champagne. I followed Lilly as she floated around the vast numbers of heads and bodies, as I too weaved myself around the periphery trying my best not to lose sight of her. Tonight, she wore red, her hair down, curled into waves. I'd never seen her like this before, I was used to an off-camera Lilly, I hadn't seen how flawless she was up close, her teeth whiter, her lips redder, her eyes brighter.

I watched her sit at a busy table, it felt strange having no walls, no fences between us, how easy it would be to get even closer, or even talk to her, but there may as well have been a wall – no matter how close I was, it was still the same distance. She began to talk to the man next to her, white hair, white beard, I recognized him from the cottage, Jonathan Barton-Hughes, her director. After a few minutes, they both stood up and he led her to the dance floor, I watched them for a few minutes, it looked sweet, the odd couple, wondered what they might be talking about, what it must be like to dance with her, to be able to glide in her arms.

I wanted to order whisky, but the car keys in my pocket told me otherwise. A guy took a stool beside me, he wasn't as posh as my last company, but he was definitely as drunk, if not more. He talked for a long time, the state of British cinema mostly, I pretended to listen, he offered tequila, offered me a line of coke. He said his goodbyes, moved onto someone more his own speed, he was OK, a different time I may have accepted both, but tonight I was still on the job.

I checked my phone, message from Mum, more doctors, more

tests with no results. I scrolled my phone, no messages, no Max Salter and worse, the party had started to unwind, I glimpsed over my shoulder and half the hall had now cleared. For all the excitement and fascination, for all intents and purposes I'd come away with nothing of any value tonight, nothing tangible, nothing Vince would smile about. Tonight had to be a big night, the last five days had not been the best, for all my trying, for all my initial enthusiasm, it hadn't gotten me any closer to a big pay cheque. Lilly and London were beating me, I couldn't keep up, for all my planning, all my predictions, Lilly and Max may as well have been back in LA, I still would never have found them together in the same place.

I checked the time. It was just past eleven, I could just go back to my hotel, I thought, that felt the best option, forget tonight, reassess tomorrow, take the wrath of Vince, accept it and move on, leave the warmth of glamour and celebrity and go out into the cold of London, back with the worthless and disreputable, prowling taxis and stumbling drunks, back to a world where I belonged, one that felt more comfortable. Instead I went to the toilet.

Where was Max?

It kept going round and round in my head.

Where was Max?

He was here in London, Heathrow, Terminal 3, I'd seen the images clear as day. Reporters and journos said he was here for business, but in my gut the only business he was truly here for was Lilly, that was why I couldn't figure out why he hadn't showed.

If I were Max, where would I meet Lilly? Her hotel? His hotel? No, both would be swarming with paps. If he wanted to encourage a frenzy of media attention then he would have just shown up here, which clearly, he hadn't.

I did have one hunch, literally a stab in the dark, founded on only assumptions and guesses, one Vince thought ridiculous but worth a go if all else failed, which so far it had. As I washed my hands I decided I'd go back and keep an eye on Lilly a little longer, wait till she called it a night, then decide once and for all whether to go with my last shot of the night. Wasn't like I had anything to lose, just pride and petrol.

I'd lost my seat at the bar, despite being quiet, the ones left only had drink on their minds. I squeezed myself back to where I was sat before, quickly looked over into the corner of the room, thank God Lilly was still here, talking to the same people, worried I'd come back and she'd have already left. I tried to get the barman's attention but he was busy pouring shots to people who quite clearly didn't need any more shots, when suddenly I felt someone come up beside me. I looked to my right, it was Lilly, stood shoulder to shoulder, trying to get the barman's attention, which of course she immediately got, and mine too, as I looked forward, trying to work out what to do next and what words to say. No walls, no fences, no camera lenses, close enough to smell her perfume, to feel her arm touch mine.

18

"Vince? Vince? Can you hear me?"

"Tommy?"

"What's going on?"

"Nephew's christening today. Got half my family here. It feels like fucking Little Italy. Can this wait till later? I'm kinda tied up."

"I wanted to tell you straight away."

"I can't hear you. What you say?"

"You're not gonna believe this, Vince. I've only gone and done it."

"Done what?"

"I got it, Vince. I got the shot."

"Serious?"

"I've just pinged it across to you."

"Give me a minute, let me just get this pancake batter off my hands and get someone to take over my frying pan."

I could hear him over the line, shouting Italian at someone, things rattling, the noise of his breath as I heard him pace around his house.

"Have you got the email yet?"

"I'm just loading up my laptop. Is it from the Awards bash?"

"No, after."

"Where? Max's hotel?"

"No, the place I thought."

"No fucking shit. Nice work."

"Has it come through yet?"

"Nearly, it's just finding a server."

He went quiet for a few seconds.

"Where is this place, some park?"

"Some bit of grass in the middle of Westminster."

"She looks pretty fucking pissed, man. They arguing?"

"Yeah. I couldn't hear them from where I was, but it looked pretty heated."

"And you're sure there was no one else there?"

"I'm positive."

The line went quiet.

"You still there, Vince?"

"You've only gone and done it, Tommy. You've only gone and fucking done it."

"Are they good?"

"Oh, these are good. Better than good."

"What do you think?"

"I think this is gonna make us a lot of green."

"How much will it make?"

"Did you get any video footage?"

"No."

"Shame. We'd get more dough if it wasn't stills. I need to speak to my office straight away. Like now. We need to get these on print ASAP, they're gonna want these sold damn quick. What time is it your end? Is it Sunday?"

"Sunday lunchtime."

"Well it's past six here. Why didn't you ring me last night?"

"Sorry, I feel asleep. I got back pretty late."

"We've lost a lot of time then."

"How much will this make us?"

"Taking off expenditure, sorting out my informers. It will leave us about 60%."

"That seems a lot taken off."

"Don't worry, Galella, you'll do well out of this."

"How well?"

"Your cut. About twenty gees."

"Sterling?"

"No, dollars. Sterling you'll be looking at just under twelve thousand give or take."

"Oh."

"You don't sound happy?"

"I thought it might make more."

"Hey, man. You did well. This is the fucking start, Tommy."

"Surely now we can stop? We got the shot. I've made enough to start over. That's all I ever wanted."

"This is far from over. This is finally starting. The girl is crumbling. She's been drinking all over Hollywood, her man Frank is over my side of the pond. She is ours for the taking. And it gets better. My sources tell me she is back down to Devon next week and it doesn't look like Frank is going back any time soon. She's got no security, no bodyguard. You can get close man."

"I can't get any fucking closer, Vince."

"You can always get closer. Cheer up, Tommy. This is a good day. You did good, man. You fucking stepped up to the plate. I'm a happy man."

"Good for you."

"Grab some balls, man. You just made yourself a lot of cheddar. That's money you can take home to your Mom and Molly. You should be fucking proud. You've become a man. And this is only the start. There is so much money to be had out of that girl."

"I'm tired, Vince. I'll call you tomorrow."

"Sleep well, my Prince. You did me proud today. Soon as I know money I'll holler at you."

"Night, Vince."

"I'm not sleeping tonight, man. I'm celebrating. I better go. I've got people to ring. Today is all about negotiation."

"What about your nephew's christening?"

"Fuck that. Baptism can wait. My nephew wants a cheque for his first car, not fucking balloons and cake. Besides, business comes first."

"Vince?"

"What?"

"Who is your informer?"

"My what?"

"Your informer."

"I got more than one, my friend, my little stool pigeons are all over. I got girls on perfume counters, men in baggage claims, some office clerk over at NBC. I got ears and eyes everywhere. All you need to know is, they are close enough."

PART FOUR

LILLY

Berkeley Square/May/Shot 409

19

I finished a few more sit-ups by the foot of my bed, attempted another set of press-ups before giving up. I looked in the mirror, analysed my stomach's side profile, they say TV added a few pounds, which was fucking fantastic seeing as I'd spent the last two days sat on every presenter's couch in London, least they were fun, nothing too serious, nothing too Diane Sawyer. My hosts, all funny and sweet and all gay from what I could gather, were harmless, treated me kindly, asked me easy questions when I'm sure they could've asked far worse.

There was a knock at my door. Room service, jeez those guys worked fast and without instruction he put the tray over by the balcony, just like he had the last time. I told him I felt bad making him work so hard, he smiled and left, I'm not sure they were allowed to talk to 'upstairs'. I was having a lazy day, pampering myself, it had been a busy time since my return, busier than I'd liked and yet again I felt me and London would never get to know each other in the way I'd have liked.

Felt like I'd seen lots, though. I'd even done some filming over at Pinewood, some underwater work which was a first. Apparently, I drown very well. It was pretty intense, all the flames and lighting, didn't require much acting, I'd never been the strongest swimmer so flapping about in a panic didn't involve stepping out of character too much. Of course, I was saved, the dashing Chris Rogan, on hand for all the required heroics, as always. Even wet he looked perfect.

I'd had an audition, too, all very last minute, I only had a day to learn my scene, didn't even have time to print off a hard copy, nor take my coloured pen to it. Despite my change in routine I felt I did enough, didn't feel like I nailed it, but I didn't feel like I made a fool out of myself either. I knew the casting director, we'd talked briefly at a black-tie event last year and he said that the screen test was more of a formality than an audition as he knew my work already, still felt like one to me. I liked the script, least what I'd read. I was down to play the wife of a blue-collar worker suffering from alcoholism. I'd never been a wife before, though I knew alcohol dependency pretty well and it was set in New York, which was great as I'd never been. Quite a gritty movie, no make-up, probably have to lose a few pounds, get gaunt and frail, leave the romance to the youngsters, time for me to grow ugly. It seemed to be the hot trend right now, becoming ugly for a role, every actress worth her salt had done it. Perhaps it was just my turn, or I was past being cast as young, hot-bodied love interest, those days were over, now I was left with being an alcoholic's dowdy other half. Men like Chris Rogan as they grew old and grey would be allowed to command armies and run criminal organizations, the more years that passed the grander an actor's role and the more we have to take them seriously. Me, I was just a wife, and hopefully if I aged gracefully I might be lucky enough to be typecast as a mother, and possibly one day a grandma. I'm Diane Keaton – not a bad thing I suppose.

I poured myself a tea, watched the teabag do its thing. It was a shame there weren't more days like these, indulgence in the simplest of terms, a good book, a long bath, and time to enjoy them both without being bothered. I'd even managed a little sleep, not long, but long enough, I was going to need it, tonight would be a late affair. Beside my pot of tea, I noticed a plate of biscuits, a gesture I didn't ask for and didn't want. Though a waste, I threw them in the bin. If I was hungry enough to go through bins for calories, then getting into a dress was the least of my worries.

It felt like all I'd done since I'd arrived in the capital was eat hors d'oeuvre, amuse-bouches, taster menus, aperitifs, petits fours, not to mention cheese and port. I'd decided not to eat today, hence the copious amounts of herbal tea, and I'd taken a laxative, I know I shouldn't have, but I needed to cleanse the system. Downside was I kept having to go to the bathroom, not very glamorous I know, my cheat's colonic, but there was a red gown in my wardrobe that I needed to get into in less than a few hours. Make-up and hair were coming soon and it would be embarrassing enough not getting into the dress, even more when I have to explain to the team who had spent several weeks hand-picking it.

It was a beautiful dress, the stylist brought a rail of options the previous night. I never quite know where they come from, the stylist or the dresses. Not that I was complaining, the jewellery I'd be wearing tonight could have bought me a small condo in Claremont, made me nervous, I hoped they were insured.

I was actually looking forward to tonight, I hadn't gotten dressed up in ages. I couldn't even remember the last carpet event I'd been to and it would be the first time I'd be back in the glare of photographers and microphones again. On the phone, I jokingly asked Sally if I had won an award, she didn't even reply. Don't worry, I told her, I knew the drill well enough, look the part, don't fall over, not too much Moët. If only real life was that simple.

I walked over to my balcony, past the piano. Yes, this room had its very own piano, I had no idea why. I didn't know who the hotel was catering for, as it certainly wasn't any of my doing. I kept feeling the urge to tap a few keys, attempt to play it, but I hadn't yet. A waste for something so beautiful to be sat unused. It may not even work, it might have been for display only, like me. I'm kidding.

Outside the window it still looked gloomy. I hoped it would brighten up for this evening as there is nothing worse than an awards show in the rain. I looked across London, regardless of the weather it always looked so tempting, like something was happening and I was about to miss it. Technically today was my day off, I should have gone and seen the sights, a bit of shopping, a bit of adventure, something a bit more cultural than shaving my legs and watching a weeks' worth of *Coronation Street*. I'd missed quite a lot about England, more than I thought, not just their TV. I was looking forward to seeing my little cottage again and turning back into Betty Crocker.

In LA I'd hardly cooked, hardly read either. My Englishness, like my jet lag, disappeared after a few days and it wasn't long before I fell back into my old ways of sushi breakfast and liquid lunches. But it wasn't all glitz and glamour, I saw a lot of family and friends, got all the cuddles and love I needed before I had to wave them all off again.

The flight back to LA wasn't great, bad turbulence over the Atlantic. I've never flown well at the best of the times, especially when alone, with no one to cling onto, but I had other reasons to be anxious, knowing a lot of people would not be happy or impressed with my decision to run home without warning or reason. I did my best to not think about it, caught up on sleep, drank the free champagne, read a little. I even bumped into a photographer I'd worked with before, he was sat a few rows behind from me, we talked briefly as we stretched our legs in the aisle. He was nice, kept calling me sister, telling me his favourite gay bars in Silver Lake – apparently, he's taking me to Faultline. I agreed but we both knew it was a promise neither of us would be expected to keep.

With my return home so unplanned I was surprised there were paparazzi as I walked my luggage through the foyer. They couldn't have all been there for me, which quite quickly I found they weren't, a pop star had just landed at another terminal, Britney Spears, so I was told. I was just their pleasant surprise, and even though I was hassled, it was a level of harassment I could cope with and I managed to get home with minimal fuss. Felt sorry for Miss Spears, taking the brunt of the chaos, though I was sure she was more used to it than me.

It was so nice to be at home, saw a lot of my old friends, drank far too much wine, went to a few clubs, what else? Dad took me out in the car I got him for his birthday, drove up San Gabriel Valley with the top down. Didn't see a lot of Dad whilst I was back, most days he was busy with work, or finding work should I say. I rang my sister too, spoke for hours, cried a bit, both of us booked time in our diaries to visit, be nice to see my little niece before she gets too old for me to recognize.

Had some quality time with my mom, we did have a little argument halfway through the day, something trivial, made up soon after. Mine and my mother's relationship was a strange one, we are better apart, better in small doses, we've never had that typical bond. I didn't want an older sister, I already had one of those, what I wanted was a mother, a normal one, not a drinking buddy, or someone to go to a bar with. But as I said, all in all I had a nice day with her, got her full, undivided attention for a change. It started with taking Ringo for a nice walk over at Runyon Canton, where just like a typical Goodridge male he attempted to dry hump anything that moved. Later I took Mom to the ArcLight for a touch of nostalgia, a late showing of *Kelly's Heroes*, sneaked in, disguised in our flats and hats. My late grandpa was big into cinema, fought the Nazis too, meant as a family we'd watched a lot of war movies over the years and westerns too. It was fair to say that, with a mom who danced, a dad who acted and Gramps the war vet, over the years I'd sat on many laps, watched a hell of a lot of movies, an unhealthy amount.

I still got excited by the movies, even my own, the trailers, the smell of popcorn, the end credits. To see my name roll down the screen, whilst the audience left their seats, always gave me goosebumps. That love doesn't change when you become a famous actress, in fact I was worse than ever, it doesn't diminish just because you're up there yourself.

What else happened whilst I was home? I pottered around the house a lot, swam in the pool, tried to get my tan back. I'd become an English rose and my paleness didn't suit the West Coast, so I tried to stay outdoors at every opportunity. I did cook a little I suppose, made us *huevos rancheros* one morning, cooked up a few mean T-bones in the smoker the night before I flew back. I joked with Mom I'd buy them an Aga, it's the only way to warm socks I told her.

I managed to get a bit of one-to-one time with Mom and Dad separately, too. Their divorce is already a done deal, both of them hell-bent on seeing it through and quickly too. Didn't know what to expect, thought Mom would be in tears, Dad a broken man, but they were all smiles and happiness. Too happy, splitting up should not be so amicable, I'd have preferred to come back to tears and tantrums and custody battles. Least it would have showed a bit of passion, like hearts had been broken, rather than handshakes and high fives. I didn't think Mom and Dad realised how much it had affected me and big sis, for them it was all bright futures, but for us it was the fucking end of the world. It should have been their end of world too, when in fact they acted like it was the start.

I ended up going out that night, went a bit crazy, ended up getting with some hot ball player, which was silly – one, he was far too young for me; two, he had a girlfriend, a pretty famous one too. More drama, more front pages.

What else? I had to sort my shit out too, money wise, bills and more bills. I tell you the more money I earned the less grasp I had of where it went. I had a feeling I was being robbed by someone, probably the state, the IRS, probably my agent. I never read contracts, so I had no idea legally how much he was allowed to screw me over, I didn't want to know, it was better to be robbed blind. He rang me whilst I was back in LA, I'd been offered a lucrative commercial for TV in Japan, some drink full of caffeine, I didn't ask too much. Big money apparently so I'd probably have no choice but to do it, even though I'd said before I never trusted artists who sold out. People are suspicious enough of us already, we are supposed to be role models, the embodiment of someone to be looked up to. I shouldn't be telling people what toilet paper to buy or what fizzy drinks to rot their teeth with.

Sad that I had more offers for advertising than I did movie roles. I'd become a trademark, a commodity, a face on a mug, a pencil case, one day I might even be a doll. I'd always wanted to be a doll, see it on the shelves of Kitson's. Princess Lilly, Ballerina Lilly, Safari Lilly. I wouldn't put it past my publicist, as long as it made money they couldn't care less how I was sold, as long as it promoted my brand. Brand was the big word in the Goodridge Camp, I never liked it, made me feel like a barcode. Still, for the sake of taking a sip of something fizzy, saying "*Konichiwa*" to a camera, I could sort myself out financially, take a year out, invest, do something for me. As if that would happen, my career was a wheel that wouldn't stop turning, there was too much money to be made, for far too many people.

It was sad to say goodbye though, Mom came to the airport with me, Dad wasn't around, audition or golf, I couldn't remember the lie he'd made up. Still, Mom waved me off, I cried a little, not in front of her. Luckily, I slept through most of the flight, arrived in London feeling fuzzy and cold. I already missed home, thankfully my homesickness didn't last long, I was too busy to be homesick, too busy for most things. Could be a good thing, I thought, with all the shit going on with Frank.

Still no news on that one. We hadn't talked for over a week, not since the morning I left, not since our big argument, I thought it would've blown over, they normally did, but it hadn't. Frank was a stubborn old mule, and I'd never been one to back down either, I had tried to make up, honestly I had, tried to ring a few times, dropped him a few messages from my cell. Made me sad that he never responded, I guess he still saw me as guilty, no matter how much I told him otherwise.

It all started the morning after Kate's visit, surprisingly I wasn't hung over, and even more surprisingly I was up at sunrise with a mop and bucket. I'd managed to clean a fair amount the night before but the remains of mine and Kate's drunken festivities extended throughout the whole house, not just the kitchen.

Frank arrived not long after I'd woken up, he brought with him pop tarts and fresh juice, and although at first shocked at the trail of mess, after his first coffee he was helping me clean too. He was in quite a talkative mood, sounded like he and Sally had a nice evening, trying new food and old brandy. Took her for a walk afterwards, past the boats, found a pub, drank some more. I asked if there was any romance, he neither agreed nor disagreed. It was nice cleaning the house with Frank, dustpan and brush, buckets of soapy water. It didn't feel like a chore as we talked, stopping for more coffee, talking some more, then cleaning again. Till he found something in the wash room.

I tried to explain it wasn't mine, I tried to explain I never took any. I tried to explain it must've been Kate's, that she must have taken it without me knowing, but Frank wouldn't listen. He thought the worst of me, to him I'd broken a promise and betrayed his trust. Things got a bit heated and I said some horrible things. It was a strange argument, it wasn't even an argument, Frank hardly spoke a word, it was his eyes that did most of his talking. I'd never seen him look so disappointed in me and that was saying something as I had a way of disappointing people, especially Frank.

Well, he left, so did I, he went off in his car, I went off in an aeroplane.

Sally said to leave him be, said she'd speak to him, get him to calm down and come to his senses, which I thought by now he would have, but he hasn't. So, for the time being I was Frank-less, left to fend for myself. I thought Sally may have demanded that I had some additional security, that she wouldn't feel comfortable me being so isolated, so vulnerable. But so far, she hadn't. We both knew my agent wanted Frank out for a new younger model – if he caught a whiff of this then Frank would be unemployed and neither me nor Sally wanted that, this was our little secret, one we had to sort out quickly.

Thank God Sally had my back, I explained it all and she believed me, I couldn't see why Frank couldn't have done the same. Sally wasn't best pleased with me running back off to LA at the time, but she could see it wasn't up for discussion, even sorting out flights and transfers for me so I could leave on the same day. I even offered for Sally to come back too, she could stay with my family, or go back to New York but she decided instead to stay. Had things that needed sorting with her family in England so I promised her I'd be back in a week.

I'm still super-pissed with Kate and I told her so. She apologized, said it was clumsy and stupid, but before I had a chance to get mad she told me she was pregnant. She was over the moon of course, she couldn't believe it, complete shock she said, I guessed it wasn't planned. Apparently, morning after our little party she found herself throwing up a lot, thought it was alcohol we'd drunk or something she'd eaten, few days later she was still being sick, it was then she took a pregnancy test. She actually got quite upset on the phone, said she was embarrassed, said it was shameful, the thought of putting cocaine into her body knowing there would've been a tiny baby inside her. She knew she'd done wrong and agreed it was stupid, it didn't need me to make her feel worse. Kate's life was always full of drama, most of it her own doing. She may have worn her pearls and French braid but she certainly was no preacher's daughter. She wasn't shy about her wealth, though she talked of it like a burden. Her father owned one of the largest vineyards in Napa County and without knowing it you've probably held, or owned or shared a bottle with her surname on the label. Kate had always gone out of her way to not be what was expected of her, the good little rich girl, she was anything but. But now she was reformed, funny what a blue line on a pregnancy stick could do, crazy how things can change in such a short space of time, one minute Tequila shots on my kitchen table, coke off my toilet seat, the next mat leave and trimesters. I was happy for her, she would be a great Mom, well I hoped so, this baby would be the reality check she needed, if this didn't change her then nothing would. In the end, I managed to twist Kate's arm to ring Frank to explain the situation, but he didn't answer any of her calls, so she sent a letter instead, explaining it was all her doing. I don't know if he'd received it, he hadn't replied.

It was getting cold now, so I closed the balcony door, went into the bathroom, sat on the chaise longue. I had a lot to do and not a lot of time, so the one thing I shouldn't have been doing was relaxing. My cell buzzed. Two messages.

One from Sally, wishing me good luck for the awards show, not that I needed luck, not like I was nominated for anything. It didn't sound like she was having a great time visiting family, we had a long talk a few days before, I told her to take her another week off, not that she wanted it, but I thought it was about time she spent time with this family she never talked about. I'm sure she'd have rather been in London, or travelling back down to Devon with me, but I assured her I could fend for myself, promised her to have the cottage all spick and span when she returned, balloons and banners. She regretfully agreed.

I was quite looking forward to my week on my own back at the cottage. I had many plans, making jello, reorganizing my closet, yoga. But left to my own devices I would most likely just end up trashing the place, eating junk and watching junk. That's the problem with having chaperones, having things done for you, every minor detail planned out. It's reversed me from an independent woman, back to an idle teenager. I hoped this week on my own might kick-start my adulthood again, a rehab of home baking and decluttering felt like the right thing to do.

There was a knock at the door, hair and make-up, I let them in and they started to set up all their equipment as I checked the other message on my cell.

Another one from Kate, she'd been messaging me all day,

probably something to do with nausea. I'd already prescribed her all things ginger, ginger tea, ginger biscuits, grated ginger. God knows why I was suddenly the expert. I read her message, a warning that Max was in town, a warning I'd heard days before, still didn't mean I wanted to be reminded.

20

I was in the limousine, took another sip of champagne, then another. I'd been in a complete mess the last few hours, the stylist came and went, the make-up girl too, I'm sure I looked wonderful but I'd neither noticed nor looked.

Whatever precautions I'd taken to get through tonight without losing my shit had failed. I thought I'd psyched myself up, given myself the pep talk, but the closer we got to the Opera House the more I felt like bursting into tears. When I first heard Max would be in London I did ask Sally if I could give tonight a miss, make out I was ill, food poisoning, anything contagious. But none of my threats were taken seriously and as Sally kept reassuring me, he probably wouldn't even be there. Kate agreed too.

A small part of me very nearly rang him, to avoid all the guesswork and just flat out ask him if he was coming. But I didn't – one, it would inflate his ego and two, it would undo all my hard work this past month. Besides deep down I knew Max wouldn't choose here and now for us to meet in public for the first time since that drama at the party, why would Max want to bring scandal and front-page news to his own front door? But there were many sides to Max and I didn't know which one had flown to London or what were his intentions, be it avoid me or find me. I just had to prepare myself for the slim chance that he might at least try. Turned out I hadn't prepared enough, judging by my heart rate as the car stopped and the screams started.

The rest was a blur, flashing lights, my name shouted, smiling, waving. Men in suits ushered me somewhere else, towards a wall of press and reporters, microphones put in my face, questions fired, then more questions. I answered them but I didn't know how well, I'd probably be slated, I'm sure they'd write I looked dazed and confused, out of it, they'll say, probably say I was on drugs. I wished I was on drugs.

I was ushered inside, handed a glass of champagne as I searched for a face I might know, or know too well, luckily, I didn't have to wait for long.

★ ★ ★

"How do I look, Miss Goodridge?"

"No corduroy tonight then, Jon?"

"No, I felt this a tad more appropriate, be it dreadfully uncomfortable. I do feel like Fred Astaire, though I doubt I'm as agile in this get-up, feel like I'm about to burst out of my cummerbund."

"Let's hope you dance like him later."

"We scrub up well, don't we? Bit different than chastity belts and cavalier boots," he said looking over at our little group.

"Everyone looks so posh, you included." I took another sip of bubbles. "I can't see Rogan anywhere."

"And you won't. Flew back yesterday, franchise business I expect."

"Getting his cape measured, hey? Sorry about my sudden disappearance the other week."

"You don't need to keep apologizing, Lilly, I assure you. How are you, darling?"

"I'm fine."

"You looking for someone in particular?"

"No."

"Lilly, for a damn fine actress you can't lie for toffee."

"That obvious?"

"Afraid so."

"Someone I know might be here."

"It wouldn't be a certain Mr Salter would it?"

"How do you know?"

"One doesn't have to be P D James to work that out. Anyhow I was aware he was in town."

"I wish he wasn't."

"I doubt he'll be here. He doesn't strike me as someone who would frequent this sort of occasion. He is far too busy and important to waste his evening receiving adulation and praise. Probably working on his next masterpiece."

"Let's hope so."

"You don't sleep with all your director's, do you?" he smiled under his beard.

"I do actually."

"I am a bit old. Not very mobile."

"Older the better."

"Even a sixty-one-year-old?"

"Especially sixty-one-year-olds."

Soon we were all escorted to somewhere else to sip champagne, the men separated off, as did the women. The men to talk about whatever it was that men talked about, women probably. And us girls were left to find a table, talk about whatever girls are supposed to talk about, which turned out was also women. And jeez did this place have some women in it, the most amazing women. Taller than me, in both height and ability, and in dress sense. Nude gowns, plunging necklines, floor-length chiffon, they looked breathtaking.

We drank some more, laughed a lot, deliberated over other actresses' breasts and more importantly how they controlled their breasts, where invisible bras started and where they ended. I chatted to Carey Mulligan, told I loved her hair all short and blonde. Kirsten Stewart, too, even met David Bowie's son, he was nice, we both apologized for not seeing each other's movies. There were so many dishy men on display that night, in particular Jeremy Renner, who smiled at me as he walked past with his entourage. The girls dared me to go on and talk to George Clooney, too. I never did, I was drunk but not that drunk, though the night was early.

After a while I forgot about Max, plied myself with more liquor, even Jon told me to slow down, which was rich seeing the whisky he had knocked back himself. Not long after I was called over by suits in earpieces with instructions and directions of where I had to be and how long I had to do it in.

It was show time.

* * *

Backstage was surprisingly non-chaotic, must be the British way of getting things done, calm and collected, just like Jon, the elegant way of dealing with panic. The dressing room was nice, white lilies, drinks and fruit. I took a few deep breaths, sipped some water, ate an apple, a croissant. I hadn't eaten all day, I ate a second croissant. I remembered Sally telling me food soaked up the alcohol, despite all the pastry and rehydration, I still felt drunk. There was a knock at the door, Marla Miller.

The Marla Miller.

She went over, past me and to the nearest chair. One of the runners asked her if she'd like a cup of tea, she laughed and coughed.

"Tea is for nice old ladies. I ain't no lady and I ain't that nice either, doll. Get me a pack of Winston's," she said as he left the room, more confused than he was offended.

I looked over at Marla, hoping she would say something, but she didn't, as she fiddled with her skirt and bra.

"Nice to meet you, Mrs Miller. I'm Lilly," I said. "I'm looking forward to presenting an award with you." I went over to shake her hand.

"Darling, let me take a look at you," she said, holding my hand, bringing me in close as she looked me up and down. She smelt stale, old smoke and perfume.

"You have a very good nose. Is it real?"

I laughed. "My grandpa was a big fan of yours, Mrs Miller. How many movies have you made. Must be a lot?"

"Oh, I've made a bunch. I've been a bit quiet these last few years. Been busy getting old. Here's hoping my next one will be my big break. Be a doll and fetch me a glass of something." She pointed to the table. "Nothing fizzy or sweet, or you'll be presenting the award on your own."

We both went quiet, as she sipped her drink and I looked over my lines. The runner came back to the door, apologized to Marla, tried to explain smoking was not allowed indoors.

"You heard of prohibition, boy? Didn't stop me drinking then, so I'm as sure some sign on a door ain't gonna stop me smoking either." The runner disappeared. Marla took a cigarette from her purse, lit it up and began to smoke, with a frown.

"Have you seen any of my movies, darling?" she asked me.

"Oh, lots of times. My dad loves all the old black and white shows."

"I've starred with all the greats, you know. Elvis, Joan Crawford. I should write my memoirs, that would ruffle a few feathers in Hollywood. You heard of Errol Flynn?"

"He was Robin Hood, right?"

"He was a bit of swine that one."

"You live in Hollywood now, Mrs Miller?"

She nodded. "You heard of Thunderbird?"

"I haven't sorry. Is it a show?"

"No, it's a house. It's where they send movie stars to die in peace, argue over fame and who has the most of it. If you think I'm bad you ain't seen nothing. A lot of strong women in there, strong perfume too. The men are pussies, we eat them for breakfast. Gloria Stuart, one of my dearest friends, she lives there too, hundred years old, bless her. Met her when we both worked for Universal Studios. She's got a star on the south side of Boulevard. You know Gloria Stuart? *Gold Diggers of 1935*? *Kiss Before the Mirror*? *Titanic*?"

"She was on the Titanic?"

"No sweetheart, the film. Old Rose."

"Oh, I loved that film."

"So, did the critics. She wouldn't have got that Academy award or that bloody star on Boulevard if it wasn't for that movie. And I told her that, she agreed with me too. That's what I need. Some big-shot director to give one old girl a second crack of the whip."

"You haven't got a star then?" I asked, regretting it straight away. From her reaction, it was obviously a subject to be avoided.

"There is still time, honey, not much of it, but enough. Might get one when I die, that's worked for some."

I didn't say anything. It looked like we were about to be called to the stage.

"I could always die on stage tonight, keel over."

"I'd rather you didn't, Mrs Miller."

"Call me Marla. And less of the Mrs. I'm no one's wife," she snarled before smiling. "Don't worry, kid. I was only teasing you. I didn't always look like this you know." She took a photo from her purse and handed it over, black and white and crumpled. "That's when I was most beautiful. I keep this for the non-believers. When I had the best tits in the business."

"My grandpa always thought you were the most beautiful woman in pictures."

"I'd like to meet your grandpa. He sounds like a fun night."

"He died last fall. He was ninety-four."

"I'll have to meet him upstairs then. Or downstairs depending on how good we've both been. I'm probably headed downstairs, heaven has always felt a little too high for me."

"My grandpa would be hard to miss. Flirting with Garbo or smoking cigarillos with Telly Savalas."

Marla laughed. "I like you, Lilly. You remind me of me. Don't let these fuckers chip away at you. It can be lonely being a female in this business. It's a world run by men and by youth, too. The first one you can handle easily, the second is trickier. Everyone I know is dead or dying, me included."

"You're still beautiful, Marla."

"Thank you. darling. I appreciate the sentiment, even if it's a load of BS."

We started to be ushered towards the stage, we were handed the trophy.

"You know your lines?" she said, as I started to walk her up the steps to the stage.

"Yep. Stand and smile. Don't fuck up."

"Sums up my career so far, darling."

"Mine too."

"Let's give 'em a bit of sass," she coughed. "Wake up the cheap seats."

★ ★ ★

All of us were sat round a large round table, a mess of empty glasses and bottles and plates, the ladies had taken their shoes off, men had undone their bow ties. The table may have been without a trophy, but no one cared by now, if they had before then the food and liquor had filled them up enough to forget. A few of the mad ones were still licking salt and sucking limes. Me, I was as inebriated as I wanted to be without the need for more tequila, the croissants and water must've worked. I wasn't the stumbling mess I was before and although I still felt a little giddy I wasn't the drunkest in the room, which was the measure I'd always tended to use to consider stopping or carrying on.

I had no idea of the time, it must've been nearing the end, I was told there were a few after-parties in various clubs and hotel rooms around the city. The younger me would've snapped that up, the new me was very different. In fact, I was genuinely looking forward to taking my shoes off and losing the eyelashes.

Jon came over, put his drink down on the table.

"Would you care for a dance, Miss Rogers. Make an old man's day."

"Certainly, Mr Astaire. You lead the way."

"You assume I can lead."

We walked across the dance floor, as I took Jon's hands and put them where they were supposed to be.

"Apologies in advance if I step on your feet," he said as we began to sway to the music.

"Jon, do you know what they said about Fred Astaire on his first screen test?"

"I haven't a clue."

"Can't act. Slightly bald. Also dances."

Jon laughed loudly. "That doesn't surprise me. We are in a business surrounded by educated people with not one brain between them. Years ago, I sent a script over to my production company."

"Was it a film I would know?"

"Not unless you have access to my office cabinet. It never made it to camera."

"Shame."

"Not really. It wasn't my best work. Anyway, where was I?"

"People with education but not brains."

"Oh yes. So, the executives weren't too keen on this script I'd given them, so they sent it back to me, told me to do an urgent rewrite. Now I loved my script as it was. I'd already rewritten it three damn times. It was as close to perfect as it was ever going be."

"So, what did you do?"

"I sent it back, with a new front cover."

"What, exactly the same screenplay?"

"Yep, damn same thing."

"What did they say."

"They said it was perfect."

"That's so funny."

"I wouldn't take anything people say too seriously. Film

companies just see dollar signs, they don't think about the craft that goes into it."

"I think everything is run by dollar signs, Jon. Depressing really."

"Only if you let it impact your decisions."

"OK, Jon, why did you choose this film? Why eighteenth-century England?"

"I could say immorality, the role of women in society, manipulation."

"I'm guessing it's not one of those things?"

"It was a little. But I just like films with sex and tits in them. There was a lot of that about back then. That's me being honest. I'm just a dirty old man really. What about you?"

"What about me?"

"Why did you choose this film?"

"Cos I wanted to run away."

He smiled.

"You're not offended are you, Jon?"

"No, course not. I'd hoped it was my dazzling script and reputation."

"Sorry."

"You do a lot of running away, don't you?"

"Seems that way."

"Why?"

"I wish I knew. I nearly didn't come tonight."

"What, because of Max Salter?"

"It's not even him, it's more what people and situations like Max bring out in me."

"And what do they bring out?"

"My worst attributes. I just roll over, say yes to anything. I'm easily influenced. I just do whatever someone tells me to do. Running away always seems the sensible choice to avoid both."

"You could just try staying put. Charge towards the things you're scared of. There's nothing wrong with a bit of passivity, and

I can think of worse traits than being easy-going. You've just got to be careful who you are being influenced by."

"That's the problem. I'm an awful judge of character."

"True. I mean you trust me for a start and I'm an awful human being. You don't like being directed by me, do you? Be honest, now."

"Like isn't the right word, Jon. I enjoy working with you."

"But?"

"But it's just different to what I'm used to, that's all."

"And what are you used to?"

"I'm used to criticism. Doing things over and over, getting it right, making things better. Being stretched to the limit, physically and emotionally."

"And you enjoy this type of torture? Suffering for your art."

"I don't feel I've worked hard enough till my voice is hoarse or my feet are covered in corns and blisters."

"Art should be enjoyable, darling. It doesn't always need such intensity."

"But that is what I'm used to. A decade of dancing has taught me nothing else. And Max, of course."

"Well, I can try to be more of a brute for the next few weeks if it would help. Throw something at you, use profanity."

"No, that's fine, Jon. You don't have to be an arsehole. Leave that the Max Salters of this world."

"I've met a lot of Max Salters. I used to be one."

"What changed?"

"Confidence."

"What, in yourself?"

"No, in others. If you pick the right people to do the right job, then you can trust them to do what is required without all the shouting and hollering. Look, I'm just an old man, I've been round the block a few times. Met a lot of different people from various walks of life. There are heroes and cunts out there, and a lot in between. There is no magic formula to recognizing the

229

differences. I just tend to go with my gut, if something smells off at the start, it most likely means it will be full of shit."

"Is that Walt Whitman?"

"Jon Noble. I'm better than Whitman. He never knew when to shut up."

"I'd have to disagree."

"Look. Take my advice. The same advice I give to the heathen that is my personal trainer."

"And what advice is that?"

"Stop running. Nothing good comes from running."

"I've been given a lot of advice today. Is this what happens when you get old? You feel the need to educate everyone you encounter on all the mistakes you've made?"

"Well, are you going to listen to any of it?"

"I'll try."

"Good. Can we stop dancing now? My legs might seize up."

"Mine too. I haven't danced in ages."

"You're a good person, Lilly. Hollywood needs people like you."

"You too."

"You do need to focus on people your own age. You can't hang around with folks like me and Marla Miller all night."

"I love people like you and Marla Miller."

"Why?"

"People like you and her, they don't give a shit. You don't care who they upset."

"And you like that? Upsetting people?"

"Not upsetting them, but giving them the honesty they deserve. I think the more time I spend in this industry the more I feel strangled by it all. What happened to all the characters out there? Doesn't seem like anyone has a voice any more. Every interview I'm told what to say, what not to say and why."

"Well, perhaps you should change that."

"What, become the femme fatale? The new Lana Turner?"

"If that's who you are."

"I don't know who I am really."

"You seem to surround yourself with old people."

"Because I always need reassurance that I'm not fucking things up."

"Fucking up is the best part. And believe me, all ages fuck up."

"You are right. I'm not ditching Frank and Sally though. I couldn't."

"I'm not saying that. I'm just saying it's about time you started being Lilly Goodridge again. Whoever that is. If you say being passive and easily influenced are the worst of traits, then bring out the opposite."

"What, Lilly Goodridge, confrontational and opinionated?"

"If that is you, then yes. Sounds a lot more fun, too."

"Easier said than done."

"Go grab us a port from the bar please, darling. I haven't the legs for the steps. There's a young gent at the bar, he looks like he needs the company," he said, pointing to a man sat head down into his drink. "He looks young. Go be a bit wild."

"He hardly looks wild, does he?"

"Then that's your first challenge."

"Thank you, Jon." I kissed him on the cheek.

"Remember, Lilly. Confrontational and opinionated."

I grinned and in my best Lana Turner impression I turned to Jon. "I'm going up and up and up. And nobody is going pull me down."

"And you said you couldn't do accents."

"I still can't."

"You're better than you think you are. Enjoy occupying your pedestal."

"I'll wave from the top I promise," I said, blowing him a kiss as I headed towards the bar, toward the man slumped at his stool.

Less than an hour later I was on my way to meet Max.

21

He told me to meet him at his hotel at midnight. I was running late, back in my room, changing out of red carpet. I wasn't rushing, he deserved to wait, I was taking my time.

How do you dress to meet an ex, I thought, though looking in the mirror my approach was obvious. Unashamedly, with no new man on my arm, no big news, no new shiny trophy, the only thing I had left to flaunt was myself. Breaking every fashion law possible, every asset I had, arse, tits and legs were all in full view. I'd even sprayed my legs with perfume, which I never did, nor would ever do again. I looked at my reflection once more. What the fuck was I doing?

Quickly I changed dresses, removed some make-up, rubbed off the perfume with a wet cloth. One last time I checked myself in the mirror; it was better, less desperate, less slut. I was the best I could be.

I rang down for my car and made my way down in the elevator.

★ ★ ★

I asked the driver if it was far. He laughed, immediately apologizing.

Strangely, I was genuinely excited. People forget, even me, that we were once inseparable. Yes, it ended badly, a lot of awful shit happened, but also a lot of good. Like most relationships I guessed. Fuck, this was going to be awkward. What do I do when I see him? Do we shake hands, do we kiss cheeks, do I punch him?

My car stopped. I'd expected it to be further, it was so short, I could've walked – both coincidental and deliberate. I looked through my tinted windows, his hotel looked as pretty as mine, grand and lit up.

My door opened, the night air hit me like a slap. A suit greeted me, helped me out of the car.

"Good evening, Miss Goodridge."

"You remind me of Charlie Chaplin with that hat." I had no clue why I said that, it was neither appropriate nor true.

"Apologies, Miss Goodridge."

"Oh, don't be silly, it was a compliment I promise," I said, trying to recover. "Sorry, I feel a bit drunk all of a sudden."

"Would you like me to fetch you a water, or would you like to sit down?"

"No, I'll be fine. Think it's the fresh air."

"Fresh air can do that, Miss Goodridge. Change in temperature and circulation. Would you like to come inside and rest for a few minutes before you venture downstairs?"

"I'm fine, honest. I'm due to meet with…"

"Mr Salter is waiting for you in the Cigar Room, Miss Goodridge. Shall I take you to him?"

"Yes please."

22

"Hello there, Lilly G." He stood up to take off my coat, before pulling out the chair next to him so I could sit down. "I thought this was a nice spot. I hope it's to your taste."

I looked around. "It's very you."

"I'll order you a new drink, your ice has melted."

"Oh, I don't mind a warm drink."

"Nonsense. It'll be more water than liquor." He ushered a barman over. "I'll have the same again, and the lady will have your house Martini. So," he looked at me, his eyes big and blue.

"So."

"You look pretty."

"Where were you tonight, Max? I thought you may have showed up. I mean, you were nominated. Or are you too cool for school now?"

"Ceremonials aren't really me, you know that."

"And there was me thinking you loved playing the man about town."

"People celebrate victory in different ways."

"How do you celebrate yours?"

"By moving on."

"No one's allowed to celebrate their success, then?"

"Awards shows aren't a celebration, it's advertising."

"It could just be a chance to dress up and a have a drink, Max."

"Isn't that what we are doing now?"

"You know what I mean. A chance to meet like-minded people, network, meet our heroes and peers."

"And which hero did you meet tonight?"

"I met plenty."

"Win anything?" he smiled, a cocky one, it was an answer he already knew. "You'll be fine, darling, you just need the right film, that's all."

"Is that so?"

"It is so. I don't think any studio has been overly generous with the quality of work they've given you."

"Go on."

"I don't think you've acted badly, as such. But at the same time, I don't think you've acted particularly well either."

"Can we change the subject, Max? I think I've had as much advice as I can take in one evening. How come you're in London? New job as a film critic?"

"I had a few meetings. I've got to pop over to Paris in a few days."

"Is that on business too?"

"Maddy is getting married."

"Is that to the same man she was with when I met her at Thanksgiving? Ross, is it?"

"Yes, that's him. I'm not his biggest fan. He's not a bad guy, he's just all hat and no cattle."

"How old is your sister now? Must be around my age."

"Bit older."

"Why Paris?"

"I don't think there is a reason. They just like France. Well, Maddy does, well at least she likes the idea of a French wedding. Ross, well he just does what he's told."

"All the family will be there? Salters on tour?"

"Not many, actually. My mom, stepfather, few aunties."

"Shame your father couldn't be there."

"Don't think it would've made a difference, he and Maddie had never got on. I'm the makeshift Father of the Bride."

The barman returned with our drinks.

"A Monte Cristo for the lady." He placed my drink in front of me. "And a Domaine de Rieston for yourself, sir. Would either of you like to see our cigar selection?"

"It's a bit early, friend. Don't want to smoke out my guest. She's not one for cigars."

"I don't mind, honest. I mean, we are in a cigar bar."

"Come back later and I assure you I will try the best you have to offer."

"Honestly, you can have one," I said. "It wouldn't feel like an authentic night out with you without the smell of cigar smoke in the air."

Max smiled at the waiter. "Bring over a couple of blends in about an hour."

"An hour?" I sniffed. "Do we have a lot to talk about?"

"Lilly, I could talk to you for days, let alone hours."

"Let's start with the hour and see where we go from there. It's been a long day, I might not last that long, depending."

"Depending on what?" he smiled.

"How long I can keep my eyes open and how long I can go without punching you again."

"The first one I can fix, we'll need more drinks. The second, I can't promise."

He ushered the barman over again, telling him the same again.

"At least you are being honest, Max."

"I've always been honest with you. That's been the problem."

"Well, just be prepared for mild violence."

"I always have been with you, Lilly."

★ ★ ★

A few drinks had passed, in the toilet I reapplied my lipstick and checked my mascara. Max and the barman were discussing tobacco in a language I couldn't understand, it felt a good time to leave them to it, take some time out and breathe, take a moment to work out what might happen next. Max looked good tonight, a vampire, dangerous, even tempting. This place suited Max too, felt like a secret, dark and subdued, purples and neons, quiet too.

One last time I checked my eyes in my reflection. I looked tired, it had been a long day. Was I drunk? I couldn't tell. I'd been drunk on and off all evening. I should go home soon, I thought. So far it had been pleasant, like old times. I didn't want it spilling over into something nasty, I hadn't the energy for it. But there was still a lot unsaid. I took a deep breath and headed back towards fresh drinks and Max, who was all smiles and cigars as I sat back down at the table.

"Romeo y Julieta. I thought this a fitting brand."

"What, love and tragedy?"

"'Love is a smoke made with the fume of sighs'."

"Wow, that's impressive."

"I was a Montague in our college production."

"Romeo?"

"Benvolio." He stood up. "'Alas, that love, so gentle in his view, should be so tyrannous and rough in proof!'" He took a bow.

"What did that all mean?"

"Rough translation..." he lit the end of his cigar, "love isn't always easy. Full of hardships."

"Well, I'll try and keep tonight civil, but don't think you can romance your way out of everything."

"I'll try not to, Lilly." He blew smoke into the ceiling. "With you I've always found it unavoidable."

And he gave me a look that suggested he wasn't joking at all. He was a hard man, not someone to be seduced by.

"So how is Lilly Goodridge? Winning?"

"I think so. You? You seem like you are getting a lot of female attention."

"That's all paper talk."

"I've seen the pictures, Max."

"They are friends, plus ones."

"Then you haven't slept with any of them?"

"A few. And what about you, Lilly? I hear you and the hottest lefty in MLB have been getting cosy?"

"With keeping things civil in mind, let's change the subject. Haven't seen you make a movie in a little while. Writers' block?"

"Oh, I'm writing. Just nobody biting. But it'll come, I just have to be patient. Get my head round what they want."

"Wish it was as simple as just making movies. Make a movie, take some time off, make another."

"It can be done, pretty rare these days. Don't think the world likes it that way, likes to have every piece of us."

"To be fair, if I was someone else I'd be reading about me and you too. It beats a book."

"You think me and you are a story?"

"I guess."

"How does it end? Happy, kids and a dog?" Max realised quickly, his choice of words was a mistake.

"Let's just hope it's happy."

"Don't think the natives will be too satisfied. Far too predictable."

"I don't care if they are satisfied. I'm not in this for the long game. Smash and grab."

"That surprises me. I had you down as more ambitious than that."

"Oh, I'm ambitious Max, just not everyone needs to see mine. Ambitions just for me." I sipped my drink. "I take you are in it for life, directing movies with a white beard and a big belly, young actresses falling at your knees to work with the legend that is Max Salter?"

"I don't think too far ahead. The game changes too much to predict."

"What do you want right now, Max? Happy carrying on living like a lothario?"

"I don't know. Ask me again in a few years. I like the sound of legend, but how I become one is up for debate. I hope to think my future will involve you."

"You do, do you?" God his eyes were delicious.

"I don't think I have much choice. It's what the people want."

"Do we get a say?"

"If we are smart."

"I'm not that clever, I'm afraid."

"Don't worry, I'll do the thinking for us both."

"No change there then, Max."

23

We'd walked for a few minutes through a deserted London, the only things that moved were black cabs, speeding to and fro. But there was no one on foot, just us. Perhaps people didn't walk in London. Only the mad ones, or drunk ones.

"Have you missed LA?"

"Not as much as I thought I would've."

"You look cold. Here, take this." Max took off his suit jacket and wrapped it around me. I still felt as cold but I appreciated the gesture. "When is the last time you danced?"

"I can't even remember. Apart from dancing around my house, it would have to have been on set when we made our first film."

"That's not true, Lilly. We danced in Vegas."

"I can't remember."

"You do, surely. It took three of us to get you off the dance floor. That night was certainly noteworthy. You looked wonderful. That white dress. Like Princess Odette herself."

"Didn't we have a big argument that night?"

"Probably."

"I miss dancing."

"I try to at least once a week. More like once a month. I just don't get the time. Life in the director's chair is pretty full throttle."

"When I get back to LA I'll start up again. May even go back to my old studio. Hope I can still remember all the techniques."

"Your body may have forgotten and it will hurt all over. But your brain will know what to do. If you need assistance I don't mind being your *ballerino*."

"I'd rather find another, thank you, Max. Athletic and dumb, with big shoulders and big brown eyes. Preferably mute so he doesn't ruin it by talking."

"Sounds like most actors in Hollywood so you'll have lots to choose from."

"I'm surprised I've not been offered roles involving dance. Have film studios stopped making musicals?"

"There's not many about. Someone will remake *Flashdance* soon. They're remaking most things. I've been offered to direct a few myself."

"Which ones?"

"Let's just say it involved the word 'Kellerman's'."

"Oh my God. I'm in. I bet the script was awful though. Were you going to do it?"

"No. I don't think anyone will now either. Not with Swayze passing away last fall. The whole remake was built around him. He was the movie."

"That was so sad."

"I went to high school with his youngest brother. He and his family lived close by. He was a lot older than me so we never actually met."

"Have you said yes to any of the other remakes?"

"Not yet. When I'm poor and all dried up. There is one I'm undecided on. It's not a remake, but it would be interesting if I pull it off."

"Which one?"

"I'm not telling you just yet."

"More secrets. Just what I need."

We came to a little patch of green amongst all the houses and parked cars. An oval of grass, little red phone box, a fence surrounding it, as high as my shoulder.

"Not as big as Central Park, is it?" I laughed.

"It's not a park, Lilly, it's a garden. Berkeley Square."

"Can we go in?"

"I think it's closed."

"I'm sure I could manage the climb."

"I think that would be deemed as trespassing."

"There's no one around. I'm game if you are."

"'With love's light wings did I o'erperch these walls'. Apologies. Armagnac brings out my inner thespian."

"Makes you sound pretty gay as well." I jumped over the iron railings. "As does what you are doing now."

"Give me a break." Max was struggling.

"Have you climbed a fence before? You're not very cat-like, are you?"

"Lilly, you try it when you've got a three-piece suit on. Savile Row doesn't tend to cut my suits with this in mind."

"James Bond manages just fine."

"Well, I must get the number of his tailor," he said as he landed on his feet.

"I feel very Julia Roberts right now."

"I am no Hugh Grant."

"Not much of a garden, is it? I thought gardens normally had flowers in? I might move out of the city when I go back home."

"What? Like Laguna?" Max brushed his trousers.

"No, I mean literally out of LA entirely. Somewhere more remote. Fields and grass, no buildings. What about you?"

"You're kidding. I spent my whole life trying to get out of rodeo country. I prefer concrete and smog."

"Shall we sit on one of these benches for a minute? My feet are killing me. Feels like I've worn heels all day."

We didn't talk for a few minutes, we just sat, a statue in front of us. We were in the middle of the gardens, felt like the rest of London was probably pitch-black whilst street lamps circled us like floodlights.

"It's a bit 'Friday night at Chavez Ravine'."

"Do you reckon we have an audience?"

"Doubt it. Think everyone's in bed. Even the paparazzi have to sleep at some point. What time is it? Is it as late as I think it is?"

He checked his watch. "It's pretty late, darling."

"That's the watch I got you, isn't it? Nice you still wear it."

"I rarely take it off."

We were sat pretty close now, shoulder to shoulder, felt like he was about to put his arm around me.

"I'm cold, Max. Whatever you've got to say, can you say it now? You've lured me here with promises of redemption and answers."

"I feel on the spot now."

"Good, it's about time you were interrogated."

"This is hard for me, Lilly. I haven't really talked about this with anyone. I've told you parts of it, but not the full story."

"Go on."

"You know I've always said I hated my father?"

"Yes."

"Well, that is still true, but there is a lot more to it. I may have mentioned this before but Salter was a name quite well known where I grew up. There were two things we were good at, always have been: football and horses. A Salter male was expected to be good at at least one, sometimes even both, like my dad. My dad was a big deal in Oak Forest. He played college football briefly, till he bust his knee, some say he was best player ever to play at Waltrip. But that wasn't his first love – it was horses he loved the most. Around our house were trophies and photos, winning rodeos at various shows. I had a cowboy as a father, and anyone who didn't know that, I was the first to remind them of it."

Max took out his wallet and passed me a small photograph.

"You can tell he's a Salter," I said, passing him it back. "Looks like a Sergio Leone movie."

"Mum always joked he was born in the wrong century. He should have been in stand offs and saloon bars, riding off across horizons."

"What happened then?"

"Well, I happened. My sister happened. There wasn't enough

243

money in rodeo shows to support a wife and children. My old man did what he thought the right thing to do."

"What, leave?"

"No, give up on his dream. Dad gave two things up, the football he was fine with, his knee meant he wouldn't play again, but giving up being a cowboy, he never quite got over."

"Surely you weren't that poor? You could've made do, got by even?"

"I don't remember a lot. I was quite young, but Mom says it was pretty hard. I didn't know any different at the time. It wasn't till I went to school I realized how little we had. I got teased a lot for how I looked, what I wore. Though it made me tough. In the end Dad felt he had no choice but to find more money. I remember him crying when he sold his horse, Duke, he was a beautiful thing, an Arabian white, Dad must have had him for twenty years. He ended up selling him to a farmer as breeding stock. Mom said he didn't have to sell Duke, but Dad was a proud man and knowing we didn't have enough for food or clothes meant his horse had to go. Eventually, Dad got some pen-pushing job in town, did quite well, became Regional Manager, but it always looked like he wore that suit and tie like a shackle. Now, you're probably thinking my dad was this real hard-arse, he wanted his son to be just like him – but he never pushed me and anything I chose to do I did of my own accord and free will. I too loved horses, not as much as Dad, I rode a little, but I loved football more and I could tell my dad was proud of me whenever he saw me playing in the red and white of Waltrip. But my one true love was dancing and I don't think my dad has ever been as proud as when I was on stage performing. I can still remember his face when I got my invitation to join Disney on Parade."

"What's that?"

"It's like a travelling show, a circus really. Go around the whole country, Canada too. Saw some amazing places. I was twenty and I'd never been out of Houston. It was hilarious when I told Dad I'd been chosen for it. He showed everyone, literally drove down Ella Boulevard in his truck telling anyone that passed by. I think Dad just wanted me to be passionate about something and he didn't care what it was. Even though everyone in Oak Forest probably thought I was a fag. Dad was just overjoyed I was getting out of Texas, he always talked of the amazing places he'd been, he always said Salters were at their best when not standing still."

"He sounds like a good Dad, Max."

"He was. It all changed when I was in New York. At the time, I was in New York on a dance scholarship when I got the phone call from my dad saying he was coming to visit. And he did, a few days later he turned up at my little apartment on West Seventeenth Street. He never looked so out of place, he still had his cowboy hat on like *Midnight Cowboy*. We went for a walk around Madison Square Park and that's when he told me he was leaving my mom."

"What, for another woman?"

"No, for another life."

"I don't get it."

"Nor did I. Nor did Mom."

"What did he say?"

"He just said it was time to go. Said now I was a man and Maddie was off to college soon that he had things that needed to be done."

"Sounds surreal."

"Felt pretty fucking surreal too."

"What things needed to be done? Where?"

"That's what I asked him. He just said it was time to move on. He had no idea where or how or why. Just knew it was time to move on."

"How could he leave your Mom like that?"

"I think he always loved her, and he probably still did when he left her. I just think he'd given up so much of his life that he'd forgotten who he really was."

"Were you angry at him?"

"At first I was. More for Mom than for me. But I understood Dad's perspective. Maddie didn't, she hated him before and still hates him know. She didn't even go to his funeral."

"I agree with Maddie. What he did sounds cowardly."

"I did at first. But Dad explained and I understood. Dad gave up so much when he became a father, and he worked hard in a job he loathed to be able to support the four of us."

"That's the job of most fathers."

"Well, my Dad wasn't like most fathers. He was a man meant to roam."

"A gypsy."

"If that's how you want to put it. I just think he reached a point in his life when he had to do things for himself."

"How was your Mom?"

"Bad at first, but remarried not long after. Deep down she must've known that one day he would leave, it was more of a question of when. And when Dad thought me and my sister were old enough to support ourselves, he thought that was the right time to get back on his horse. I think he was brave. At first, I didn't. I hated him, but over time I admired him for it. It hit me hard when he died, I drank a lot, a hell of a lot, should have got help, but where I'm from it's a 'breathe in, chest out' mentality. Men aren't supposed to buckle. No matter the weight on their shoulders."

"And you think what he did was brave?"

"Yes, I do."

"I don't."

"You didn't see his face every time he had to put that shirt and tie on, do his nine to five. He never said it, he loved us all very much, but to him it must've been like living in a cage."

"And you think having a child with me would feel like being trapped? Is that what you are saying, Max? Like, seriously?"

"What I'm saying, Lilly, is I never wanted to look at you or look at my children and wish I was somewhere else. I'm just saying, at that point in my life I had to follow what was right for me. At that moment, a child was not the right timing."

"I'm sorry the timing was an inconvenience, Max. If you remember, it was you who put his dick in me."

"Don't be crass, Lilly."

"What now then, Max? Are ready for fatherhood yet? Or shall I wait a bit longer, till the time suits?"

"You are being childish, Lilly."

"OK, so what I'll do is wait ten years when you've done all your womanising, got all your Oscar trophies, your star on the walk of fame, and then maybe, just maybe if I'm lucky, you might then consider settling down. That's very big of you and so brave."

"You make it sound vulgar."

"Well, it is."

"Perhaps I haven't explained well enough."

"Oh, I think you've explained it just fine."

"I want you, Lilly. I want children. That has never changed."

"That's the problem, Max. The bit you don't understand. The dream should have been me and our child, not your career. Being a family shouldn't feel like a punishment."

"Don't go, Lilly. Please."

"I should have had that baby, Max. I made a mistake. I made a mistake ever letting you get close to me. I made a mistake getting into movies. But I won't make any mistakes again, I assure you of that. I won't let you affect my life any more. I'm tired of being broken."

"You think I didn't hit rock bottom when you had the abortion? It was my child too. My pain was no different than yours."

"Fuck off. You didn't feel it move in your stomach, you didn't feel how empty it felt inside after. You didn't feel the guilt of choosing to kill something living."

"It was the right thing to do."

"It was the cowardly thing to do. Which you Salter men seem

to thrive on. I want to go home now, Max. You look after yourself. Good luck living outside of the cage."

"I don't want it to end like this."

"I do. That is exactly what I want. I want this to be the end."

"I can't keep apologizing, not when I'm not the only one to blame here. It was a joint decision."

"Joint decision? You knew the control you had over me. I would've done anything you said, Max. Gone anywhere and done anything. I would've had that baby. I just wanted you to be as excited as me. You knew that."

"Then you should have been stronger. You should have kept it if that's what you felt was right."

I was about to hit him.

"Lilly, stop." He tried to hold me. "Lilly, I didn't want this. This wasn't my intention."

"What was your intention, Max? Sweep me back off my feet?"

"There was no intention. I just wanted to see you. Give you an explanation. I'm as confused as you right now with all this. I'm not used to all this attention either."

"You fucking thrive on it, Max. You love the attention."

"Not this attention."

"Oh, you'll adapt I'm sure. You always do. Why the fuck did you even want to meet me tonight? Just to fuck me up again?"

"I just wanted to see you."

"Why? Because you are bored?"

"I have never been bored with you. I'm allowed to still care about you, Lilly."

"No, you are not, Max. Care about someone else." I burst into tears as Max took me in his arms, let me cry into his chest.

"Why don't we just get out of all this, Max. Escape, find some beautiful island where we can watch movies all day and dance at night."

"One day we will, Lilly. I need to get my house in order, bull strong and horse high. Work out the best way of looking after you, how to protect our futures."

It was then that I kissed him. A kiss I should never have offered and he should never have accepted.

24

I was in my trailer, spread out across my bed. It hadn't been a particularly long day, but one of the hardest, which might have been why it had been my favourite day on set so far. Nice to be outside, too, all the horses and hounds, the little boys in knickerbockers, the sunrise over the hills, men riding and women swooning. I could only imagine how beautiful the dailies would look.

I checked the air con. Women had it hard in the 1900s – as men on horseback hunted anything that moved, us girls were left to sweat it out in bonnets on the lawn, with tiny umbrellas and even tinier dogs yapping at our feet. So much fabric on one body, under-dresses and overdresses, I looked down at myself, I resembled a duvet, engulfed by my own dress. I picked up my call sheet, checked how long I had till I'd be summoned again, I had a good hour to kill. I really should go over my lines, I thought, eyeing the script on the side.

* * *

My trailer door knocked. Then knocked again.

"I'm up. I'm up," I said, scrambling to the door, expecting some girl with a clipboard.

"Oh, Jon. It's you." My eyes were still half closed.

"The mystery of your whereabouts has finally been revealed."

"So sorry. I must have fallen asleep. I'm not late for my scene, am I?"

"A little, yes. I can call off the search party."

"I've been in here the whole time."

"I know. You must be a heavy sleeper, I think half the crew have taken a turn knocking on your door. I must just have the knack."

"I'm so sorry, Jon. I've not been sleeping too well with you-know-what. Can you give me a couple of minutes to get my shit together?"

"Lilly, would you mind if you and I could catch up at some point?"

"Sure. Later today?"

"No, today is a bit hectic. Tomorrow is less stretched. I'm over in Salcombe, actually, perhaps we could have a quick catch-up and a bit to eat?"

"That would be lovely."

"Anyhow, must dash."

"I'll be literally five minutes, Jon. I'm so sorry." He closed my door behind him. I felt like I had just been summoned to the principal's office.

25

I'd gotten to Salcombe a little earlier than I needed to, which did me a favour as I needed to pick up a few bits for later that night. It wasn't the first time I'd been here, came a little while back with Frank and Sally to fish for crab, but the weather meant we didn't stick around too long, ended up leaving with our nets and empty buckets.

It was nice today to be able to take my time, casually stroll in the sunshine, look in every shop window, mosey around the harbour with the gulls and boats. Also meant I had more time to spend money, which was dangerous for me and my accountant. Ended up with a ton of meat, some cute pumps, a little floral dress, by the time it came to meeting Jon I was more than ready for my first glass of wine, in fact I pretty much necked it in one.

"How's the frittata?" Jon asked, picking at his food, like he couldn't find what he was looking for.

"Lovely, thank you. How's your salad?"

"Boring. To be fair, as far as salads go, it's rather pleasant. I'm just a little bored of eating like a slug. Though Mrs Barton-Hughes is rather adamant I get my five a day."

"Is she here in Devon then?"

"No, she is home. East Sussex. That's why she is worried. Thinks me being here on my own unchaperoned means I'll revert to fried breakfasts and cheese suppers."

"And have you reverted?"

"Take a wild guess." He grabbed his belly. "She's coming to visit next week. Hence the urgent detox."

We both concentrated on our food, taking it in turns to

look out across the decking at a horizon of masts and sails, how it reminded Jon of Capri, how idyllic he thought the town was, how he planned to buy a place out here, a little holiday home, a memento.

It continued, this small talk, little jokes and stories, but it was obvious that today's lunch was more than a catch-up. By the time our desserts came out I could sense Jon had run out of anecdotes and quips, and had no choice but to get down to why we were both really here.

"Oh, I haven't asked. How was your time off back home? Did you manage to dissuade your parents from going their separate ways?"

"No unfortunately not," I said mid-cheesecake. "They are proceeding as planned."

"Oh dear. And how do you feel about that?"

"I'm gutted, obviously. But what can I do? Crying and moping won't solve anything. Thanksgiving will be interesting, not sure how it will pan out, them being on the opposite sides of the city now."

"Can't be nice for you, though, darling."

"I've done all the tears. I'm glad I got time to understand why they were doing it. Thanks again for being so cool with me running off."

"You didn't leave me much choice, Lilly."

"Sorry. I did throw you in it. Hope it wasn't too traumatic."

"There were a few angry faces, most of which from the second AD, so I think you may have to buy him a case of ale for his late-night reshuffling."

"You must regret hiring me, Jon."

"You are definitely one of the more challenging women I've worked with, but I wouldn't say regret, no."

"Am I doing OK, though? I do worry I'm not giving you enough out there."

Jon took a mouthful of fruit salad. "You do seem to have a lot on your plate right now, even more so since London."

"I try not to think about all that is going on out there."

"And that's the best way to be, Lilly darling. Chew it up, but don't swallow, that's what I always say. Must still be hard to not let it affect you."

"Do you think it has affected me? Is that why I'm here?"

"I think you're doing your best with all that has gone on. I just wanted you to know that you can ask for help. You don't have to pretend you are fine when you are not."

"Is this about me falling asleep yesterday? That won't happen again, I swear. Think I just hadn't recovered from the long flight and the whole London stuff."

"I'm just worried you are spreading yourself too thin, darling. A few of the girls have mentioned how tired you look, then there was the incident with the hair."

"How did you know about that?"

"I hear things, Lilly. It's my job to hear things."

"I promise I'll get my head back in the game. Trust me."

"Oh, of course I know you will do your best. I just wonder if there was anything I could do – have a rethink? Lose some of your dialogue?"

"Jon, I don't want you to have to move your script around just for me. I hardly have enough lines as it is – any fewer, I'd be in a silent movie."

"Lilly, you look cross. This wasn't my intention."

"You obviously think I'm doing a shit job."

"I didn't say that, did I?"

"You might as well have done."

"Look, Lilly, let's draw a line in the sand on all this. You've got today and tomorrow to get your head sorted till you're back on set. Have a rest and we'll take stock of things then, see how you are feeling and if we need to…" Jon stopped.

"Need to what, Jon? Fire me?"

"Oh God no, Lilly. See if we need to change things to make it better."

I downed the last of the wine.

"Let's change the subject." Jon smiled. "Something a tad lighter. What plans have you for the weekend?"

I laughed. "Probably best you don't know."

"That sounds rather ambiguous."

"You won't like it."

"Probably best I don't know, then."

Just then the manager came over, I assumed with the bill.

"Sorry to bother you, madam, but there seems to be some commotion out the front."

"A commotion, where?" I said looking behind me.

"Lots of men with cameras. I don't want to rush you, Miss Goodridge but it may be best for you to leave, before it turns nasty out there.

I looked at Jon. I could tell by his face he didn't know how to deal with the situation.

"Thank you," I said. "Can we leave round the back?"

"Yes, of course. Through the kitchen, I'd suggest."

"Might be worth the calling the…" as I heard a police siren wail.

I looked at the manager and then to Jon, looked at all the children eating their cakes, the old ladies sipping their tea, their faces filled with fear, their little village turned from calm to chaos.

"I'm so sorry, Jon," I said, getting up from my chair. "I'm so sorry everyone," I added, as the manager started to guide me towards my escape.

26

I have a candle problem. That's what I thought to myself as I stood back and looked at my assortment around the fireplace, the table, the windowsill. And it didn't end there, they were all around the house, the kitchen, the bathroom, even the backyard. I don't quite know how the obsession started, I blamed the cottage entirely, I never had this addiction back in LA, probably because I never stocked candles, or candle holders, or lighting matches. Here I had all three, and they were everywhere, scattered amongst various cupboards. Now I found it difficult to enjoy an evening without it being candlelit. Worse still, now I was buying the fucking things, as if I needed more, they had shops here dedicated to all things wax and wick. Now I was bringing home bigger candles, more elaborate holders and jars, now I even had a snuffer. But it looked pretty, inviting, human sacrifice may have sprung to mind, but it was cosy and at least it wouldn't be me, it was normally the virgins that went first, or goats.

I walked back through the house, gave the beans another stir, opened the Aga to check the ribs, nearly grabbed a beer but didn't as I stepped back outside, into the garden. The smell was grass, fresh cut, it stuck to my bare feet as I sank back down into my lounger. I took a deep breath. The sky was tinted, the sun was so bright today I'd spent most of it hidden behind my shades, think I'd even managed to burn my shoulders. England, I never knew you had it in you.

I looked down at my tummy, patted it with my hand. I'd lost weight, my boobs looked smaller too. Great, I'm sure the press would have a field day talking about how I'd lost a dress size, trying to work out what crazy-ass fad diet I'd been on so they could copy it. I'm sure publicists would decide one for me, some blood type or caveman diet. I guarantee they wouldn't be honest, they wouldn't tell the public it was down to stress and anxiety. Instead they'd lie and make out it was exercise and portion control, controlled anorexia has always been more socially acceptable than a poor emotional state, though both had the same desired result. Who gives a fuck as long as we were all thin, hey? I wouldn't be after this meal, I had more barbecue in my oven than Bludso's.

I felt myself yawn. Today had taken its toll, I started to count the tasks completed in my head: marinaded the meat, axed some wood, the lawn, packed the fridge with cold beers, unpacked the cold beers. Probably for the best, the records showed we weren't at our best when intoxicated. I felt like the night needed to be one where our heads were clear and focused. I decided to move all the alcohol in the house into the pantry, somewhere out of reach, out of sight.

To my complete and utter shock, I'd found out too that the house didn't have a barbecue – got a shitload of coal, but no barbecue. It was my own fault, I forgot momentarily I was in England, they probably never cooked outside. I had to go next door and ask the old guy if he had one, which luckily, he did, said he was surprised I hadn't found one. He was really sweet, went out of his way to help carry it across. It looked like it was the highlight of his day, he told me about the area, intrigued by my house and garden, kept looking through the windows, said he hadn't set foot in it in years, said it felt a little odd. I could tell he wanted to stop and chat and I'm sure if I'd have offered a pot of tea he would never have left, but I had too much to do, so thanked him for his help and the constant supply of eggs as he headed back towards his tiny cottage and clucking chickens.

Thank God for being busy, managed to take my mind off what happened earlier. I messaged Jon as soon as I got home, checked he got out unscathed, which thankfully he did. I was stupid going out on my own, sometimes I forget how much I need people like Frank, someone who could diffuse a situation, scare people off with just their sheer size. I hoped Sally would not catch wind of this, I certainly wouldn't tell her, I didn't need another telling-off today.

I looked across my garden, the whole me-and-Max thing in London had turned me a little paranoid, a little on edge, constantly felt like at any minute I would be found out. First few days I arrived back from London I checked around the perimeter of my garden, even climbed over the fence, walked around the back and front of the house, past all the sheep shit and mulch. But I never saw anything that proved someone might have been watching me, or had been. Didn't help with my sleep either, which Jon had already seen first-hand.

It was a strange sensation to feel watched, to look out of my window and know amongst those trees and bushes and fields was a camera lens pointing back at me, maybe more than one, maybe none at all. But there was a comfort in it, too, knowing I might not be out here all alone. Though not in knowing who it was or how close they were willing to come.

I knew that must have sounded odd, I knew most people would've been ringing the police or checking in to the nearest hotel and most people would probably be right, I might indeed end up stabbed or murdered in my sleep and that would be my own fault. If this was a movie I would be screaming at the screen to run away too, but this was no horror movie. Instead I felt a comfort in knowing that there was someone out there, in fact I hoped there was someone out there. It would be more depressing if it was all just my own imagination, my mind playing tricks on me, that I'd made the whole thing up, that I was turning mad. That is what it does to people, after all, turns people deranged and senseless, it's just a matter of when and how.

I'd need a quick shower soon, smelling my own armpit, not to mention the coal dust in my hair, the smell of raw meat still on my hands. Gotta sort my face out, it wasn't ready for guests, or guest, I should say. I felt my hair, still felt as awful, my own fault, what was it with me and taking it out on my scalp? I have no idea where it stemmed from, but ever since Junior High I'd hacked at it, turned it red, orange, purple once when I was in my Limp Bizkit phase, surprised Mom didn't send me off to rehab. She just knew it was my way of dealing with things, my little coping mechanism when things went bad, self-harm but not that leaves a scar.

Hence why, on the day I arrived back from London, for a total of four hours I had peroxide hair. Don't ask me how or why, I just felt like doing something drastic, make myself feel better. I thought turning myself Monroe would do the trick, which predictably, it didn't. What the fuck had I done? I had filming the next day, I was an eighteenth-century duchess, not a fifties pin-up girl. I scrolled through my cell and luckily, I knew someone from the crew I could call, and with instructions and directions, one of the girls from hair and make-up arrived at my front door with a suitcase full of chemicals. She was brilliant, a life saver, spent the next few hours with my head over a bath whilst she fiddled with her potions till my hair resembled what it once was before. I felt such a dick, I apologized, offered to pay her, but she said not to worry, said it was our secret, asked instead for an autograph for her sister. I waved her off at the door, as she wheeled her trolley back to her car.

Panic over, my mini breakdown resolved, blonde back to brunette, no harm done. I didn't think Jon would find out, but somehow, he had. At least Sally didn't know, another secret she wouldn't need to concern herself with. It would only worry her and she had enough to worry about, she was pretty occupied at the moment with the media shit storm back home.

I missed her not being here, but I suppose it was my own fault, it wasn't her who kissed Max out in the open and I left her with no choice but to fly back to LA and defend my corner. Though from what she said it was all good news, apparently me and Max are what everyone is talking about; apparently, I may even have to fly back, put a voice to all the stories, let Jimmy Fallon interrogate me with a smile, let SNL poke fun at what my life had become, as long as the audience laughed.

Sally was quite pleased though – polarizing opinions, worshipped or detested, it was making all the right people smile, the fans, my agent, just not me. Me, I felt my career was going in a direction I didn't want it to travel in. I'd need to sit down with everyone once this film wrapped, sort out where this career of mine was headed. Good luck on that one, Lilly, I thought. I got the impression my opinion was of the least concern in the world of profit and loss.

On a brighter note, Frank and I had talked, briefly. I asked him what he'd been up to, fishing mainly by the sound of it, charter fishing and reading, even gardening. Said his backyard was too grey, too much concrete and not enough colour and life. I agreed with him, I should know, I'd seen his backyard, forgotten pot plants and dead surfboards. Said living in an English cottage had turned him all green-fingered, he didn't say but I think he missed us, or missed here, or both.

I'd never tell him this but I still felt let down by Frank, how he dealt with our argument. I'm sure when he returned we would both apologize for things we thought we did or did not say, explain both our actions. Only speaking for myself but the whole situation had left a bad taste. At first, I thought it was trust, but it wasn't, I would always be able to trust Frank. I thought he would trust me a little more than he did, but we both knew I'd lied before, so I didn't blame him for thinking I would again. What hurt the most for me was that he left, or didn't follow me. And that was something he swore he would never do.

It's funny the things you remember. Last year in his hospital bed, granted he was still probably pumped full of meds, I told him off for nearly dying and he swore he would never leave me, that no matter where, he would always be there and it wasn't just words, he meant what he said, and I believed it.

Mine and Frank's relationship was a unique one, it would be easy for a father and daughter comparison, me being the daughter he'd never had and he being the father I'd always wanted, so I would agree that it was similar. I just think we needed each other, that's all. It wasn't always like that. At first, I hated him and I don't think he was very fond of me either. Party girl meets ex-navy, it was destined to be volatile and for the first month it was pretty horrendous for everyone involved.

Last March was when I first met Frank, when we were officially introduced. I was doing all manner of naughty things, management thought I was on a downward spiral, as did Sally, who for all her trying couldn't keep me under control. Like a bad puppy, passed from owner to owner, they thought I needed a dog whisperer. So, in came Frank, the new pack leader with his whistle.

I actually read Cesar Millan's book, you know, before I met Frank. My mom had it lying around the house the same time she was attempting to teach little Ringo good toilet etiquette. I doubt Mom read it as Ringo was and still is shitting and pissing in any room he sees fit. Well, I read it and I guess Frank must have at some point, too, judging by the similarities.

He didn't say it but it was clear my new life with Frank consisted of exercise, discipline and affection. Day one, Frank read me the riot act, which I ignored. He'd reread the riot act and again, I would ignore it, deliberately and with intent, but still his three-pronged attack continued. Frank knew how and when I should be educated, told off or praised and he repeated it throughout the first few months of our time together. I resented it of course, but it continued regardless. Soon, rather than going out to parties, we would read together; instead of spending a night in a police cell, we would watch old movies together; instead of ignoring him, we started to talk. Frank was patient with me and the transition from wild child to angel was a gradual one, but one that brought us closer than either of us would have expected.

People tell me I could hire someone younger, even Frank told me the same thing. I've joked he's no Kevin Costner, I've joked he's too small and in truth I'm sure there were much more qualified bodyguards out there. But Frank has always looked larger them himself and I honestly felt he would do anything to protect me, fling himself off some cliff, take a bullet, or just hug me when I needed a hug, or tell me when I was being an arsehole. You'd be surprised how much I need to be told that. I have always appreciated people's honesty, and the longer my career has gone on, the less I got of it. I get over-praised, to a point sometimes I start to believe it all, believe my own self-importance.

I thought I loved Frank, I loved him more than my own father, which is horrible but true. I mean, don't get me wrong, I loved my parents to death, they have always been very liberated and free, a 'live your life through your heart' mentality, which was a lovely way to live, I suppose, and I always felt loved and they truly made me feel I could be anything I wanted to be, conquer the world and all that shit.

But in a right-and-wrong sense, actions-and-consequences sense, they fell short. Frank was the father I needed and still needed. Tell me how it is, tell me "No" without explanation or discussion, just "No". Not that I always listened of course.

I thought I'd lost him once, heart attack, lots of scans and tests, scared the life out of me, he was nearly a goner, his arteries closed up, had to go up through his groin. Doctor said they asked him who his next of kin was, he said me, made me realise how important I was to him, and he was to me. I visited him every day in hospital, paid for all the medical bills, which wasn't cheap, had to make an awful movie to foot the cost. He told me off for that, said I owed him his life now, and that was a vow he took very seriously, so seriously it nearly got him into trouble. Paparazzi got too close to me once, I got flustered and fell, that was the only time I saw Frank ever lose it. I don't know how many men he hit and shoved, but enough to make the cops throw him in a cell, enough to have to be bailed out, enough to buy the best lawyer I could find. It should have made me angry with him, his violent outburst, but it only made me love him more.

Honesty and security, that was all I have ever wanted, and Frank gave me both. That was why it upset me when he left, and how he had left me since. I felt safe when Frank was around, not so much in the physical sense, but in that my actions and choices were ones made together. I hadn't a wise head, I could be easily influenced, without Frank I felt I could easily self-destruct and Frank knew that. That's why he shouldn't have promised to never leave and then do the complete opposite, no matter what he thought I'd done. When the time was right we would talk it through, we couldn't let this fester. And at least he was now coming back, and then I could feel safe again. Until then I would have to fend for myself.

I don't think Frank would approve of tonight's plans. If Frank was around this would not be happening. Didn't really know how it might pan out, round two, or was it round three? I'd lost count.

Good choice or bad choice, inviting him here was a choice made on my own, without Frank or Sally. We needed to talk, about what happened, about us, try and figure out what to do next so we would both come out of it in one piece and our careers intact. You never know, this could be the night that brings us together again. I've had time to reflect, about what he said, what I said, I still think he's a bastard, but he was my bastard and the story of me and Max wasn't quite over. Maybe it was worth giving us a second shot.

★ ★ ★

Three hours later I was still looking out of the window, into the dark and gales, all dressed up, dinner ready, candles lit, everything ready except Max. I was trying not to pace, my hand felt empty without a wine glass or bottle of beer. I went to the kitchen, added more sauce to the ribs, kept the beans on a low heat, much longer and they'd be ruined, too.

I checked the clock, he was late, later than I thought. Perhaps he was lost, I thought, the roads here were a labyrinth, even GPS didn't know how to find this place, roads here weren't even roads, hardly a street light in sight.

I walked over to the patio doors, checking if I'd had any missed calls but I hadn't, I could try him again, I thought, though what was the point in sending a second voicemail? I looked out into the garden, the evening had turned darker than I'd hoped, and the weather had made eating outside impossible.

Come on, Lilly, I said to myself. Don't let this shit drag you down. Trying to remind myself the night could still yet be salvaged.

It was at that exact moment all the lights went, every single one. I very nearly laughed, in fact I think I did. The house turned to complete black, nothing but the flicker of a million scented candles and the smell of burning meat.

27

Max pulled a face, chewing and chewing, swallowing like it was a relief.

"Sorry again, Max. I didn't realise how long it had been in the oven."

Max put down his fork and pushed his plate away, even though there was still half a dinner he'd hardly touched.

"And you're sure you have no beer?"

"Sorry, all out."

"Nothing at all?"

"Don't you think you've had enough?"

"I didn't know I'd come to a kids' party. You bringing out a piñata next?" he said, picking at his teeth. "I'm gonna take a leak," he said, taking a torch with him.

Believe it or not I did try and fix the light situation, spent half an hour on my knees in a dark cupboard trying to work out the circuit board. When Max arrived, I asked if he could take a look, a job a man could fix in a blink. Though Max wasn't in the mood to help, said electrics wasn't his forte, which I was sure was a lie having watched him pretty much rewire his own games room.

"Your house smells of candyfloss, by the way." Max did up his fly. "And not in a good way."

"Sorry, Lucky I'm addicted to candles hey," I smiled, pointing at all the shadows and darkness.

Max started to walk around, picking things up, putting them down.

"You like it? Cute isn't it."

"It's got more steps than the Trinità dei Monti. What is that?"

"That's an Aga."

"A what?" He walked over to it.

"It's like an oven with no dials. You wanna sit down? I've got peach cobbler if you are still hungry."

"No, I'm not hungry. You eat it, looks like you need to eat more. You've lost weight again, Lilly, and it looks rather disagreeable. Gaunt doesn't suit you. I've told you this before. Are you sure you haven't any beer? Liquor? This is one big place. I'm sure there is some somewhere. What was it you used to say, Lilly? If you're not drinking, you're not playing."

"Sorry, no playing tonight. Besides, you've had enough. I'm surprised you even drove."

"I drive better drunk, believe it or not." He was opening cupboards, inspecting my mail.

"Shall we go through to the front room, then? I've got the fire going, we should be able to see a lot more through there."

Max neither agreed nor disagreed. He followed me through to the next room, our torches aimed at our feet so as not to trip on any steps on the way.

"How was Maddy and Ross's wedding? I bet France was beautiful."

"France was, the French weren't."

"What about your speech?"

"I can't remember. I didn't offend anyone as far as I know."

"I wish I could've been there. I've never been to Paris."

Max sat himself down on the couch, rubbed his eyes like he was in pain.

"Are you OK, Max?"

"Tired. I've had an horrendous week. And driving here was hardly a day at the races."

"Because of me and you, I take it? All the shit in the press?"

"No, my problem right now is investors, fucking bane of my life having to beg to those pricks. No one dares gamble any more. They just want safe bets."

266

"What's wrong with a safe bet?"

Max sniffed. "Safe bets aren't fun to make and they ain't fun to watch either."

"I take it mine and your antics have made you less of a sellable commodity?"

He laughed.

"Why's that funny?"

"Sometimes I forget how naive you are."

"Look, I invited you here to talk, not be mean, thought we needed to work out a way of how to deal with all this attention."

"Don't worry, I'm dealing with it, honey."

"By drinking yourself to death. Do you even have a plan where we go from here, or is your plan just to carry on making friends with the bottom of a whiskey bottle?"

"You want to hear my plan, Lilly? Let's give them their fucking interview. Me and you, let them fire all the questions at us."

"And tell them what? Everything?"

"If they ask the right question then I don't see why not."

"That is ridiculous. Why would you want to do that? We don't have to justify ourselves to people."

"Because it sells, Lilly. It makes money, makes things happen, makes boardrooms sign cheques."

"You serious, Max?"

"Deadly serious. Controversy carries a lot more weight than credibility and talent. That's the one thing I've learnt from all the shit me and you have been through this past few months. Why do you think I drink, Lilly? I drink because the fact of the matter is, I'm famous by association, not for all the years I've trained and studied. I'm famous because I make headlines. We make headlines."

"You want to be a legend, Max. That is what you have always wanted."

"Based on my work, not on who I chose to fuck and fight with."

"I don't get it, Max. The truth, the abortion, the drugs, it wouldn't paint you in a good light. Is that what you really want?"

"I don't know what I want right now."

"The truth would ruin your career. Turn you into public enemy number one."

"People live off such titles."

"God, you sound like Sally."

"Sally knows business. She always has."

"Well, I'm sorry I don't share both your views that self-destruction is something to be proud of."

"Oh, don't play the innocent, Lilly. You bring controversy on yourself. You play the game better than I ever have."

"Not deliberately."

"Then what is your plan, Lilly, hold hands and make up? Don't you know how a good story should pan out? We need a few more lows before we give them their happy ending."

"Is there an alternative?"

"I'm gonna find some beer and go outside, that's my alternative suggestion. It's too hot in here with that fire and these fucking candle fumes."

"There isn't any beer, Max."

"I'm sobering up, Lilly. You should know that I'm nicer when I'm drunk than when I'm sober."

"We could watch a movie? Just like we used to. I've got one I know you'll love. Might take your mind of off things."

"No thanks. I'm not one for pyjama parties."

"Come on, I'll take you outside." I grabbed a jumper from off the back of the couch. "The fresh air might clear your head, Max, stop you being an arsehole." I put the torch to my face. "I'm scared to close my eyes. I'm scared to open them," I said in my best *Blair Witch* impression.

Even Max laughed, his first smile since he arrived.

"With the number of fucking steps in this house, a corner of the room is probably the safest place to be."

* * *

We walked across the grass.

"Unbelievable." I said.

"What?"

"The storm has stopped. I had a barbecue planned."

"Still pretty windy out here. I doubt a fire would stay lit for long."

We both walked out into the centre of the garden, lit only by the candle flames that survived the weather. We both sat together on the bench facing the walled stream.

"I like storms," I said, eyes to the sky, taking a deep breath. "Everything settles after a good storm. Do you like the lawn? I mowed it today, not that you can see all the effort I put in."

"Haven't you got gardeners?"

"I'm self-reliant, Max."

"So it seems."

"I need to be. There's no one around here I can rely on."

"Including me?"

"Including you, yes."

"That's not fair. One thing I've always been is dependable."

"You're right, Max. I can always relay on you to fuck things up, can't I?"

"I assure you it's never intentional."

"I don't think anyone fucks up intentionally so don't use that as an attribute."

"And what attributes do you want from a man these days?"

"What question is that?"

"The kind drunk men ask."

"I don't know, Max. What do you want me to say? Tall, dark and handsome, family man, gentle but firm, rugged, passionate, driven, strong."

"I'm all of those things."

"You're tall. You're not gentle, certainly not a family man."

"Gentle but firm, what does that even mean? Men aren't

269

Dobermans. Is this what you want in a man? A well-behaved dog?"

"Course it's not, Max. I'm being trivial."

"Then what is it you want?"

"I just want to be happy."

"Happy?" Max smiled. "How fucking Disney."

"Yes, happy. I don't care if that's alone or beside someone. Alone sounds easier."

"And what would make you happy? Did I make you happy?"

"I don't want to play this shit. Can we go back inside? I'm cold."

"Play what?"

"Do you even want to be with me? You flirt like you want to, you tell me you love me one week, that you want to be with me again."

"And you made it quite clear in London that was not going to happen."

"I kissed you, Max. Of course I want you, but not on your terms."

"What you want changes like this fucking weather."

"Because I never know what Max I will get. The real Max, or the one like tonight, who turns up half cut and acting like a fucking retard. That is why we shouldn't be together. No couple could survive this."

"I agree."

"You agree. Good, then we go our separate ways now. Ride this storm, protect our necks, move on, meet new partners, have different lives. We don't have to be enemies, Max, we can both have happy lives without resenting the one who gets there first."

"It's not that simple, I'm afraid."

"Why can't it be?"

Max stood up. "You know what London taught me, Lilly, our little kiss for all to see? Taught me how much you impact my career, how important it is for me and you to stay in those headlines. The sad fact is, I need you, otherwise I'm off the boil. That is why I drink."

"You are being dramatic. You have a career without me. You had one before I ever came along."

"Lilly, before you I was a nobody. No studio would touch me."

"Max, you are selling yourself short."

"Lilly, we can't stop now. Not when it just got interesting. Not while we have people's attention."

"You can't tell me what I can and can't do. I'm sorry if this mucks up your plans."

He sniggered. "Of course I can. I've been telling you what to do since the day we met."

"You are evil, Max."

"I'm just an opportunist, that's all."

"Well, I'm not taking part in whatever grand scheme you have been plotting. I will move on without you. See who I want. Fuck who I want."

"And who would fuck you right now, Lilly? You are damaged. You want someone to fix you, but no one is ever going to fix you or find a solution because you are beyond help. It's inevitable that you will end up alone. An old, washed-up actress with nothing left but fucking gold and cancer. But you know what, taking that all into consideration, I'm still in love with you. Despite all your flaws and issues, I still see a future for us. That's the mad thing in all this. I still want to be with you."

"You are fucking delusional. I want you to leave."

Max got up, started to walk off. "I won't let anyone else have you, not for the short term. This Lilly and Max show is far too important right now. A lot rides on it."

"Is that a threat?"

"No, just a statement of fact. I just hope you choose the easy way, the hard way is far too expensive and will end up with the same result, I assure you."

"Just go!" I screamed.

271

"I'll let myself out. But I do request you play long."

"Play along with what?"

"Just do as I say. Trust me, it will be to your advantage. We'll both come out if it on top if we do it my way. I'll make us folklore if you let me handle this right. Be a good girl. Do as you are told. Not that you were ever too good at following direction. The only time you've ever done as you were told was when I made you have that fucking abortion you still cry so much about."

It was then I slapped him. Hard across his face.

★ ★ ★

I didn't watch Max drive off, but I heard his tyres ripping up gravel and stone, his engine race across the bridge as I stumbled through the garden, sobbing and shaking. This was all too much. I screamed till it hurt, screamed till there was nothing left, my head tilted back, my eyes fixed to the sky. It was a scream a long time coming, built up over weeks and months, over lots of different reasons, though when I stopped, there was no release, my anger was not emptied. One deep breath and I was filled up with the same confusion, embarrassed by my past, a hatred for my future. I'd fallen short, everything in my life was going wrong and I had no way to fix it. I would just watch it all crumble around me, till anyone important had left, till I ended up broken beyond repair.

I didn't remember stumbling across towards the water's edge, but I remembered the current, violent and fierce, black and unforgiving, loud like a roar, like it could take anything it wanted with it, like it could suck you under or spit you out. I looked over, it wasn't a long way down, but high enough, if the fall didn't do the trick then the water would. I wobbled on my feet, climbing onto the cobbled wall, the wind and spray pulling and pushing, holding me back, helping me fall.

This is it, Lilly. They'd get what they wanted all along. They would finally have their headline. It just wouldn't be pretty. The world would be able to clamber over my coffin, salivating over opinions and blame, dissected and discussing my mental state. I would become a 'what if,' a 'what a shame,' a 'what a waste,' I would die young and fast and pretty, better than the alternative, sorry Marla but that just wasn't me, I'm too tired for that road and I wouldn't have the energy even if I wanted to.

I closed my eyes, pictured finality and already felt lighter, heard myself apologizing, to whom, I wasn't sure, to myself, to everyone. It would be a comfort regardless, for them and me, they were used to my running away, this time my escape would be permanent. I felt myself counting down from five, my fist clenched, my teeth gritted. I knew what I was about to do, but had no idea what I was doing.

5,4,3,2...

The moment I felt my feet leave the wall there was no time for pain as bone hit rock, no gasps as my skin felt the waters sting, but still I heard my name.

Lilly! Stop!

As a hand grabbed mine.

As I felt myself being dragged from water back to mud.

Coughing. Breathing. Gasping.

Felt myself being lifted. My head against his chest.

Our clothes stuck together, wet and cold.

A man out of breath, asking if I was OK.

My eyes closed, as I let myself be saved.

To be continued...